THE BERNARD SHAW LIBRARY

GETTING MARRIED
AND
PRESS CUTTINGS

Bernard Shaw was born in Dublin in 1856. Essentially shy, yet he created the persona of G.B.S., the showman, satirist, controversialist, critic, pundit, wit, intellectual buffoon and dramatist. Commentators brought a new adjective into English: Shavian, a term used to embody all his brilliant qualities.

After his arrival in London in 1876 he became an active Socialist and a brilliant platform speaker. He wrote on many social aspects of the day; on *Commonsense about the War* (1914), *How to Settle the Irish Question* (1917) and *The Intelligent Woman's Guide to Socialism and Capitalism* (1928). He undertook his own education at the British Museum and consequently became keenly interested in cultural subjects. Thus his prolific output included music, art and theatre reviews: which were collected into several volumes; *Music in London 1890–1894* (3 vols., 1931); *Pen Portraits and Reviews* (1931); and *Our Theatres in the Nineties* (3 vols., 1931). He wrote five novels and some shorter fiction including *The Black Girl in Search of God and Some Lesser Tales* and *Cashel Byron's Profession*, both published in Penguin.

He conducted a strong attack on the London theatre and was closely associated with the intellectual revival of British theatre. His many plays fall into several categories: 'Plays Pleasant'; 'Plays Unpleasant'; comedies; chronicle-plays; 'metabiological Pentateuch', (*Back to Methuselah*, a series of plays) and 'political extravaganzas'. G.B.S. died in 1950.

GETTING MARRIED

AND

PRESS CUTTINGS

BY

Bernard Shaw

DEFINITIVE TEXT
under the editorial supervision of
Dan H. Laurence

PENGUIN BOOKS

PENGUIN BOOKS

Published by the Penguin Group
Penguin Books Ltd, 27 Wrights Lane, London W8 5TZ, England
Viking Penguin, a division of Penguin Books USA Inc.
375 Hudson Street, New York, New York 10014, USA
Penguin Books Australia Ltd, Ringwood, Victoria, Australia
Penguin Books Canada Ltd, 2801 John Street, Markham, Ontario, Canada L3R 1B4
Penguin Books (NZ) Ltd, 182–190 Wairau Road, Auckland 10, New Zealand

Penguin Books Ltd, Registered Offices: Harmondsworth, Middlesex, England

Getting Married first published in English in 1911
Press Cuttings first published in English in 1909
Published together in Penguin Books 1986
3 5 7 9 10 8 6 4 2

Printed in England by Clays Ltd, St Ives plc

All business connected with Bernard Shaw's plays is in the Hands of The Society of Authors,
84 Drayton Gardens, London SW10 9SB (Telephone 071–373 6642), to which all enquires and
applications for licences to perform should be addressed and performing fees paid. Dates and places
of contemplated performances must be precisely specified in all applications.
Applications for permission to give stock and amateur performances of Bernard Shaw's plays in the
United States of America and Canada should be made to Samuel French Inc., 45 West 25th Street,
New York, New York 10010.

CONTENTS

Getting Married   7
    Preface   11

Press Cuttings   223

Getting Married:
A Disquisitory Play

WITH

Preface

N.B.—There is a point of some technical interest to be noted in this play. The customary division into acts and scenes has been disused, and a return made to unity of time and place as observed in the ancient Greek drama. In the foregoing tragedy, The Doctor's Dilemma, there are five acts; the place is altered five times; and the time is spread over an undetermined period of more than a year. No doubt the strain on the attention of the audience and on the ingenuity of the playwright is much less; but I find in practice that the Greek form is inevitable when drama reaches a certain point in poetic and intellectual evolution. Its adoption was not, on my part, a deliberate display of virtuosity in form, but simply the spontaneous falling of a play of ideas into the form most suitable to it, which turned out to be the classical form. Getting Married, in several acts and scenes, with the time spread over a long period, would be impossible.

Composition begun 5 August 1907; completed 14 March 1908. First published in German translation, as *Die Ehe*, 1910. Published in *The Doctor's Dilemma, Getting Married, & The Shewing-up of Blanco Posnet*, 1911. First presented at the Haymarket Theatre, London, on 12 May 1908, for six matinées.

Alice (Mrs Alfred) Bridgenorth   *Mary Rorke*
Alderman William Collins   *E. Holman Clarke*
General "Boxer" Bridgenorth   *Charles Fulton*
Lesbia Grantham   *Beryl Faber*
Reginald Bridgenorth   *William Farren (Jun.)*
Leo (Mrs Reginald) Bridgenorth   *Marie Löhr*
Alfred Bridgenorth, Bishop of Chelsea
                                    Henry Ainley
St John Hotchkiss   *Robert Loraine*
Cecil Sykes   *Berte Thomas*
Edith Bridgenorth   *Auriol Lee*
Rev. Oliver Cromwell Soames ("Father Anthony")   *James Hearn*
Joseph Wallaston (The Beadle)   *Albert Sims*
Zenobia Alexandrina (Mrs George) Collins
                                    Fanny Brough

Period—12 May 1908. Forenoon

Scene—*The Norman Kitchen in the Palace of the Bishop of Chelsea*

The play is not divided into acts or scenes. It is played with two intervals: "The Audience is respectfully requested to regard these interruptions as intended for its convenience, and not as part of the Author's design."

Preface

Contents

The Revolt against Marriage, 452
Marriage nevertheless Inevitable, 453
What does the Word Marriage Mean?, 454
Survivals of Sex Slavery, 457
The New Attack on Marriage, 460
A Forgotten Conference of Married Men, 461
Hearth and Home, 466
Too Much of a Good Thing, 468
Large and Small Families, 469
The Gospel of Laodicea, 471
For Better for Worse, 474
Wanted: An Immoral Statesman, 476
The Limits of Democracy, 478
The Science and Art of Politics, 480
Why Statesmen Shirk the Marriage Question, 481
The Question of Population, 482
The Right to Motherhood, 483
Monogamy, Polygyny, and Polyandry, 485
The Male Revolt Against Polygyny, 486
Difference between Oriental and Occidental
Polygyny, 487
The Old Maid's Right to Motherhood, 489
Ibsen's Chain Stitch, 490
Remoteness of the Facts from the Ideal, 493
Difficulty of obtaining Evidence, 493
Marriage as a Magic Spell, 495
The Impersonality of Sex, 496
The Economic Slavery of Women, 499
Unpopularity of Impersonal Views, 501

Impersonality is not Promiscuity, 502
Domestic Change of Air, 503
Home Manners are Bad Manners, 505
Spurious "Natural" Affection, 505
Carrying the War into the Enemy's Country, 507
Shelley and Queen Victoria, 508
A Probable Effect of Giving Women the Vote, 509
The Personal Sentimental Basis of Monogamy, 511
Divorce, 515
Importance of Sentimental Grievances, 517
Divorce without Asking Why, 518
Economic Slavery again the Root Difficulty, 520
Labor Exchanges and the White Slavery, 520
Divorce Favorable to Marriage, 522
Male Economic Slavery and the Rights of
Bachelors, 524
The Pathology of Marriage, 527
The Criminology of Marriage, 529
Does it Matter?, 530
Christian Marriage, 532
Divorce a Sacramental Duty, 534
Othello and Desdemona, 535
What is to Become of the Children?, 537
The Cost of Divorce, 542
Conclusions, 544

THE REVOLT AGAINST MARRIAGE

There is no subject on which more dangerous nonsense is talked and thought than marriage. If the
mischief stopped at talking and thinking it would be
bad enough; but it goes further, into disastrous
anarchical action. Because our marriage law is inhuman and unreasonable to the point of downright

abomination, the bolder and more rebellious spirits form illicit unions, defiantly sending cards round to their friends announcing what they have done. Young women come to me and ask me whether I think they ought to consent to marry the man they have decided to live with; and they are perplexed and astonished when I, who am supposed (heavens knows why!) to have the most advanced views attainable on the subject, urge them on no account to compromise themselves without the security of an authentic wedding ring. They cite the example of George Eliot, who formed an illicit union with Lewes. They quote a saying attributed to Nietzsche, that a married philosopher is ridiculous, though the men of their choice are not philosophers. When they finally give up the idea of reforming our marriage institutions by private enterprise and personal righteousness, and consent to be led to the Registry or even to the altar, they insist on first arriving at an explicit understanding that both parties are to be perfectly free to sip every flower and change every hour, as their fancy may dictate, in spite of the legal bond. I do not observe that their unions prove less monogamic than other people's: rather the contrary, in fact; consequently, I do not know whether they make less fuss than ordinary people when either party claims the benefit of the treaty; but the existence of the treaty shews the same anarchical notion that the law can be set aside by any two private persons by the simple process of promising one another to ignore it.

MARRIAGE NEVERTHELESS INEVITABLE

Now most laws are, and all laws ought to be, stronger than the strongest individual. Certainly the marriage law is. The only people who successfully evade it are those who actually avail themselves of its shelter by pretending to be married when they are not, and by Bohemians who have no position to lose and no career to be closed. In every other case open violation of the marriage laws means either downright ruin or such inconvenience and disablement as a prudent man or woman would get married ten times over rather than face. And these disablements and inconveniences are not even the price of freedom; for, as Brieux has shewn so convincingly in Les Hannetons, an avowedly illicit union is often found in practice to be as tyrannical and as hard to escape from as the worst legal one.

We may take it then that when a joint domestic establishment, involving questions of children or property, is contemplated, marriage is in effect compulsory upon all normal people; and until the law is altered there is nothing for us but to make the best of it as it stands. Even when no such establishment is desired, clandestine irregularities are negligible as an alternative to marriage. How common they are nobody knows; for in spite of the powerful protection afforded to the parties by the law of libel, and the readiness of society on various other grounds to be hoodwinked by the keeping up of the very thinnest appearances, most of them are probably never suspected. But they are neither dignified nor safe and comfortable, which at once rules them out for normal decent people. Marriage remains practically inevitable; and the sooner we acknowledge this, the sooner we shall set to work to make it decent and reasonable.

WHAT DOES THE WORD MARRIAGE MEAN ?

However much we may all suffer through marriage, most of us think so little about it that we regard it as a fixed part of the order of nature, like gravitation. Except for this error, which may be regarded as constant, we use the word with reckless looseness, meaning a dozen different things by it, and yet always assuming that to a respectable man it can have only one meaning. The pious citizen, suspecting the Socialist (for example) of unmentionable things, and asking him heatedly whether he wishes to abolish marriage, is infuriated by a sense of unanswerable quibbling when the Socialist asks him what particular variety of marriage he means: English civil marriage, sacramental marriage, indissoluble Roman Catholic marriage, marriage of divorced persons, Scotch marriage, Irish marriage, French, German, Turkish, or South Dakotan marriage. In Sweden, one of the most highly civilized countries in the world, a marriage is dissolved if both parties wish it, without any question of conduct. That is what marriage means in Sweden. In Clapham that is what they call by the senseless name of Free Love. In the British Empire we have unlimited Kulin polygamy, Muslim polygamy limited to four wives, child marriages, and, nearer home, marriages of first cousins: all of them abominations in the eyes of many worthy persons. Not only may the respectable British champion of marriage mean any of these widely different institutions; sometimes he does not mean marriage at all. He means monogamy, chastity, temperance, respectability, morality, Christianity, anti-socialism, and a dozen other things that have no necessary connection with marriage. He often means something that he dare not avow: ownership of the person of another human being, for instance. And he never tells the truth about his own marriage either to himself or anyone else.

With those individualists who in the nineteenth

century dreamt of doing away with marriage altogether
on the ground that it is a private concern between the
two parties with which society has nothing to do,
there is now no need to deal. The vogue of "the self-
regarding action" has passed; and it may be assumed
without argument that unions for the purpose of
establishing a family will continue to be registered
and regulated by the State. Such registration is
marriage, and will continue to be called marriage long
after the conditions of the registration have changed so
much that no citizen now living would recognize
them as marriage conditions at all if he revisited the
earth. There is therefore no question of abolishing
marriage; but there is a very pressing question of
improving its conditions. I have never met anybody
really in favor of maintaining marriage as it exists in
England today. A Roman Catholic may obey his
Church by assenting verbally to the doctrine of
indissoluble marriage. But nobody worth counting
believes directly, frankly, and instinctively that when
a person commits a murder and is put into prison for
twenty years for it, the free and innocent husband or
wife of that murderer should remain bound by the
marriage. To put it briefly, a contract for better for
worse is a contract that should not be tolerated. As a
matter of fact it is not tolerated fully even by the
Roman Catholic Church; for Roman Catholic marriages can be dissolved, if not by the temporal Courts,
by the Pope. Indissoluble marriage is an academic
figment, advocated only by celibates and by comfortably married people who imagine that if other couples
are uncomfortable it must be their own fault, just as
rich people are apt to imagine that if other people are
poor it serves them right. There is always some means
of dissolution. The conditions of dissolution may vary

widely, from those on which Henry VIII procured
his divorce from Katharine of Aragon to the pleas on
which American wives obtain divorces (for instance,
"mental anguish" caused by the husband's neglect
to cut his toe-nails); but there is always some point at
which the theory of the inviolable better-for-worse
marriage breaks down in practice. South Carolina has
indeed passed what is called a freak law declaring that
a marriage shall not be dissolved under any circumstances; but such an absurdity will probably be re-
pealed or amended by sheer force of circumstances
before these words are in print. The only question to
be considered is, What shall the conditions of the
dissolution be ?

SURVIVALS OF SEX SLAVERY

If we adopt the common romantic assumption that the
object of marriage is bliss, then the very strongest
reason for dissolving a marriage is that it shall be
disagreeable to one or other or both of the parties. If
we accept the view that the object of marriage is to
provide for the production and rearing of children,
then childlessness should be a conclusive reason for
dissolution. As neither of these causes entitles married
persons to divorce it is at once clear that our marriage
law is not founded on either assumption. What it is
really founded on is the morality of the tenth com-
mandment, which Englishwomen will one day succeed
in obliterating from the walls of our churches by
refusing to enter any building where they are publicly
classed with a man's house, his ox, and his ass, as his
purchased chattels. In this morality female adultery is
malversation by the woman and theft by the man,
whilst male adultery with an unmarried woman is not

an offence at all. But though this is not only the theory of our marriage laws, but the practical morality of many of us, it is no longer an avowed morality, nor does its persistence depend on marriage; for the abolition of marriage would, other things remaining unchanged, leave women more effectually enslaved than they now are. We shall come to the question of the economic dependence of women on men later on; but at present we had better confine ourselves to the theories of marriage which we are not ashamed to acknowledge and defend, and upon which, therefore, marriage reformers will be obliged to proceed.

We may, I think, dismiss from the field of practical politics the extreme sacerdotal view of marriage as a sacred and indissoluble covenant, because, though reinforced by unhappy marriages as all fanaticisms are reinforced by human sacrifices, it has been reduced to a private and socially inoperative eccentricity by the introduction of civil marriage and divorce. Theoretically, our civilly married couples are to a Catholic as unmarried couples are: that is, they are living in open sin. Practically, civilly married couples are received in society, by Catholics and everyone else, precisely as sacramentally married couples are; and so are people who have divorced their wives or husbands and married again. And yet marriage is enforced by public opinion with such ferocity that the least suggestion of laxity in its support is fatal to even the highest and strongest reputations, although laxity of conduct is winked at with grinning indulgence; so that we find the austere Shelley denounced as a fiend in human form, whilst Nelson, who openly left his wife and formed a *ménage à trois* with Sir William and Lady Hamilton, was idolized. Shelley might have had an illegitimate child in every county in England if he had done so frankly as a sinner. His unpardonable offence was that he attacked marriage as an institution. We feel a strange anguish of terror and hatred against him, as against one who threatens us with a mortal injury. What is the element in his proposals that produces this effect?

The answer of the specialists is the one already alluded to: that the attack on marriage is an attack on property; so that Shelley was something more hateful to a husband than a horse thief: to wit, a wife thief, and something more hateful to a wife than a burglar: namely, one who would steal her husband's house from over her head, and leave her destitute and nameless on the streets. Now, no doubt this accounts for a good deal of anti-Shelleyan prejudice: a prejudice so deeply rooted in our habits that, as I have shewn in my play, men who are bolder freethinkers than Shelley himself can no more bring themselves to commit adultery than to commit any common theft, whilst women who loathe sex slavery more fiercely than Mary Wollstonecraft are unable to face the insecurity and discredit of the vagabondage which is the masterless woman's only alternative to celibacy. But in spite of all this there is a revolt against marriage which has spread so rapidly within my recollection that though we all still assume the existence of a huge and dangerous majority which regards the least hint of scepticism as to the beauty and holiness of marriage as infamous and abhorrent, I sometimes wonder why it is so difficult to find an authentic living member of this dreaded army of convention outside the ranks of the people who never think about public questions at all, and who, for all their numerical weight and apparently invincible prejudices, accept social changes today as tamely as their forefathers accepted the Reformation under Henry and Edward, the Restoration under Mary, and, after Mary's death, the shandygaff which Elizabeth compounded from both doctrines and called the Articles of the Church of England. If matters were left to these simple folk, there would never be any changes at all; and society would perish like a snake that could not cast its skins. Nevertheless the snake does change its skin in spite of them; and there are signs that our marriage-law skin is causing discomfort to thoughtful people and will presently be cast whether the others are satisfied with it or not. The question therefore arises: What is there in marriage that makes the thoughtful people so uncomfortable?

THE NEW ATTACK ON MARRIAGE

The answer to this question is an answer which everybody knows and nobody likes to give. What is driving our ministers of religion and statesmen to blurt it out at last is the plain fact that marriage is now beginning to depopulate the country with such alarming rapidity that we are forced to throw aside our modesty like people who, awakened by an alarm of fire, rush into the streets in their nightdresses or in no dresses at all. The fictitious Free Lover, who was supposed to attack marriage because it thwarted his inordinate affections and prevented him from making life a carnival, has vanished and given place to the very real, very strong, very austere avenger of outraged decency who declares that the licentiousness of marriage, now that it no longer recruits the race, is destroying it.

As usual, this change of front has not yet been noticed by our newspaper controversialists and by the

suburban season-ticket holders whose minds the
newspapers make. They still defend the citadel on the
side on which nobody is attacking it, and leave its
weakest front undefended.

The religious revolt against marriage is a very old
one. Christianity began with a fierce attack on marriage; and to this day the celibacy of the Roman
Catholic priesthood is a standing protest against its
incompatibility with the higher life. St Paul's reluctant sanction of marriage; his personal protest that he
countenanced it of necessity and against his own conviction; his contemptuous "better to marry than to
burn" is only out of date in respect of his belief that
the end of the world was at hand and that there was
therefore no longer any population question. His
instinctive recoil from its worst aspect as a slavery to
pleasure which induces two people to accept slavery
to one another has remained an active force in the
world to this day, and is now stirring more uneasily
than ever. We have more and more Pauline celibates
whose objection to marriage is the intolerable indignity of being supposed to desire or live the married
life as ordinarily conceived. Every thoughtful and
observant minister of religion is troubled by the
determination of his flock to regard marriage as a
sanctuary for pleasure, seeing as he does that the
known libertines of his parish are visibly suffering
much less from intemperance than many of the
married people who stigmatize them as monsters of
vice.

A FORGOTTEN CONFERENCE OF MARRIED MEN

The late Hugh Price Hughes, an eminent Method-
ist divine, once organized in London a conference of

respectable men to consider the subject. Nothing came of it (nor indeed could have come of it in the absence of women); but it had its value as giving the young sociologists present, of whom I was one, an authentic notion of what a picked audience of respectable men understood by married life. It was certainly a staggering revelation. Peter the Great would have been shocked; Byron would have been horrified; Don Juan would have fled from the conference into a monastery. The respectable men all regarded the marriage ceremony as a rite which absolved them from the laws of health and temperance; inaugurated a lifelong honeymoon; and placed their pleasures on exactly the same footing as their prayers. It seemed entirely proper and natural to them that out of every twenty-four hours of their lives they should pass eight shut up in one room with their wives alone, and this, not birdlike, for the mating season, but all the year round and every year. How they settled even such minor questions as to which party should decide whether and how much the window should be open and how many blankets should be on the bed, and at what hour they should go to bed and get up so as to avoid disturbing one another's sleep, seemed insoluble questions to me. But the members of the conference did not seem to mind. They were content to have the whole national housing problem treated on a basis of one room for two people. That was the essence of marriage for them.

Please remember, too, that there was nothing in their circumstances to check intemperance. They were men of business; that is, men for the most part engaged in routine work which exercized neither their minds nor their bodies to the full pitch of their capacities. Compared with statesmen, first-rate professional men, artists, and even with laborers and artisans as far as muscular exertion goes, they were underworked, and could spare the fine edge of their faculties and the last few inches of their chests without being any the less fit for their daily routine. If I had adopted their habits, a startling deterioration would have appeared in my writing before the end of a fortnight, and frightened me back to what they would have considered an impossible asceticism. But they paid no penalty of which they were conscious. They had as much health as they wanted: that is, they did not feel the need of a doctor. They enjoyed their smokes, their meals, their respectable clothes, their affectionate games with their children, their prospects of larger profits or higher salaries, their Saturday half holidays and Sunday walks, and the rest of it. They did less than two hours work a day and took from seven to nine office hours to do it in. And they were no good for any mortal purpose except to go on doing it. They were respectable only by the standard they themselves had set. Considered seriously as electors governing an empire through their votes, and choosing and maintaining its religious and moral institutions by their powers of social persecution, they were a black-coated army of calamity. They were incapable of comprehending the industries they were engaged in, the laws under which they lived, or the relation of their country to other countries. They lived the lives of old men contentedly. They were timidly conservative at the age at which every healthy human being ought to be obstreperously revolutionary. And their wives went through the routine of the kitchen, nursery, and drawing room just as they went through the routine of the office. They had all, as they called it, settled down, like balloons that had lost their lifting margin of gas; and it was evident that the process of settling down would go on until they settled into their graves. They read old-fashioned newspapers with effort, and were just taking with avidity to a new sort of paper, costing a halfpenny, which they believed to be extraordinarily bright and attractive, and which never really succeeded until it became extremely dull, discarding all serious news and replacing it by vapid tittle-tattle, and substituting for political articles informed by at least some pretence of knowledge of economics, history, and constitutional law, such paltry follies and sentimentalities, snobberies and partisaneries, as ignorance can understand and irresponsibility relish.

What they called patriotism was a conviction that because they were born in Tooting or Camberwell, they were the natural superiors of Beethoven, of Rodin, of Ibsen, of Tolstoy and all other benighted foreigners. Those of them who did not think it wrong to go to the theatre liked above everything a play in which the hero was called Dick; was continually fingering a briar pipe; and, after being overwhelmed with admiration and affection through three acts, was finally rewarded with the legal possession of a pretty heroine's person on the strength of a staggering lack of virtue. Indeed their only conception of the meaning of the word virtue was abstention from stealing other men's wives or from refusing to marry their daughters.

As to law, religion, ethics, and constitutional government, any counterfeit could impose on them. Any atheist could pass himself off on them as a bishop, any anarchist as a judge, any despot as a Whig, any sentimental socialist as a Tory, any philtre-monger or witch-finder as a man of science, any

phrase-maker as a statesman. Those who did not
believe the story of Jonah and the great fish were all
the readier to believe that metals can be transmuted
and all diseases cured by radium, and that men can
live for two hundred years by drinking sour milk.
Even these credulities involved too severe an intellectual effort for many of them: it was easier to grin and
believe nothing. They maintained their respect for
themselves by "playing the game" (that is, doing what
everybody else did), and by being good judges of hats,
ties, dogs, pipes, cricket, gardens, flowers, and the
like. They were capable of discussing each other's
solvency and respectability with some shrewdness,
and could carry out quite complicated systems of
paying visits and "knowing" one another. They felt a
little vulgar when they spent a day at Margate, and
quite distinguished and travelled when they spent it at
Boulogne. They were, except as to their clothes, "not
particular": that is, they could put up with ugly sights
and sounds, unhealthy smells, and inconvenient
houses, with inhuman apathy and callousness. They
had, as to adults, a theory that human nature is so
poor that it is useless to try to make the world any
better, whilst as to children they believed that if they
were only sufficiently lectured and whipped, they
could be brought to a state of moral perfection such
as no fanatic has ever ascribed to his deity. Though
they were not intentionally malicious, they practised
the most appalling cruelties from mere thoughtless-
ness, thinking nothing of imprisoning men and women
for periods up to twenty years for breaking into their
houses; of treating their children as wild beasts to be
tamed by a system of blows and imprisonment which
they called education; and of keeping pianos in their
houses, not for musical purposes, but to torment their

daughters with a senseless stupidity that would have revolted an inquisitor.

In short, dear reader, they were very like you and me. I could fill a hundred pages with the tale of our imbecilities and still leave much untold; but what I have set down here haphazard is enough to condemn the system that produced us. The corner-stone of that system was the family and the institution of marriage as we have it today in England.

HEARTH AND HOME

There is no shirking it: if marriage cannot be made to produce something better than we are, marriage will have to go, or else the nation will have to go. It is no use talking of honor, virtue, purity, and wholesome, sweet, clean English home lives when what is meant is simply the habits I have described. The flat fact is that English home life today is neither honorable, virtuous, wholesome, sweet, clean, nor in any creditable way distinctively English. It is in many respects conspicuously the reverse; and the result of withdrawing children from it completely at an early age, and sending them to a public school and then to a university, does, in spite of the fact that these institutions are class warped and in some respects quite abominably corrupt, produce sociabler men. Women, too, are improved by the escape from home provided by women's colleges; but as very few of them are fortunate enough to enjoy this advantage, most women are so thoroughly home-bred as to be unfit for human society. So little is expected of them that in Sheridan's School for Scandal we hardly notice that the heroine is a female cad, as detestable and dishonorable in her repentance as she is vulgar and silly in her naughtiness. It was left to an abnormal critic like George Gissing to point out the glaring fact that in the collection of life studies of Victorian women to be found in the novels of Dickens, the most convincingly real ones are either vilely unamiable or comically contemptible; whilst his attempts to manufacture admirable heroines by idealizations of homebred womanhood are not only absurd but not even pleasantly absurd: one has no patience with them.

As all this is corrigible by reducing home life and domestic sentiment to something like reasonable proportions in the life of the individual, the danger of it does not lie in human nature. Home life as we understand it is no more natural to us than a cage is natural to a cockatoo. Its grave danger to the nation lies in its narrow views, its unnaturally sustained and spitefully jealous concupiscences, its petty tyrannies, its false social pretences, its endless grudges and squabbles, its sacrifice of the boy's future by setting him to earn money to help the family when he should be in training for his adult life (remember the boy Dickens and the blacking factory), and of the girl's chances by making her a slave to sick or selfish parents, its unnatural packing into little brick boxes of little parcels of humanity of ill-assorted ages, with the old scolding or beating the young for behaving like young people, and the young hating and thwarting the old for behaving like old people, and all the other ills, mentionable and unmentionable, that arise from excessive segregation. It sets these evils up as benefits and blessings representing the highest attainable degree of honor and virtue, whilst any criticism of or revolt against them is savagely persecuted as the extremity of vice. The revolt, driven under ground and exacerbated, produces debauchery veiled by hypocrisy, an overwhelming demand for licentious theatrical entertainments which no censorship can stem, and, worst of all, a confusion of virtue with the mere morality that steals its name until the real thing is loathed because the imposture is loathsome. Literary traditions spring up in which the libertine and profligate— Tom Jones and Charles Surface—are the heroes, and decorous, law-abiding persons—Blifil and Joseph Surface—are the villains and butts. People like to believe that Nell Gwynne has every amiable quality and the Bishop's wife every odious one. Poor Mr Pecksniff, who is generally no worse than a humbug with a turn for pompous talking, is represented as a criminal instead of as a very typical English paterfamilias keeping a roof over the head of himself and his daughters by inducing people to pay him more for his services than they are worth. In the extreme instances of reaction against convention, female murderers get sheaves of offers of marriage; and when Nature throws up that rare phenomenon, an unscrupulous libertine, his success among "well brought-up" girls is so easy, and the devotion he inspires so extravagant, that it is impossible not to see that the revolt against conventional respectability has transfigured a commonplace rascal into a sort of Anarchist Savior. As to the respectable voluptuary, who joins Omar Khayyam clubs and vibrates to Swinburne's invocation of Dolores to "come down and redeem us from virtue," he is to be found in every suburb.

TOO MUCH OF A GOOD THING

We must be reasonable in our domestic ideals. I do not think that life at a public school is altogether good for a boy any more than barrack life is altogether good for a soldier. But neither is home life altogether good. Such good as it does, I should say, is due to its freedom from the very atmosphere it professes to supply. That atmosphere is usually described as an atmosphere of love; and this definition should be sufficient to put any sane person on guard against it. The people who talk and write as if the highest attainable state is that of a family stewing in love continuously from the cradle to the grave, can hardly have given five minutes serious consideration to so outrageous a proposition. They cannot have even made up their minds as to what they mean by love; for when they expatiate on their thesis they are sometimes talking about kindness, and sometimes about mere appetite. In either sense they are equally far from the realities of life. No healthy man or animal is occupied with love in any sense for more than a very small fraction indeed of the time he devotes to business and to recreations wholly unconnected with love. A wife entirely preoccupied with her affection for her husband, a mother entirely preoccupied with her affection for her children, may be all very well in a book (for people who like that kind of book); but in actual life she is a nuisance. Husbands may escape from her when their business compels them to be away from home all day; but young children may be, and quite often are, killed by her cuddling and coddling and doctoring and preaching: above all, by her continuous attempts to excite precocious sentimentality, a practice as objectionable, and possibly as mischievous, as the worst tricks of the worst nursemaids.

LARGE AND SMALL FAMILIES

In most healthy families there is a revolt against this tendency. The exchanging of presents on birthdays and the like is barred by general consent, and the relations of the parties are placed by express treaty on an unsentimental footing.

Unfortunately this mitigation of family sentimentality is much more characteristic of large families than small ones. It used to be said that members of large families get on in the world; and it is certainly true that for purposes of social training a household of twenty surpasses a household of five as an Oxford College surpasses an eight-roomed house in a cheap street. Ten children, with the necessary adults, make a community in which an excess of sentimentality is impossible. Two children make a doll's house, in which both parents and children become morbid if they keep to themselves. What is more, when large families were the fashion, they were organized as tyrannies much more than as "atmospheres of love." Francis Place tells us that he kept out of his father's way because his father never passed a child within his reach without striking it; and though the case was an extreme one, it was an extreme that illustrated a tendency. Sir Walter Scott's father, when his son incautiously expressed some relish for his porridge, dashed a handful of salt into it with an instinctive sense that it was his duty as a father to prevent his son enjoying himself. Ruskin's mother gratified the sensual side of her maternal passion, not by cuddling her son, but by whipping him when he fell downstairs or was slack in learning the Bible off by heart; and this grotesque safety-valve for voluptuousness, mischievous as it was in many ways, had at least the advantage that the child did not enjoy it and was not debauched by it, as he would have been by transports of sentimentality.

But nowadays we cannot depend on these safeguards, such as they were. We no longer have large families: all the families are too small to give the children the necessary social training. The Roman father is out of fashion; and the whip and the cane are becoming discredited, not so much by the old arguments against corporal punishment (sound as these were) as by the gradual wearing away of the veil from the fact that flogging is a form of debauchery. The advocate of flogging as a punishment is now exposed to very disagreeable suspicions; and ever since Rousseau rose to the effort of making a certain very ridiculous confession on the subject, there has been a growing perception that child whipping, even for the children themselves, is not always the innocent and highminded practice it professes to be. At all events there is no getting away from the facts that families are smaller than they used to be, and that passions which formerly took effect in tyranny have been largely diverted into sentimentality. And though a little sentimentality may be a very good thing, chronic sentimentality is a horror, more dangerous, because more possible, than the erotomania which we all condemn when we are not thoughtlessly glorifying it as the ideal married state.

THE GOSPEL OF LAODICEA

Let us try to get at the root error of these false domestic doctrines. Why was it that the late Samuel Butler, with a conviction that increased with his experience of life, preached the gospel of Laodicea, urging people to be temperate in what they called goodness as in everything else? Why is it that I, when I hear some well-meaning person exhort young people to make it a rule to do at least one kind action every day, feel very much as I should if I heard them persuade children to get drunk at least once every day? Apart from the initial absurdity of accepting as permanent a state of things in which there would be in this country misery enough to supply occasion for several thousand million kind actions per annum, the effect on the character of the doers of the actions would be so appalling, that one month of any serious attempt to carry out such counsels would probably bring about more stringent legislation against actions going beyond the strict letter of the law in the way of kindness than we have now against excess in the opposite direction.

There is no more dangerous mistake than the mistake of supposing that we cannot have too much of a good thing. The truth is, an immoderately good man is very much more dangerous than an immoderately bad man: that is why Savonarola was burnt and John of Leyden torn to pieces with red-hot pincers whilst multitudes of unredeemed rascals were being let off with clipped ears, burnt palms, a flogging, or a few years in the galleys. That is why Christianity never got any grip of the world until it virtually reduced its claims on the ordinary citizen's attention to a couple of hours every seventh day, and let him alone on week-days. If the fanatics who are preoccupied day in and day out with their salvation were healthy, virtuous, and wise, the Laodiceanism of the ordinary man might be regarded as a deplorable shortcoming; but, as a matter of fact, no more frightful misfortune could threaten us than a general spread of fanaticism. What people call goodness has to be kept in check just as carefully as what they call badness; for the human constitution will not stand very much of either without serious psychological mischief, ending in insanity or crime. The fact that the insanity may be privileged, as Savonarola's was up to the point of wrecking the social life of Florence, does not alter the case. We always hesitate to treat a dangerously good man as a lunatic because he may turn out to be a prophet in the true sense: that is, a man of exceptional sanity who is in the right when we are in the wrong. However necessary it may have been to get rid of Savonarola, it was foolish to poison Socrates and burn St Joan of Arc. But it is none the less necessary to take a firm stand against the monstrous proposition that because certain attitudes and sentiments may be heroic and admirable at some momentous crisis, they should or can be maintained at the same pitch continuously through life. A life spent in prayer and almsgiving is really as insane as a life spent in cursing and picking pockets: the effect of everybody doing it would be equally disastrous. The superstitious tolerance so long accorded to monks and nuns is inevitably giving way to a very general and very natural practice of confiscating their retreats and expelling them from their country, with the result that they come to England and Ireland, where they are partly unnoticed and partly encouraged because they conduct technical schools and teach our girls softer speech and gentler manners than our comparatively ruffianly elementary teachers. But they are still full of the notion that because it is possible for men to attain the summit of Mont Blanc and stay there for an hour, it is possible for them to live there. Children are punished and scolded for not living there; and adults take serious offence if it is not assumed that they live there.

As a matter of fact, ethical strain is just as bad for us as physical strain. It is desirable that the normal pitch of conduct at which men are not conscious of being particularly virtuous, although they feel mean when they fall below it, should be raised as high as possible; but it is not desirable that they should attempt to live above this pitch any more than that they should habitually walk at the rate of five miles an hour or carry a hundredweight continually on their backs. Their normal condition should be in nowise difficult or remarkable; and it is a perfectly sound instinct that leads us to mistrust the good man as much as the bad man, and to object to the clergyman who is pious extra-professionally as much as to the professional pugilist who is quarrelsome and violent in private life. We do not want good men and bad men any more than we want giants and dwarfs. What we do want is a high quality for our normal: that is, people who can be much better than what we now call respectable without self sacrifice. Conscious goodness, like conscious muscular effort, may be of use in emergencies; but for everyday national use it is negligible; and its effect on the character of the individual may easily be disastrous.

FOR BETTER FOR WORSE

It would be hard to find any document in practical daily use in which these obvious truths seem so stupidly overlooked as they are in the marriage service. As we have seen, the stupidity is only apparent: the service was really only an honest attempt to make the best of a commercial contract of property and slavery by subjecting it to some religious restraint and elevating it by some touch of poetry. But the actual result is that when two people are under the influence of the most violent, most insane, most delusive, and most transient of passions, they are required to swear that they will remain in that excited, abnormal, and exhausting condition continuously until death do them part. And though of course nobody expects them to do anything so impossible and so unwholesome, yet the law that regulates their relations, and the public opinion that regulates that law, is actually founded on the assumption that the marriage vow is not only feasible but beautiful and holy, and that if they are false to it, they deserve no sympathy and no relief. If all married people really lived together, no doubt the mere force of facts would make an end to this inhuman nonsense in a month, if not sooner; but it is very seldom brought to that test. The typical British husband sees much less of his wife than he does of his business partner, his fellow clerk, or whoever works beside him day by day. Man and wife do not, as a rule, live together: they only breakfast together, dine together, and sleep in the same room. In most cases the woman knows nothing of the man's working life and he knows nothing of her working life (he calls it her home life). It is remarkable that the very people who romance most absurdly about the closeness and sacredness of the marriage tie are also those who are most convinced that the man's sphere and the woman's sphere are so entirely separate that only in their leisure moments can they ever be together. A man as intimate with his own wife as a magistrate is with his clerk, or a Prime Minister with the leader of the Opposition, is a man in ten thousand. The majority of married couples never get to know one another at all: they only get accustomed to having the same house, the same children, and the same income, which is quite a different matter. The comparatively few men who work at home—writers, artists, and to some extent clergymen—have to effect some sort of segregation

within the house or else run a heavy risk of overstrain-
ing their domestic relations. When the pair is so poor
that it can afford only a single room, the strain is
intolerable: violent quarrelling is the result. Very few
couples can live in a single-roomed tenement without exchanging blows quite frequently. In the leisured
classes there is often no real family life at all. The boys
are at a public school; the girls are in the schoolroom
in charge of a governess: the husband is at his club or
in a set which is not his wife's; and the institution of
marriage enjoys the credit of a domestic peace which
is hardly more intimate than the relations of prisoners
in the same gaol or guests at the same garden party.
Taking these two cases of the single room and the
unearned income as the extremes, we might perhaps
locate at a guess whereabout on the scale between
them any particular family stands. But it is clear
enough that the one-roomed end, though its conditions enable the marriage vow to be carried out with
the utmost attainable exactitude, is far less endurable
in practice, and far more mischievous in its effect on
the parties concerned, and through them on the
community, than the other end. Thus we see that the
revolt against marriage is by no means only a revolt
against its sordidness as a survival of sex slavery. It
may even plausibly be maintained that this is precisely
the part of it that works most smoothly in practice.
The revolt is also against its sentimentality, its
romance, its Amorism, even against its enervating
happiness.

WANTED: AN IMMORAL STATESMAN

We now see that the statesman who undertakes to
deal with marriage will have to face an amazingly

complicated public opinion. In fact, he will have to leave opinion as far as possible out of the question, and deal with human nature instead. For even if there could be any real public opinion in a society like ours, which is a mere mob of classes, each with its own habits and prejudices, it would be at best a jumble of superstitions and interests, taboos and hypocrisies, which could not be reconciled in any coherent enactment. It would probably proclaim passionately that it does not matter in the least what sort of children we have, or how few or how many, provided the children are legitimate. Also that it does not matter in the least what sort of adults we have, provided they are married. No statesman worth the name can possibly act on these views. He is bound to prefer one healthy illegitimate child to ten rickety legitimate ones, and one energetic and capable unmarried couple to a dozen inferior apathetic husbands and wives. If it could be proved that illicit unions produce three children each and marriages only one and a half, he would be bound to encourage illicit unions and discourage and even penalize marriage. The common notion that the existing forms of marriage are not political contrivances, but sacred ethical obligations to which everything, even the very existence of the human race, must be sacrificed if necessary (and this is what the vulgar morality we mostly profess on the subject comes to) is one on which no sane Government could act for a moment; and yet it influences, or is believed to influence, so many votes, that no Government will touch the marriage question if it can possibly help it, even when there is a demand for the extension of marriage, as in the case of the recent long-delayed Act legalizing marriage with a deceased wife's sister. When a reform in the other direction is needed (for example, an extension of divorce), not even the existence of the most unbearable hardships will induce our statesmen to move so long as the victims submit sheepishly, though when they take the remedy into their own hands an inquiry is soon begun. But what is now making some action in the matter imperative is neither the sufferings of those who are tied for life to criminals, drunkards, physically unsound and dangerous mates, and worthless and unamiable people generally, nor the immorality of the couples condemned to celibacy by separation orders which do not annul their marriages, but the fall in the birth-rate. Public opinion will not help us out of this difficulty: on the contrary, it will, if it be allowed, punish anybody who mentions it. When Zola tried to repopulate France by writing a novel in praise of parentage, the only comment made here was that the book could not possibly be translated into English, as its subject was too improper.

THE LIMITS OF DEMOCRACY

Now if England had been governed in the past by statesmen willing to be ruled by such public opinion as that, she would have been wiped off the political map long ago. The modern notion that democracy means governing a country according to the ignorance of its majorities is never more disastrous than when there is some question of sexual morals to be dealt with. The business of a democratic statesman is not, as some of us seem to think, to convince the voters that he knows no better than they as to the methods of attaining their common ends, but on the contrary to convince them that he knows much better than they do, and therefore differs from them on every possible question of method. The voter's duty is to take care that the Government consists of men whom he can trust to devize or support institutions making for the common welfare. This is highly skilled work; and to be governed by people who set about it as the man in the street would set about it is to make straight for "red ruin and the breaking up of laws." Voltaire said that Mr Everybody is wiser than anybody; and whether he is or not, it is his will that must prevail; but the will and the way are two very different things. For example, it is the will of the people on a hot day that the means of relief from the effects of the heat should be within the reach of everybody. Nothing could be more innocent, more hygienic, more import-ant to social welfare. But the way of the people on such occasions is mostly to drink large quantities of beer, or, among the more luxurious classes, iced claret cup, lemon squashes, and the like. To take a moral illustration, the will to suppress misconduct and secure efficiency in work is general and salutary; but the notion that the best and only effective way is by complaining, scolding, punishing, and revenging is equally general. When Mrs Squeers opened an abcess on her pupil's head with an inky penknife, her object was entirely laudible: her heart was in the right place: a statesman interfering with her on the ground that he did not want the boy cured would have deserved impeachment for gross tyranny. But a statesman tolerating amateur surgical practice with inky penknives in school would be a very bad Minister of Education. It is on the question of method that your expert comes in; and though I am democrat enough to insist that he must first convince a repre-sentative body of amateurs that his way is the right way and Mrs Squeers's way the wrong way, yet I would not have them assume that Mrs Squeers's amateur way is likely to be the right way because she belongs to the democracy and the Minister to the bureaucracy, or that any other test is to be applied to it except the test of its effect on human welfare.

THE SCIENCE AND ART OF POLITICS

Political Science means nothing else than the devizing of the best ways of fulfilling the will of the world; and, I repeat, it is skilled work. Once the way is discovered, the methods laid down, and the machinery provided, the work of the statesman is done, and that of the official begins. To illustrate, there is no need for the police officer who governs the street traffic to be or to know any better than the people who obey the wave of his hand. All concerted action involves subordination and the appointment of directors at whose signal the others will act. There is no more need for them to be superior to the rest than for the keystone of an arch to be of harder stone than the coping. But when it comes to devizing the directions which are to be obeyed: that is, to making new institutions and scrapping old ones, then you need aristocracy in the sense of government by the best. A military state organized so as to carry out exactly the impulses of the average soldier would not last a year. The result of trying to make the Church of England reflect the notions of the average churchgoer has reduced it to a cipher except for the purposes of a petulantly irreligious social and political club. Democracy as to the thing to be done may be inevitable (hence the vital need for a democracy of supermen); but democracy as to the way to do it is like letting the passengers drive the train: it can only end in collision and wreck. As a matter of fact, we obtain reforms (such as they are), not by allowing the electorate to draft statutes, but by persuading it that a certain minister and his cabinet are gifted with sufficient political sagacity to find out how to produce the desired result. And the usual penalty of taking advantage of this power to reform our institutions is defeat by a vehement "swing of the pendulum" at the next election. Therein lies the peril and the glory of democratic statesmanship. A statesman who confines himself to popular legislation—or, for the matter of that, a playwright who confines himself to popular plays—is like a blind man's dog who goes wherever the blind man pulls him, on the ground that both of them want to go to the same place.

WHY STATESMEN SHIRK THE MARRIAGE QUESTION

The reform of marriage, then, will be a very splendid and very hazardous adventure for the Prime Minister who takes it in hand. He will be posted on every hoarding and denounced in every Opposition paper, especially in the sporting papers, as the destroyer of the home, the family, of decency, of morality, of chastity and what not. All the commonplaces of the modern anti-Socialist Noodle's Oration will be hurled at him. And he will have to proceed without the slightest concession to it, giving the noodles nothing but their due in the assurance "I know how to attain our ends better than you," and staking his political life on the conviction carried by that assurance, which conviction will depend a good deal on the certainty with which it is made, which again can be attained only by studying the facts of marriage and understanding the needs of the nation. And, after all, he will find that the pious commonplaces on which he and the electorate are agreed conceal an utter difference in the real ends in view: his being public, far-sighted, and impersonal, and those of multitudes of the electorate narrow, personal, jealous, and corrupt. Under such circumstances, it is not to be wondered at that the mere mention of the marriage question makes a British Cabinet shiver with apprehension and hastily pass on to safer business. Nevertheless the reform of marriage cannot be put off for ever. When its hour comes, what are the points the Cabinet will have to take up?

THE QUESTION OF POPULATION

First, it will have to make up its mind as to how many people we want in the country. If we want less than at present, we must ascertain how many less; and if we allow the reduction to be made by the continued operation of the present sterilization of marriage, we must settle how the process is to be stopped when it has gone far enough. But if we desire to maintain the population at its present figure, or to increase it, we must take immediate steps to induce people of moderate means to marry earlier and to have more children. There is less urgency in the case of the very poor and the very rich. They breed recklessly: the rich because they can afford it, and the poor because they cannot afford the precautions by which the artisans and the middle classes avoid big families. Nevertheless the population declines, because the high birth-rate of the very poor is counterbalanced by a huge infantile-mortality in the slums, whilst the very rich are also the very few, and are becoming sterilized by the spreading revolt of their women against excessive childbearing—sometimes against any childbearing.

This last cause is important. It cannot be removed by any economic readjustment. If every family were provided with £10,000 a year tomorrow, women would still refuse more and more to continue bearing children until they are exhausted whilst numbers of others are bearing no children at all. Even if every woman bearing and rearing a valuable child received a handsome series of payments, thereby making motherhood a real profession as it ought to be, the number of women able or willing to give more of their lives to gestation and nursing than three or four children would cost them might not be very large if the advance in social organization and conscience indicated by such payments involved also the opening up of other means of livelihood to women. And it must be remembered that urban civilization itself, insofar as it is a method of evolution (and when it is not this, it is simply a nuisance), is a sterilizing process as far as numbers go. It is harder to keep up the supply of elephants than of sparrows and rabbits; and for the same reason it will be harder to keep up the supply of highly cultivated men and women than it now is of agricultural laborers. Bees get out of this difficulty by a special system of feeding which enables a queen bee to produce 4000 eggs a day whilst the other females lose their sex altogether and become workers supporting the males in luxury and idleness until the queen has found her mate, when the queen kills him and the quondam females kill all the rest (such at least are the accounts given by romantic naturalists of the matter).

THE RIGHT TO MOTHERHOOD

This system certainly shews a much higher development of social intelligence than our marriage system;

but if it were physically possible to introduce it into human society it would be wrecked by an opposite and not less important revolt of women: that is, the revolt against compulsory barrenness. In this two classes of women are concerned: those who, though they have no desire for the presence or care of children, nevertheless feel that motherhood is an experience necessary to their complete psychical development and understanding of themselves and others, and those who, though unable to find or unwilling to entertain a husband, would like to occupy themselves with the rearing of children. My own experience of discussing this question leads me to believe that the one point on which all women are in furious secret rebellion against the existing law is the saddling of the right to a child with the obligation to become the servant of a man. Adoption, or the begging or buying or stealing of another woman's child, is no remedy: it does not provide the supreme experience of bearing the child. No political constitution will ever succeed or deserve to succeed unless it includes the recognition of an absolute right to sexual experience, and is untainted by the Pauline or romantic view of such experience as sinful in itself. And since this experience in its fullest sense must be carried in the case of women to the point of childbearing, it can only be reconciled with the acceptance of marriage with the child's father by legalizing polygyny, because there are more adult women in the country than men. Now though polygyny prevails throughout the greater part of the British Empire, and is as practicable here as in India, there is a good deal to be said against it, and still more to be felt. However, let us put our feelings aside for a moment, and consider the question politically.

MONOGAMY, POLYGYNY, AND POLYANDRY

The number of wives permitted to a single husband or of husbands to a single wife under a marriage system, is not an ethical problem: it depends solely on the proportion of the sexes in the population. If in consequence of a great war three-quarters of the men in this country were killed, it would be absolutely necessary to adopt the Mohammedan allowance of four wives to each man in order to recruit the population. The fundamental reason for not allowing women to risk their lives in battle and for giving them the first chance of escape in all dangerous emergencies: in short, for treating their lives as more valuable than male lives, is not in the least a chivalrous reason, though men may consent to it under the illusion of chivalry. It is a simple matter of necessity; for if a large proportion of women were killed or disabled, no possible readjustment of our marriage law could avert the depopulation and consequent political ruin of the country, because a woman with several husbands bears fewer children than a woman with one, whereas a man can produce as many families as he has wives. The natural foundation of the institution of monogamy is not any inherent viciousness in polygyny or polyandry, but the hard fact that men and women are born in about equal numbers. Unfortunately, we kill so many of our male children in infancy that we are left with a surplus of adult women which is sufficiently large to claim attention, and yet not large enough to enable every man to have two wives. Even if it were, we should be met by an economic difficulty. A Kaffir is rich in proportion to the number of his wives, because the women are the breadwinners. But in our civilization women are not paid for their social work in the bearing and rearing of children and the ordering of households: they are quartered on the wages of their husbands. At least four out of five of our men could not afford two wives unless their wages were nearly doubled. Would it not then be well to try unlimited polygyny; so that the remaining fifth could have as many wives apiece as they could afford? Let us see how this would work.

THE MALE REVOLT AGAINST POLYGYNY

Experience shews that women do not object to polygyny when it is customary: on the contrary, they are its most ardent supporters. The reason is obvious. The question, as it presents itself in practice to a woman, is whether it is better to have, say, a whole share in a tenth-rate man or a tenth share in a first-rate man. Substitute the word Income for the word Man, and you will have the question as it presents itself economically to the dependent woman. The woman whose instincts are maternal, who desires superior children more than anything else, never hesitates. She would take a thousandth share, if necessary, in a husband who was a man in a thousand, rather than have some comparatively weedy weakling all to herself. It is the comparatively weedy weakling, left mateless by polygyny, who objects. Thus, it was not the women of Salt Lake City nor even of America who attacked Mormon polygyny. It was the men. And very naturally. On the other hand, women object to polyandry, because polyandry enables the best women to monopolize all the men, just as polygyny enables the best men to monopolize all the women. That is why all our ordinary men and women are unanimous in defence of monogamy, the men because it excludes polygyny, and the women because it excludes polyandry. The women, left to themselves, would tolerate polygyny. The men, left to themselves, would tolerate polyandry. But polygyny would condemn a great many men, and polyandry a great many women, to the celibacy of neglect. Hence the resistance any attempt to establish unlimited polygyny always provokes, not from the best people, but from the mediocrities and the inferiors. If we could get rid of our inferiors and screw up our average quality until mediocrity ceased to be a reproach, thus making every man reasonably eligible as a father and every woman reasonably desirable as a mother, polygyny and polyandry would immediately fall into sincere disrepute, because monogamy is so much more convenient and economical that nobody would want to share a husband or wife if he (or she) could have a sufficiently good one all to himself (or herself). Thus it appears that it is the scarcity of husbands or wives of high quality that leads women to polygyny and men to polyandry, and that if this scarcity were cured, monogamy, in the sense of having only one husband or wife at a time (facilities for changing are another matter), would be found satisfactory.

DIFFERENCE BETWEEN ORIENTAL AND OCCIDENTAL POLYGYNY

It may now be asked why the polygynist nations have not gravitated to monogamy, like the latter-day saints of Salt Lake City. The answer is not far to seek; their polygyny is limited. By the Mohammedan law a man cannot marry more than four wives; and by the unwritten law of necessity no man can keep more wives than he can afford; so that a man with four wives must be quite as exceptional in Asia as a man with a carriage-and-pair or a motor car is in Europe, where, nevertheless, we may all have as many carriages and motors as we can afford to pay for. Kulin polygyny, though unlimited, is not really a popular institution: if you are a person of high caste you pay another person of very august caste indeed to make your daughter momentarily one of his sixty or seventy momentary wives for the sake of ennobling your grandchildren; but this fashion of a small and intensely snobbish class is negligible as a general precedent. In any case, men and women in the East do not marry anyone they fancy, as in England and America. Women are secluded and marriages are arranged. In Salt Lake City the free unsecluded woman could see and meet the ablest man of the community, and tempt him to make her his tenth wife by all the arts peculiar to women in English-speaking countries. No Eastern woman can do anything of the sort. The man alone has any initiative; but he has no access to the woman; besides, as we have seen, the difficulty created by male licence is not polygyny but polyandry, which is not allowed.

Consequently, if we are to make polygyny a success, we must limit it. If we have two women to every one man, we must allow each man only two wives. That is simple; but unfortunately our own actual proportion is, roughly, something like $1\frac{1}{11}$ women to 1 man. Now you cannot enact that each man shall be allowed $1\frac{1}{11}$ wives, or that each woman who cannot get a husband all to herself shall divide herself between eleven already married husbands. Thus there is no way out for us through polygyny. There is no way at all out of the present system of condemning the superfluous women to barrenness, except by legitimizing the children of women who are not married to the fathers.

THE OLD MAID'S RIGHT TO MOTHERHOOD

Now the right to bear children without taking a husband could not be confined to women who are superfluous in the monogamic reckoning. There is the practical difficulty that although in our population there are about a million monogamically superfluous women, yet it is quite impossible to say of any given unmarried woman that she is one of the superfluous. And there is the difficulty of principle. The right to bear a child, perhaps the most sacred of all women's rights, is not one that should have any conditions attached to it except in the interests of race welfare. There are many women of admirable character, strong, capable, independent, who dislike the domestic habits of men; have no natural turn for mothering and coddling them; and find the concession of conjugal rights to any person under any conditions intolerable by their self-respect. Yet the general sense of the community recognizes in these very women the fittest people to have charge of children, and trusts them, as schoolmistresses and matrons of institutions, more than women of any other type when it is possible to procure them for such work. Why should the taking of a husband be imposed on these women as the price of their right to maternity? I am quite unable to answer that question. I see a good deal of first-rate maternal ability and sagacity spending itself on bees and poultry and village schools and cottage hospitals; and I find myself repeatedly asking myself why this valuable strain in the national breed should be sterilized. Unfortunately, the very women whom we should tempt to become mothers for the good of the race are the very last people to press their services on their country in that way. Plato long ago pointed out the importance of being governed by men with sufficient sense of responsibility and comprehension of public duties to be very reluctant to undertake the work of governing; and yet we have taken his instruction so little to heart that we are at present suffering acutely from government by gentlemen who will stoop to all the mean shifts of electioneering and incur all its heavy expenses for the sake of a seat in Parliament. But what our sentimentalists have not yet been told is that exactly the same thing applies to maternity as to government. The best mothers are not those who are so enslaved by their primitive instincts that they will bear children no matter how hard the conditions are, but precisely those who place a very high price on their services, and are quite prepared to become old maids if the price is refused, and even to feel relieved at their escape. Our democratic and matrimonial institutions may have their merits: at all events they are mostly reforms of something worse; but they put a premium on want of self-respect in certain very important matters; and the consequence is that we are very badly governed and are, on the whole, an ugly, mean, ill-bred race.

IBSEN'S CHAIN STITCH

Let us not forget, however, in our sympathy for the superfluous women, that their children must have fathers as well as mothers. Who are the fathers to be? All monogamists and married women will reply hastily: either bachelors or widowers; and this solution will serve as well as another; for it would be hypocritical to pretend that the difficulty is a practical one. None the less, the monogamists, after due reflection, will point out that if there are widowers enough the superfluous women are not really superfluous, and therefore there is no reason why the parties should not marry respectably like other people. And they might in that case be right if the reasons were purely numerical: that is, if every woman were willing to take a husband if one could be found for her, and every man willing to take a wife on the same terms; also, please remember, if widows would remain celibate to give the unmarried woman a chance. These ifs will not work. We must recognize two classes of old maids: one, the really superfluous women, and the other, the women who refuse to accept maternity on the (to them) unbearable condition of taking a husband. From both classes may, perhaps, be subtracted for the present the large proportion of women who could not afford the extra expense of one or more children. I say "perhaps," because it is by no means sure that within reasonable limits mothers do not make a better fight for subsistence, and have not, on the whole, a better time than single women. In any case, we have two distinct cases to deal with: the superfluous and the voluntary; and it is the voluntary whose grit we are most concerned to fertilize. But here, again, we cannot put our finger on any particular case and pick out Miss Robinson's as superfluous, and Miss Wilkinson's as voluntary. Whether we legitimize the child of the unmarried woman as a duty to the superfluous or as a bribe to the voluntary, the practical result must be the same: to wit, that the condition of marriage now attached to legitimate parentage will be withdrawn from all women, and fertile unions outside marriage recognized by society. Now clearly the consequences would not stop there. The strongminded ladies who are resolved to be mistresses in their own houses would not be the only ones to take advantage of the new law. Even women to whom a home without a man in it would be no home at all, and who fully intended, if the man turned out to be the right one, to live with him exactly as married couples live, would, if they were possessed of independent means, have every inducement to adopt the new conditions instead of the old ones. Only the women whose sole means of livelihood was wifehood would insist on marriage: hence a tendency would set in to make marriage more and more one of the customs imposed by necessity on the poor, whilst the freer form of union, regulated, no doubt, by settlements and private contracts of various kinds, would become the practice of the rich: that is, would become the fashion. At which point nothing but the achievement of economic independence by women, which is already seen clearly ahead of us, would be needed to make marriage disappear altogether, not by formal abolition, but by simple disuse. The private contract stage of this process was reached in ancient Rome. The only practicable alternative to it seems to be such an extension of divorce as will reduce the risks and obligations of marriage to a degree at which they will be no worse than those of the alternatives to marriage. As we shall see, this is the solution to which all the arguments tend. Meanwhile, note how much reason a statesman has to pause before meddling with an institution which, unendurable as its drawbacks are, threatens to come to pieces in all directions if a single thread of it be cut. Ibsen's similitude of the machine-made chain stitch, which unravels the whole seam at the first pull when a single stitch is ripped, is very applicable to the knot of marriage.

REMOTENESS OF THE FACTS FROM THE IDEAL

But before we allow this to deter us from touching the sacred fabric, we must find out whether it is not already coming to pieces in all directions by the continuous strain of circumstances. No doubt, if it were all that it pretends to be, and human nature were working smoothly within its limits, there would be nothing more to be said: it would be let alone as it always is let alone during the cruder stages of civilization. But the moment we refer to the facts, we discover that the ideal matrimony and domesticity which our bigots implore us to preserve as the cornerstone of our society is a figment: what we have really got is something very different, questionable at its best, and abominable at its worst. The word pure, so commonly applied to it by thoughtless people, is absurd; because if they do not mean celibate by it, they mean nothing; and if they do mean celibate, then marriage is legalized impurity, a conclusion which is offensive and inhuman. Marriage as a fact is not in the least like marriage as an ideal. If it were, the sudden changes which have been made on the Continent from indissoluble Roman Catholic marriage to marriage that can be dissolved by a box on the ear as in France, by an epithet as in Germany, or simply at the wish of both parties as in Sweden, not to mention the experiments made by some of the American States, would have shaken society to its foundations. Yet they have produced so little effect that Englishmen open their eyes in surprise when told of their existence.

DIFFICULTY OF OBTAINING EVIDENCE

As to what actual marriage is, one would like evidence

instead of guesses; but as all departures from the ideal
are regarded as disgraceful, evidence cannot be ob-
tained; for when the whole community is indicted,
nobody will go into the witness-box for the prosecu-
tion. Some guesses we can make with some confidence.
For example, if it be objected to any change that our
bachelors and widowers would no longer be Galahads,
we may without extravagance or cynicism reply that
many of them are not Galahads now, and that the
only change would be that hypocrisy would no longer
be compulsory. Indeed, this can hardly be called
guessing: the evidence is in the streets. But when we
attempt to find out the truth about our marriages, we
cannot even guess with any confidence. Speaking for
myself, I can say that I know the inside history of
perhaps half a dozen marriages. Any family solicitor
knows more than this; but even a family solicitor,
however large his practice, knows nothing of the
million households which have no solicitors, and
which nevertheless make marriage what it really is.
And all he can say comes to no more than I can say:
to wit, that no marriage of which I have any knowledge is in the least like the ideal marriage. I do not
mean that it is worse: I mean simply that it is different.
Also, far from society being organized in a defence of
its ideal so jealous and implacable that the least step
from the straight path means exposure and ruin, it is
almost impossible by any extravagance of misconduct
to provoke society to relax its steady pretence of
blindness, unless you do one or both of two fatal
things. One is to get into the newspapers; and the
other is to confess. If you confess misconduct to
respectable men or women, they must either disown
you or become virtually your accomplices: that is why
they are so angry with you for confessing. If you get

into the papers, the pretence of not knowing becomes impossible. But it is hardly too much to say that if you avoid these two perils, you can do anything you like, as far as your neighbors are concerned. And since we can hardly flatter ourselves that this is the effect of charity, it is difficult not to suspect that our extraordinary forbearance in the matter of stone throwing is that suggested in the well-known parable of the woman taken in adultery which some early freethinker slipped into the Gospel of St John: namely, that we all live in glass houses. We may take it, then, that the ideal husband and the ideal wife are no more real human beings than the cherubim. Possibly the great majority keeps its marriage vows in the technical divorce court sense. No husband or wife yet born keeps them or ever can keep them in the ideal sense.

MARRIAGE AS A MAGIC SPELL

The truth which people seem to overlook in this matter is that the marriage ceremony is quite useless as a magic spell for changing in an instant the nature of the relations of two human beings to one another. If a man marries a woman after three weeks acquaintance, and the day after meets a woman he has known for twenty years, he finds, sometimes to his own irrational surprise and his wife's equally irrational indignation, that his wife is a stranger to him, and the other woman an old friend. Also, there is no hocus pocus that can possibly be devized with rings and veils and vows and benedictions that can fix either a man's or woman's affection for twenty minutes, much less twenty years. Even the most affectionate couples must have moments during which they are far more conscious of one another's faults than of one another's attractions. There are couples who dislike one another furiously for several hours at a time; there are couples who dislike one another permanently; and there are couples who never dislike one another; but these last are people who are incapable of disliking anybody. If they do not quarrel, it is not because they are married, but because they are not quarrelsome. The people who are quarrelsome quarrel with their husbands and wives just as easily as with their servants and relatives and acquaintances: marriage makes no difference. Those who talk and write and legislate as if all this could be prevented by making solemn vows that it shall not happen, are either insincere, insane, or hopelessly stupid. There is some sense in a contract to perform or abstain from actions that are reasonably within voluntary control; but such contracts are only needed to provide against the possibility of either party being no longer desirous of the specified performance or abstention. A person proposing or accepting a contract not only to do something but to like doing it would be certified as mad. Yet popular superstition credits the wedding rite with the power of fixing our fancies or affections for life even under the most unnatural conditions.

THE IMPERSONALITY OF SEX

It is necessary to lay some stress on these points, because few realize the extent to which we proceed on the assumption that marriage is a short cut to perfect and permanent intimacy and affection. But there is a still more unworkable assumption which must be discarded before discussions of marriage can get into any sort of touch with the facts of life. That assumption is that the specific relation which marriage author-

izes between the parties is the most intimate and
personal of human relations, and embraces all the
other high human relations. Now this is violently
untrue. Every adult knows that the relation in question can and does exist between entire strangers,
different in language, color, tastes, class, civilization,
morals, religion, character: in everything, in short,
except their bodily homology and the reproductive
appetite common to all living organisms. Even hatred,
cruelty, and contempt are not incompatible with it;
and jealousy and murder are as near to it as affectionate friendship. It is true that it is a relation beset with
wildly extravagant illusions for inexperienced people,
and that even the most experienced people have not
always sufficient analytic faculty to disentangle it from
the sentiments, sympathetic or abhorrent, which may
spring up through the other relations which are
compulsorily attached to it by our laws, or sentiment-
ally associated with it in romance. But the fact
remains that the most disastrous marriages are those
founded exclusively on it, and the most successful
those in which it has been least considered, and in
which the decisive considerations have had nothing to
do with sex, such as liking, money, congeniality of
tastes, similarity of habits, suitability of class, &c.,
&c.

It is no doubt necessary under existing circumstances for a woman without property to be sexually
attractive, because she must get married to secure a
livelihood; and the illusions of sexual attraction will
cause the imagination of young men to endow her
with every accomplishment and virtue that can make
a wife a treasure. The attraction being thus constantly
and ruthlessly used as a bait, both by individuals and
by society, any discussion tending to strip it of its

illusions and get at its real natural history is nervously
discouraged. But nothing can well be more unwholesome for everybody than the exaggeration and glorifi-
cation of an instinctive function which clouds the
reason and upsets the judgement more than all the
other instincts put together. The process may be
pleasant and romantic; but the consequences are not.
It would be far better for everyone, as well as far
honester, if young people were taught that what they
call love is an appetite which, like all other appetites, is
destroyed for the moment by its gratification; that no
profession, promise, or proposal made under its
influence should bind anybody; and that its great
natural purpose transcends the personal interests of
any individual or even of any ten generations of
individuals that it should be held to be an act of
prostitution and even a sort of blasphemy to attempt
to turn it to account by exacting a personal return for
its gratification, whether by process of law or not. By
all means let it be the subject of contracts with society as to its consequences; but to make marriage an
open trade in it as at present, with money, board and
lodging, personal slavery, vows of eternal exclusive
personal sentimentalities and the rest of it as the price,
is neither virtuous, dignified, nor decent. No husband
ever secured his domestic happiness and honor, nor
has any wife ever secured hers, by relying on it. No
private claims of any sort should be founded on it: the
real point of honor is to take no corrupt advantage of
it. When we hear of young women being led astray
and the like, we find that what has led them astray is a
sedulously inculcated false notion that the relation
they tempted to contract is so intensely personal, and
the vows made under the influence of its transient
infatuation so sacred and enduring, that only an

atrociously wicked man could make light of or forget them. What is more, as the same fantastic errors are inculcated in men, and the conscientious ones therefore feel bound in honor to stand by what they have promised, one of the surest methods to obtain a husband is to practise on his susceptibilities until he is either carried away into a promise of marriage to which he can be legally held, or else into an indiscretion which he must repair by marriage on pain of having to regard himself as a scoundrel and a seducer, besides facing the utmost damage the lady's relatives can do him.

Such a transaction is not an entrance into a "holy state of matrimony": it is as often as not the inauguration of a lifelong squabble, a corroding grudge, that causes more misery and degradation of character than a dozen entirely natural "desertions" and "betrayals." Yet the number of marriages effected more or less in this way must be enormous. When people say that love should be free, their words, taken literally, may be foolish; but they are only expressing inaccurately a very real need for the disentanglement of sexual relations from a mass of exorbitant and irrelevant conditions imposed on them on false pretences to enable needy parents to get their daughters "off their hands" and to keep those who are already married effectually enslaved by one another.

THE ECONOMIC SLAVERY OF WOMEN

One of the consequences of basing marriage on the considerations stated with cold abhorrence by Saint Paul in the seventh chapter of his epistle to the Corinthians, as being made necessary by the unlikeness of most men to himself, is that the sex slavery

involved has become complicated by economic
slavery; so that whilst the man defends marriage
because he is really defending his pleasures, the
woman is even more vehement on the same side
because she is defending her only means of livelihood.
To a woman without property or marketable talent a
husband is more necessary than a master to a dog.
There is nothing more wounding to our sense of
human dignity than the husband hunting that begins
in every family when the daughters become marriageable; but it is inevitable under existing circumstances;
and the parents who refuse to engage in it are bad
parents, though they may be superior individuals.
The cubs of a humane tigress would starve; and the
daughters of women who cannot bring themselves to
devote several years of their lives to the pursuit of
sons-in-law often have to expiate their mother's
squeamishness by lifelong celibacy and indigence. To
ask a young man his intentions when you know he has
no intentions, but is unable to deny that he has paid
attentions; to threaten an action for breach of promise
of marriage; to pretend that your daughter is a
musician when she has with the greatest difficulty
been coached into playing three pianoforte pieces
which she loathes; to use your own mature charms to
attract men to the house when your daughters have
no aptitude for that department of sport; to coach
them, when they have, in the arts by which men can
be led to compromize themselves; and to keep all the
skeletons locked up in the family cupboard until the
prey is duly hunted down and bagged; all this is a
mother's duty today; and a very revolting duty it is:
one that disposes of the conventional assumption that
it is in the faithful discharge of her home duties that
a woman finds her self-respect. The truth is that

family life will never be decent, much less ennobling, until this central horror of the dependence of women on men is done away with. At present it reduces the difference between marriage and prostitution to the difference between Trade Unionism and unorganized casual labor: a huge difference, no doubt, as to order and comfort, but not a difference in kind.

However, it is not by any reform of the marriage laws that this can be dealt with. It is in the general movement for the prevention of destitution that the means for making women independent of the compulsory sale of their persons, in marriage or otherwise, will be found; but meanwhile those who deal specifically with the marriage laws should never allow themselves for a moment to forget this abomination that "plucks the rose from the fair forehead of an innocent love, and sets a blister there", and then calmly calls itself, purity, home, motherhood, respectability, honor, decency, and any other fine name that happens to be convenient, not to mention the foul epithets it hurls freely at those who are ashamed of it.

UNPOPULARITY OF IMPERSONAL VIEWS

Unfortunately it is very hard to make an average citizen take impersonal views of any sort in matters affecting personal comfort or conduct. We may be enthusiastic Liberals or Conservatives without any hope of seats in Parliament, knighthoods, or posts in the Government, because party politics do not make the slightest difference in our daily lives and therefore cost us nothing. But to take a vital process in which we are keenly interested personal instruments and ask us to regard it, and feel about it, and legislate on it, wholly as if it were an impersonal one, is to make a

higher demand than most people seem capable of
responding to. We all have personal interests in
marriage which we are not prepared to sink. It is not
only the women who want to get married: the men do
too, sometimes on sentimental grounds, sometimes on
the more sordid calculation that bachelor life is less
comfortable and more expensive, since a wife pays for
her status with domestic service as well as with the
other services expected of her. Now that children are
avoidable, this calculation is becoming more common
and conscious than it was: a result which is regarded
as "a steady improvement in general morality."

IMPERSONALITY IS NOT PROMISCUITY

There is, too, a really appalling prevalence of the
superstition that the sexual instinct in men is utterly
promiscuous and that the least relaxation of law and
custom must produce a wild outbreak of licentiousness. As far as our moralists can grasp the proposition
that we should deal with the sexual relation as impersonal, it seems to them to mean that we should
encourage it to be promiscuous: hence their recoil
from it. But promiscuity and impersonality are not the
same thing. No man ever yet fell in love with the entire
female sex, nor any woman with the entire male sex.
We often do not fall in love at all; and when we do we
fall in love with one person, and remain indifferent to
thousands of others who pass before our eyes every
day. Selection, carried even to such fastidiousness as
to induce people to say quite commonly that there is
only one man or woman in the world for them, is the
rule in nature. If anyone doubts this, let him open a
shop for the sale of picture post-cards, and, when an
enamoured lady customer demands a portrait of her

favorite actor or a gentleman of his favorite actress, try to substitute some other portrait on the ground that since the sexual instinct is promiscuous, one portrait is as pleasing as another. I suppose no shopkeeper has ever been foolish enough to do such a thing; and yet all our shopkeepers, the moment a discussion arises on marriage, will passionately argue against all reform on the ground that nothing but the most severe coercion can save their wives and daughters from quite indiscriminate rapine.

DOMESTIC CHANGE OF AIR

Our relief at the morality of the reassurance that man is not promiscuous in his fancies must not blind us to the fact that he is (to use the word coined by certain American writers to describe themselves) something of a Varietist. Even those who say there is only one man or woman in the world for them, find that it is not always the same man or woman. It happens that our law permits us to study this phenomenon among entirely law-abiding people. I know one lady who has been married five times. She is, as might be expected, a wise, attractive, and interesting woman. The question is, Is she wise, attractive, and interesting because she has been married five times, or has she been married five times because she is wise, attractive, and interesting? Probably some of the truth lies both ways. I also know of a household consisting of three families, A having married first B, and then C, who afterwards married D. All three unions were fruitful; so that the children had a change both of fathers and mothers. Now I cannot honestly say that these and similar cases have convinced me that people are the worse for a change. The lady who has married and managed five husbands must be much more expert at it than most monogamic ladies; and as a companion and counsellor she probably leaves them nowhere. Mr Kipling's question

What can they know of England that only England know?

disposes not only of the patriots who are so patriotic that they never leave their own country to look at another, but of the citizens who are so domestic that they have never married again and never loved anyone except their own husbands and wives. The domestic doctrinaires are also the dull people. The impersonal relation of sex may be judicially reserved for one person; but any such reservation of friendship, affection, admiration, sympathy and so forth is only possible to a wretchedly narrow and jealous nature; and neither history nor contemporary society shews us a single amiable and respectable character capable of it. This has always been recognized in cultivated society: that is why poor people accuse cultivated society of profligacy, poor people being often so ignorant and uncultivated that they have nothing to offer each other but the sex relationship, and cannot conceive why men and women should associate for any other purpose.

As to the children of the triple household, they were not only on excellent terms with one another, and never thought of any distinction between their full and their half brothers and sisters; but they had the superior sociability which distinguishes people who live in communities from those who live in small families.

The inference is that changes of partners are not in themselves injurious or undesirable. People are not demoralized by them when they are effected according to law. Therefore we need not hesitate to alter the law merely because the alteration would make such changes easier.

HOME MANNERS ARE BAD MANNERS

On the other hand, we have all seen the bonds of marriage vilely abused by people who are never classed with shrews and wife-beaters: they are indeed sometimes held up as models of domesticity because they do not drink nor gamble nor neglect their children nor tolerate dirt and untidiness, and because they are not amiable enough to have what are called amiable weaknesses. These terrors conceive marriage as a dispensation from all the common civilities and delicacies which they have to observe among strangers, or, as they put it, "before company." And here the effects of indissoluble marriage-for-better-for-worse are very plainly and disagreeably seen. If such people took their domestic manners into general society, they would very soon find themselves without a friend or even an acquaintance in the world. There are women who, through total disuse, have lost the power of kindly human speech and can only scold and complain: there are men who grumble and nag from inveterate habit even when they are comfortable. But their unfortunate spouses and children cannot escape from them.

SPURIOUS "NATURAL" AFFECTION

What is more, they are protected from even such discomfort as the dislike of his prisoners may cause to a gaoler by the hypnotism of the convention that the natural relation between husband and wife and parent and child is one of intense affection, and that to feel any other sentiment towards a member of one's family is to be a monster. Under the influence of the emotion thus manufactured the most detestable people are spoilt with entirely undeserved deference, obedience, and even affection whilst they live, and mourned when they die by those whose lives they wantonly or maliciously made miserable. And this is what we call natural conduct. Nothing could well be less natural. That such a convention should have been established shews that the indissolubility of marriage creates such intolerable situations that only by beglamoring the human imagination with a hypnotic suggestion of wholly unnatural feelings can it be made to keep up appearances.

If the sentimental theory of family relationship encourages bad manners and personal slovenliness and uncleanness in the home, it also, in the case of sentimental people, encourages the practice of rousing and playing on the affections of children prematurely and far too frequently. The lady who says that as her religion is love, her children shall be brought up in an atmosphere of love, and institutes a system of sedulous endearments and exchanges of presents and conscious and studied acts of artificial kindness, may be defeated in a large family by the healthy derision and rebellion of children who have acquired hardihood and common sense in their conflicts with one another. But the small families, which are the rule just now, succumb more easily; and in the case of a single sensitive child the effect of being forced in a hothouse atmosphere of unnatural affection may be disastrous.

In short, whichever way you take it, the convention that marriage and family relationship produce special feelings which alter the nature of human intercourse is a mischievous one. The whole difficulty of bringing up a family well is the difficulty of making its members behave as considerately at home as on a visit in a strange house, and as frankly, kindly, and easily in a strange house as at home. In the middle classes, where the segregation of the artificially limited family in its little brick box is horribly complete, bad manners, ugly dresses, awkwardness, cowardice, peevishness, and all the petty vices of unsociability flourish like mushrooms in a cellar. In the upper class, where families are not limited for money reasons; where at least two houses and sometimes three or four are the rule (not to mention the clubs); where there is travelling and hotel life; and where the men are brought up, not in the family, but in public schools, universities, and the naval and military services, besides being constantly in social training in other people's houses, the result is to produce a set that, in comparison with the middle class, counts as a different and much more sociable species. And in the very poorest class, where people have no homes, only sleeping places crowded with lodgers, and consequently live practically in the streets, sociability again appears, leaving the middle class despised and disliked for its helpless and offensive unsociability as much by those below it as those above it, and yet ignorant enough to be proud of it, and to hold itself up as a model for the reform of the (as it considers) elegantly vicious rich and profligate poor alike.

CARRYING THE WAR INTO THE ENEMY'S COUNTRY

Without pretending to exhaust the subject, I have said enough to make it clear that the moment we lose the desire to defend our present matrimonial and family arrangements, there will be no difficulty in making out an overwhelming case against them. No doubt until then we shall continue to hold up the British home as the Holy of Holies in the temple of honorable motherhood, innocent childhood, manly virtue, and sweet and wholesome national life. But with a clever turn of the hand this holy of holies can be exposed as an Augean stable, so filthy that it would seem more hopeful to burn it down than to attempt to sweep it out. And this latter view will perhaps prevail if the idolaters of marriage persist in refusing all proposals for reform and treating those who advocate it as infamous delinquents. Neither view is of any use except as a poisoned arrow in a fierce fight between two parties determined to discredit each other with a view to obtaining powers of legal coercion over one another.

SHELLEY AND QUEEN VICTORIA

The best way to avert such a struggle is to open the eyes of the thoughtlessly conventional people to the weakness of their position in a mere contest of recrimination. Hitherto they have assumed that they have the advantage of coming into the field without a stain on their characters to combat libertines who have no character at all. They conceive it to be their duty to throw mud; and they feel that even if the enemy can find any mud to throw, none of it will stick. They are mistaken. There will be plenty of that sort of ammunition in the other camp; and most of it will stick very hard indeed. The moral is, do not throw any. If we can imagine Shelley and Queen Victoria arguing out their differences in another world, we may be sure that the

Queen has long ago found out that she cannot settle the question by classing Shelley with George IV as a bad man; and Shelley is not likely to have called her vile names on the general ground that as the economic dependence of women makes marriage a money bargain in which the man is the purchaser and the woman the purchased, there is no essential difference between a married woman and the woman of the streets. Unfortunately, all the people whose methods of controversy are represented by our popular newspapers are not Queen Victorias and Shelleys. A great mass of them, when their prejudices are challenged, have no other impulse than to call the challenger names, and, when the crowd seems to be on their side, to maltreat him personally or hand him over to the law, if he is vulnerable to it. Therefore I cannot say that I have any certainty that the marriage question will be dealt with decently and tolerantly. But dealt with it will be, decently or indecently; for the present state of things in England is too strained and mischievous to last. Europe and America have left us a century behind in this matter.

A PROBABLE EFFECT OF GIVING WOMEN THE VOTE

The political emancipation of women is likely to lead to a comparatively stringent enforcement by law of sexual morality (that is why so many of us dread it); and this will soon compel us to consider what our sexual morality shall be. At present a ridiculous distinction is made between vice and crime, in order that men may be vicious with impunity. Adultery, for instance, though it is sometimes fiercely punished by giving an injured husband crushing damages in a divorce suit (injured wives are not considered in this way), is not now directly prosecuted; and this impunity extends to illicit relations between unmarried persons who have reached what is called the age of consent. There are other matters, such as notification of contagious disease and solicitation, in which the hand of the law has been brought down on one sex only. Outrages which were capital offences within the memory of persons still living when committed on women outside marriage, can still be inflicted by men on their wives without legal remedy. At all such points the code will be screwed up by the operation of Votes for Women, if there be any virtue in the franchise at all. The result will be that men will find the more ascetic side of our sexual morality taken seriously by the law. It is easy to foresee the consequences. No man will take much trouble to alter laws which he can evade, or which are either not enforced or enforced on women only. But when these laws take him by the collar and thrust him into prison, he suddenly becomes keenly critical of them, and of the arguments by which they are supported. Now we have seen that our marriage laws will not stand criticism, and that they have held out so far only because they are so worked as to fit roughly our state of society, in which women are neither politically nor personally free, in which indeed women are called womanly only when they regard themselves as existing solely for the use of men. When Liberalism enfranchises them politically, and Socialism emancipates them economically, they will no longer allow the law to take immorality so easily. Both men and women will be forced to behave morally in sex matters; and when they find that this is inevitable they will raise the question of what behavior really should be established as moral. If they decide in favor of our present professed morality, they will have to make a revolutionary change in their habits by becoming in fact what they only pretend to be at present. If, on the other hand, they find that this would be an unbearable tyranny, without even the excuse of justice or sound eugenics, they will reconsider their morality and remodel the law.

THE PERSONAL SENTIMENTAL BASIS OF MONOGAMY

Monogamy has a sentimental basis which is quite distinct from the political one of equal numbers of the sexes. Equal numbers in the sexes are quite compatible with a change of partners every day or every hour. Physically there is nothing to distinguish human society from the farm-yard except that children are more troublesome and costly than chickens and calves, and that men and women are not so completely enslaved as farm stock. Accordingly, the people whose conception of marriage is a farmyard or slave-quarter conception are always more or less in a panic lest the slightest relaxation of the marriage laws should utterly demoralize society; whilst those to whom marriage is a matter of more highly evolved sentiments and needs (sometimes said to be distinctively human, though birds and animals in a state of freedom evince them quite as touchingly as we) are much more liberal, knowing as they do that monogamy will take care of itself provided the parties are free enough, and that promiscuity is a product of slavery and not of liberty.

The solid foundation of their confidence is the fact that the relationship set up by a comfortable marriage is so intimate and so pervasive of the whole life of the parties to it, that nobody has room in his or her life for more than one such relationship at a time. What is called a household of three is never really of three except in the sense that every household becomes a household of three when a child is born, and may in the same way become a household of four or fourteen if the union be fertile enough. Now no doubt the marriage tie means so little to some people that the addition to the household of half a dozen more wives or husbands would be as possible as the addition of half a dozen governesses or tutors or visitors or servants. A Sultan may have fifty wives as easily as he may have fifty dishes on his table, because in the English sense he has no wives at all; nor have his wives any husband: in short, he is not what we call a married man. And there are sultans and sultanas and seraglios existing in England under English forms. But when you come to the real modern marriage of sentiment, a relation is created which has never to my knowledge been shared by three persons except when all three have been extraordinarily fond of one another. Take for example the famous case of Nelson and Sir William and Lady Hamilton. The secret of this household of three was not only that both the husband and Nelson were devoted to Lady Hamilton, but that they were also apparently devoted to one another. When Hamilton died both Nelson and Emma seem to have been equally heartbroken. When there is a successful household of one man and two women the same unusual condition is fulfilled: the two women not only cannot live happily without the man but cannot live happily without each other. In every other case known to me, either from observation or record, the experiment is a hopeless failure: one of the two rivals for the really intimate affection of the third inevitably drives out the other. The driven-out party may accept the situation and remain in the house as a friend to save appearances, or for the sake of the children, or for economic reasons; but such an arrangement can subsist only when the forfeited relation is no longer really valued; and this indifference, like the triple bond of affection which carried Sir William Hamilton through, is so rare as to be practicably negligible in the establishment of a conventional morality of marriage. Therefore sensible and experienced people always assume that when a declaration of love is made to an already married person, the declaration binds the parties in honor never to see one another again unless they contemplate divorce and remarriage. And this is a sound convention, even for unconventional people. Let me illustrate by reference to a fictitious case: the one imagined in my own play Candida will do as well as another. Here a young man who had been received as a friend into the house of a clergyman falls in love with the clergyman's wife, and, being young and inexperienced, declares his feelings, and claims that he, and not the clergyman, is the more suitable mate for the lady. The clergyman, who has a temper, is first tempted to hurl the youth into the street by bodily violence: an impulse natural, perhaps, but vulgar and improper, and not open, on consideration, to decent men. Even coarse and inconsiderate men are restrained from it by the fact that the sympathy of the woman turns naturally to the victim of physical brutality and against the bully, the Thackerayan notion to the contrary being one of the illusions of literary masculinity. Besides, the husband is not necessarily the stronger man: and appeal to force has resulted in the ignominious defeat of the husband quite as often in poetic justice as conceived in the conventional novelet. What an

honorable and sensible man does when his household
is invaded is what the Reverend James Mavor Morell
does in my play. He recognizes that just as there is not
room for two women in that sacredly intimate
relation of sentimental domesticity which is what
marriage means to him, so there is no room for two
men in that relation with his wife; and he accordingly
tells her firmly that she must choose which man will
occupy the place that is large enough for one only.
He is so far shrewdly unconventional as to recognize
that if she chooses the other man, he must give way,
legal tie or no legal tie; but he knows that either one or
the other must go. And a sensible wife would act in
the same way. If a romantic young lady came into
her house and proposed to adore her husband on a
tolerated footing, she would say "My husband has
not room in his life for two wives: either you go out of
the house or I go out of it." The situation is not at all
unlikely: I had almost said not at all unusual. Young
ladies and gentlemen in the greensickly condition
which is called calf-love, associating with married
couples at dangerous periods of mature life, quite
often find themselves in it; and the extreme reluctance
of proud and sensitive people to make any assertion
of matrimonial rights, or to condescend to jealousy,
sometimes make the threatened husband or wife
hesitate to take prompt steps and do the apparently
conventional thing. But whether they hesitate or act
the result is always the same. In a real marriage of
sentiment the wife or husband cannot be supplanted
by halves; and such a marriage will break very soon
under the strain of polygyny or polyandry. What we
want at present is a sufficiently clear teaching of this
fact to ensure that prompt and decisive action shall
always be taken in such cases without any false shame

of seeming conventional (a shame to which people capable of such real marriage are specially susceptible), and a rational divorce law to enable the marriage to be dissolved and the parties honorably resorted and recoupled without disgrace and scandal if that should prove the proper solution.

It must be repeated here that no law, however stringent, can prevent polygamy among groups of people who choose to live loosely and be monogamous only in appearance. But such cases are not now under consideration. Also, affectionate husbands like Samuel Pepys, and affectionate wives of the corresponding temperament, may, it appears, engage in transient casual adventures out of doors without breaking up their home life. But within doors that home life may be regarded as naturally monogamous. It does not need to be protected against polygamy; it protects itself.

DIVORCE

All this has an important bearing on the question of divorce. Divorce reformers are so much preoccupied with the injustice of forbidding a woman to divorce her husband for unfaithfulness to his marriage vow, whilst allowing him that power over her, that they are apt to overlook the pressing need for admitting other and far more important grounds for divorce. If we take a document like Pepys' Diary, we learn that a woman may have an incorrigibly unfaithful husband, and yet be much better off than if she had an ill-tempered, peevish, maliciously sarcastic one, or was chained for life to a criminal, a drunkard, a lunatic, an idle vagrant, or a person whose religious faith was contrary to her own. Imagine being married to a liar,

a borrower, a mischief maker, a teaser or tormentor of
children and animals, or even simply to a bore!
Conceive yourself tied for life to one of the perfectly
"faithful" husbands who are sentenced to a month's
imprisonment occasionally for idly leaving their
wives in childbirth without food, fire, or attendance?
What woman would not rather marry ten Pepyses?
what man a dozen Nell Gwynnes? Adultery, far from
being the first and only ground for divorce, might
more reasonably be made the last, or wholly excluded.
The present law is perfectly logical only if you once
admit (as no decent person ever does) its fundamental
assumption that there can be no companionship
between men and women because the woman has a
"sphere" of her own, that of housekeeping, in which
the man must not meddle, whilst he has all the rest of
human activity for his sphere: the only point at which
the two spheres touch being that of replenishing the
population. On this assumption the man naturally
asks for a guarantee that the children shall be his
because he has to find the money to support them.
The power of divorcing a woman for adultery is this
guarantee, a guarantee that she does not need to
protect her against a similar imposture on his part,
because he cannot bear children. No doubt he can
spend the money that ought to be spent on her children on another woman and her children; but this is
desertion, which is a separate matter. The fact for us
to seize is that in the eye of the law, adultery without
consequences is merely a sentimental grievance,
whereas the planting on one man of another man's
offspring is a substantial one. And so, no doubt, it is;
but the day has gone by for basing laws on the assumption that a woman is less to a man than his dog, and
thereby encouraging and accepting the standards of

the husbands who buy meat for their bull-pups and leave their wives and children hungry. That basis is the penalty we pay for having borrowed our religion from the East, instead of building up a religion of our own out of our western inspiration and western sentiment. The result is that we all believe that our religion is on its last legs, whereas the truth is that it is not yet born, though the age walks visibly pregnant with it. Meanwhile, as women are dragged down by their oriental servitude to our men, and as, further, women drag down those who degrade them quite as effectually as men do, there are moments when it is difficult to see anything in our sex institutions except a *police des mœurs* keeping the field for a competition as to which sex shall corrupt the other most.

IMPORTANCE OF SENTIMENTAL GRIEVANCES

Any tolerable western divorce law must put the sentimental grievances first, and should carefully avoid singling out any ground of divorce in such a way as to create a convention that persons having that ground are bound in honor to avail themselves of it. It is generally admitted that people should not be encouraged to petition for a divorce in a fit of petulance. What is not so clearly seen is that neither should they be encouraged to petition in a fit of jealousy, which is certainly the most detestable and mischievous of all the passions that enjoy public credit. Still less should people who are not jealous be urged to behave as if they were jealous, and to enter upon duels and divorce suits in which they have no desire to be successful. There should be no publication of the grounds on which a divorce is sought or granted; and as this would abolish the only means the public now has of ascertaining that every possible effort has been made to keep the couple united against their wills, such privacy will only be tolerated when we at last admit that the sole and sufficient reason why people should be granted a divorce is that they want one. Then there will be no more reports of divorce cases, no more letters read in court with an indelicacy that makes every sensitive person shudder and recoil as from a profanation, no more washing of household linen, dirty or clean, in public. We must learn in these matters to mind our own business and not impose our individual notions of propriety on one another, even if it carries us to the length of openly admitting what we are now compelled to assume silently, that every human being has a right to sexual experience, and that the law is concerned only with parentage, which is now a separate matter.

DIVORCE WITHOUT ASKING WHY

The one question that should never be put to a petitioner for divorce is "Why?" When a man appeals to a magistrate for protection from someone who threatens to kill him, on the simple ground that he desires to live, the magistrate might quite reasonably ask him why he desires to live, and why the person who wishes to kill him should not be gratified. Also whether he can prove that his life is a pleasure to himself or a benefit to anyone else, and whether it is good for him to be encouraged to exaggerate the importance of his short span in this vale of tears rather than to keep himself constantly ready to meet his God.

The only reason for not raising these very weighty points is that we find society unworkable except on the assumption that every man has a natural right to live.

Nothing short of his own refusal to respect that right in others can reconcile the community to killing him. From this fundamental right many others are derived. The American Constitution, one of the few modern political documents drawn up by men who were forced by the sternest circumstances to think out what they really had to face instead of chopping logic in a university class-room, specifies "liberty and the pursuit of happiness" as natural rights. The terms are too vague to be of much practical use; for the supreme right to life, extended as it now must be to the life of the race, and to the quality of life as well as to the mere fact of breathing, is making short work of many ancient liberties, and exposing the pursuit of happiness as perhaps the most miserable of human occupations. Nevertheless, the American Constitution roughly expresses the conditions to which modern democracy commits us. To impose marriage on two unmarried people who do not desire to marry one another would be admittedly an act of enslavement. But it is no worse than to impose a continuation of marriage on people who have ceased to desire to be married. It will be said that the parties may not agree on that; that one may desire to maintain the marriage the other wishes to dissolve. But the same hardship arises whenever a man in love proposes marriage to a woman and is refused. The refusal is so painful to him that he often threatens to kill himself and sometimes even does it. Yet we expect him to face his ill luck, and never dream of forcing the woman to accept him. His case is the same as that of the husband whose wife tells him she no longer cares for him, and desires the marriage to be dissolved. You will say, perhaps, if you are superstitious, that it is not the same—that marriage makes a difference. You are wrong: there is no magic in marriage. If there were, married couples would never desire to separate. But they do. And when they do, it is simple slavery to compel them to remain together.

ECONOMIC SLAVERY AGAIN THE ROOT DIFFICULTY

The husband, then, is to be allowed to discard his wife when he is tired of her, and the wife the husband when another man strikes her fancy? One must reply unhesitatingly in the affirmative; for if we are to deny every proposition that can be stated in offensive terms by its opponents, we shall never be able to affirm any-thing at all. But the question reminds us that until the economic independence of women is achieved, we shall have to remain impaled on the other horn of the dilemma and maintain marriage as a slavery. And here let me ask the Government of the day (1910) a question with regard to the Labor Exchanges it has very wisely established throughout the country. What do these Exchanges do when a woman enters and states that her occupation is that of a wife and mother; that she is out of a job; and that she wants an em-ployer? If the Exchange refuse to entertain her application, they are clearly excluding nearly the whole female sex from the benefit of the Act. If not, they must become matrimonial agencies, unless, in-deed, they are prepared to become something worse by putting the woman down as a housekeeper and introducing her to an employer without making marriage a condition of the hiring.

LABOR EXCHANGES AND THE WHITE SLAVERY

Suppose, again, a woman presents herself at the Labor Exchange, and states her trade as that of a White

Slave, meaning the unmentionable trade pursued by thousands of women in all civilized cities. Will the Labor Exchange find employers for her? If not, what will it do with her? If it throws her back destitute and unhelped on the streets to starve, it might as well not exist as far as she is concerned; and the problem of unemployment remains unsolved at its most painful point. Yet if it finds honest employment for her and for all the unemployed wives and mothers, it must find new places in the world for women; and in so doing it must achieve for them economic independence of men. And when this is done, can we feel sure that any woman will consent to be a wife and mother (not to mention the less respectable alternative) unless her position is made as eligible as that of the women for whom the Labor Exchanges are finding independent work? Will not many women now engaged in domestic work under circumstances which make it repugnant to them, abandon it and seek employment under other circumstances? As unhappiness in marriage is almost the only discomfort sufficiently irksome to induce a woman to break up her home, and economic dependence the only compulsion sufficiently stringent to force her to endure such unhappiness, the solution of the problem of finding independent employment for women may cause a great number of childless unhappy marriages to break up spontaneously, whether the marriage laws are altered or not. And here we must extend the term childless marriages to cover households in which the children have grown up and gone their own way, leaving the parents alone together: a point at which many worthy couples discover for the first time that they have long since lost interest in one another, and have been united only by a common interest in their children. We may expect, then, that marriages which are maintained by economic pressure alone will dissolve when that pressure is removed; and as all the parties to them will certainly not accept a celibate life, the law must sanction the dissolution in order to prevent a recurrence of the scandal which has moved the Government to appoint the Commission now sitting to investigate the marriage question: the scandal, that is, of a great number of persons, condemned to celibacy by magisterial separation orders, and, of course, refusing to submit to the condemnation, forming illicit connections to an extent which threatens to familiarize the working classes with an open disuse of marriage. In short, once set women free from their economic slavery, and you will find that unless divorce is made as easy as the dissolution of a business partnership, the practice of dispensing with marriage will presently become so common that conventional couples will be ashamed to get married.

DIVORCE FAVORABLE TO MARRIAGE

Divorce, in fact, is not the destruction of marriage, but the first condition of its maintenance. A thousand indissoluble marriages mean a thousand marriages and no more. A thousand divorces may mean two thousand marriages; for the couples may marry again. Divorce only re-assorts the couples: a very desirable thing when they are ill-assorted. Also, it makes people much more willing to marry, especially prudent people and proud people with a high sense of self-respect. Further, the fact that a divorce is possible often prevents its being petitioned for, not only because it puts married couples on their good behavior towards one another, but because, as no room feels like a prison if the door is left open, the removal of the sense of bondage would at once make marriage much happier than it is now. Also, if the door were always open, there would be no need to rush through it as there is now when it opens for one moment in a lifetime, and may never open again.

From this point of view England has the worst civil marriage law in the world, with the exception of silly South Carolina. In every other reasonably civilized country the grounds on which divorce can be granted admit of so wide an interpretation that all unhappy marriages can be dissolved without resorting to the shameful shifts imposed by our law. Yet the figures just given to the Royal Commission shew that in the State of Washington, where there are eleven different grounds of divorce, and where, in fact, divorce can be had for the asking at a negligible cost, the divorce rate is only 184 per 100,000 of the population, which, if we assume that the 100,000 people represent 20,000 families, means less than one per cent of domestic failures. In Japan the rate is 215, which is said to be the highest on record. This is not very alarming: what is quite hideous is that the rate in England is only 2, a figure which, if we assume that human nature is much the same in Walworth as in Washington, must represent a frightful quantity of useless unhappiness and clandestine polygamy. I am not forgetting my own demonstration that the rate is kept down in Washington by the economic slavery of women; but I must point out that this is at its worst in the middle classes only, because a woman of the working class can turn to and support herself, however poorly; and a woman of the upper classes usually has some property. And in all classes we may guess that the object of many divorces is not the resumption of a single life, but a change of partners. As this change can be effected easily under the existing law in the State of Washington it is not certain that the economic emancipation of women would alter the rate there to any startling extent. What is certain is that it could not conceivably raise it to a figure at which even the most panicky alarmist could persuade sensible people that the whole social fabric was tumbling to pieces. When journalists and bishops and American Presidents and other simple people describe this Washington result as alarming, they are speaking as a peasant speaks of a motor car or an aeroplane when he sees one for the first time. All he means is that he is not used to it and therefore fears that it may injure him. Every advance in civilization frightens these honest folk. This is a pity; but if we were to spare their feelings we should never improve the world at all. To let them frighten us, and then pretend that their stupid timidity is virtue and purity and so forth, is simply moral cowardice.

MALE ECONOMIC SLAVERY AND THE RIGHTS OF BACHELORS

It must not be forgotten that the refusal to accept the indignities, risks, hardships, softships, and divided duties of marriage is not confined to our voluntary old maids. There are men of the mould of Beethoven and Samuel Butler, whom one can hardly conceive as married men. There are the great ecclesiastics, who will not own two loyalties: one to the Church and one to the hearth. There are men like Goethe, who marry late and reluctantly solely because they feel that they cannot in honest friendship refuse the status of marriage to any woman of whose attachment to them they have taken any compromizing advantage, either in fact or in appearance. No sensible man can, under existing circumstances, advise a woman to keep house with a man without insisting on his marrying her, unless she is independent of conventional society (a state of things which can occur only very exceptionally); and a man of honor cannot advise a woman to do for his sake what he would not advise her to do for anyone else's. The result is that our Beethovens and Butlers—of whom, in their ordinary human aspect, there are a good many—become barren old bachelors, and rather savage ones at that.

Another difficulty which we always think of in connection with women, but which is by no means without its application to men, is the economic one. The number of men who cannot afford to marry is large enough to produce very serious social results; and the higher the work the man is doing, the more likely he is to find himself in this class until he has reached or passed middle age. The higher departments of science, law, philosophy, poetry, and the fine arts are notoriously starved in youth and early manhood: the marriageable age there, economically speaking, is nearer fifty than twenty. Even in business the leading spirits seldom reach a position of security until they are far beyond the age at which celibacy is tolerable. Account must also be taken of the younger sons of the propertied classes, brought up in households in which the rate of expenditure, though ten times that possible on a younger son's portion, yet represents the only habit of life he has learnt.

Taking all these cases as representing a bachelor class, and bearing in mind that though a man who marries at forty is not called a bachelor, yet he has for twenty years of his adult life been one, and therefore produced all the social problems that arise out of the existence of unmarried men, we must not shrink from asking whether all these gentlemen are celibates, even though we know that the question must be answered very emphatically in the negative. Some of them marry women of property, thereby reproducing the economic dependence of women on men with the sexes reversed. But there are so few women of property available for this purpose in comparison with the number of bachelors who cannot afford to marry, that this resource does not solve the problem of the bachelor who cannot afford a wife. If there were no other resources available, bachelors would make love to the wives and daughters of their friends. This being morally inadmissible, a demand arises for a cheap temporary substitute for marriage. A class of women must be found to protect the wives and daughters of the married by keeping company with the bachelors for hire for as long or as short a time as the bachelor can afford, on the understanding that no claim is to be made on him after the hiring is ended. And such an institution, as we know, exists among us. It is commonly spoken of and thought of as an offence against our marriage morality; but all the experts who write scientific treatises on marriage seem to be agreed that it is, on the contrary, a necessary part of that morality, and must stand and fall with it.

I do not myself think that this view will bear examination. In my play, Mrs Warren's Profession, I have shewn that the institution in question is an economic phenomenon, produced by our underpayment and ill-treatment of women who try to earn an honest living. I am aware that for some reason scientific writers are perversely impatient of this view, and, to discredit it, quote police lists of the reasons given by the victims for adopting their trade, and insist on the fact that poverty is not often alleged. But this means only that the actual word is seldom used. If a prisonful of thieves were asked what induced them to take to thieving, and some replied Poverty, and others Hunger, and others Desire for Excitement, no one would deny that the three answers were really one answer—that poverty means hunger, an intolerable lack of variety and pleasure, and, in short, all sorts of privations. When a girl, similarly interrogated, says she wanted fine clothes, or more fun, or the like, she is really saying that she lacked what no woman with plenty of money need lack. The fact that, according to the testimony of men who profess experience in such matters, you may search Europe in vain for a woman in this trade who has the table manners of a lady, shews that prostitution is not a vocation but a slavery to which women are driven by the miseries of honest poverty. When every young woman has an honorable and comfortable livelihood open to her on reasonable terms, the streets will make no more recruits. When every young man can afford to marry, and marriage reform makes it easy to dissolve unions contracted by young and inexperienced people in the event of their turning out badly, or of one of the pair achieving a position neither comfortable nor suitable for the other, both prostitution and bachelordom will die a natural death. Until then, all talk of "purification" is idle. It is for that reason that I lay little stress on prostitution here, and refer readers who are curious about the psychopathy of bachelordom and spinsterhood to the monumental work of my friend Havelock Ellis.

THE PATHOLOGY OF MARRIAGE

I shall also say as little as possible of the pathology of marriage and its kerbstone breakwater. Only, as there seems to be no bottom to the abyss of public ignorance on the subject, I am compelled to warn my readers that marriage has a pathology and even a criminology. But they are both so frightful that they have been dealt with not only in such treatises as those of Havelock Ellis, Fournier, Duclaux, and many German writers, but in such comparatively popular works as The Heavenly Twins by Sarah Grand, and several of the plays of Brieux: notably Les Avariés, Les Trois Filles de M. Dupont, and Maternité. I purposely pass them by quickly, not only because attention has already been called to them by these devoted writers, but because my mission is not to deal with obvious horrors, but to open the eyes of normal respectable men to evils which are escaping their consideration.

As to the evils of disease and contagion, our consciences are sound enough: what is wrong with us is ignorance of the facts. No doubt this is a very formidable ignorance in a country where the first cry of the soul is "Dont tell me: I dont want to know," and where frantic denials and furious suppressions indicate everywhere the cowardice and want of faith which conceives life as something too terrible to be faced. In this particular case "I dont want to know" takes a righteous air, and becomes "I dont want to know anything about the diseases which are the just punishment of wretches who should not be mentioned in my presence or in any book that is intended for family reading." Wicked and foolish as the spirit of this attitude is, the practice of it is so easy and lazy and uppish that it is very common. But its cry is drowned by a louder and more sincere one. We who do not want to know also do not want to go blind, to go mad, to be disfigured, to be barren, to become pestiferous, or to see such things happening to our children. We learn, at last, that the majority of the victims are not the people of whom we so glibly say "Serve them right," but quite innocent children and innocent parents, smitten by a contagion which, no matter in what vice it may or may not have originated, contaminates the innocent and guilty alike once it is launched exactly as any other contagious disease does; that indeed it often hits the innocent and misses the guilty because the guilty know the danger and take elaborate precautions against it, whilst the innocent, who have been either carefully kept from any knowledge of their danger, or erroneously led to believe that contagion is possible through misconduct only, run into danger blindfold. Once knock this fact into people's minds, and their self-righteous indifference and intolerance soon change into lively concern for themselves and their families.

THE CRIMINOLOGY OF MARRIAGE

The pathology of marriage involves the possibility of the most horrible crime imaginable: that of the person who, when suffering from contagious disease, forces the contagion on another person by an act of violence. Such an act occurring between unmarried people would, within the memory of persons now living, have exposed the aggressor to the penalty of death; and it is still punished unmercifully by an extreme term of penal servitude when it occurs, as it sometimes does, through the hideous countryside superstition that it effects a cure when the victim is a virgin. Marriage makes this outrage absolutely legal. You may with impunity do to the person to whom you are married what you may not do to the most despised outcast of the streets. And this is only the extreme instance of the outlawry which our marriage laws effect. In our anxiety to provide for ourselves a little private Alsatia in which we can indulge ourselves as we please without reproach or interference from law, religion, or even conscience (and this is what marriage has come to mean to many of us), we have forgotten that we cannot escape restraints without foregoing rights; that all the laws that are needed to compel strangers to respect us are equally if not more necessary to compel our husbands and wives to respect us; and that society without law, whether between two or two million persons, means tyranny and slavery.

If the incorrigible sentimentalists here raise their little pipe of "Not if they love one another," I tell them, with such patience as is possible, that if they had ever had five minutes experience of love they would know that love is itself a tyranny requiring special safeguards; that people will perpetrate "for the sake of" those they love, exactions and submissions that they would never dream of proposing to or suffering from those they dislike or regard with indifference; that healthy marriages are partnerships of companionable and affectionate friendship; that cases of chronic lifelong love, whether sentimental or sensual, ought to be sent to the doctor if not to the executioner; and that honorable men and women, when their circumstances permit it, are so far from desiring to be placed helplessly at one another's mercy that they employ every device the law now admits of, from the most stringent marriage settlements to the employment of separate legal advisers, to neutralize the Alsatian evils of the marriage law.

DOES IT MATTER?

A less obviously silly evasion, and one which has a greater air of common sense, is "After all, seeing that most couples get on very well together, does it matter so much?" The same reply might be made by a lazy magistrate when asked for a warrant to arrest a burglar, or by a sleepy fireman wakened by a midnight call for his fire-escape. "After all, very few people have their houses broken into; and fewer still have them burnt. Does it matter?" But tell the magistrate that it is *his* house that has been broken into, or *his* house that has been burnt; and you will be startled by the change in his attitude. Because a mass of people have shaken down into comfort enough to satisfy them, or at least to cause them no more discomfort than they are prepared to put up with for the sake of a quiet life, less lucky and more sensitive and conscientious people should not be condemned to expose themselves to intolerable wrongs. Besides, people ought not to be content with the marriage law as it is merely because it is not often unbearably uncomfortable. Slaves are very often much more comfortable both in body and mind than fully responsible free men. That does not excuse anybody for embracing slavery. It is no doubt a great pity, from many points of view, that we were not conquered by Napoleon, or even by Bismarck and Moltke. None the less we should have been rightly despised if we had not been prepared to fight them for the right to misgovern ourselves.

But, as I have said, I am content, in this matter of the evils of our marriage law, to take care of the pence and let the pounds take care of themselves. The crimes and diseases of marriage will force themselves on public attention by their own virulence. I mention them here only because they reveal certain habits of thought and feeling with regard to marriage of which we must rid ourselves if we are to act sensibly when we take the necessary reforms in hand.

CHRISTIAN MARRIAGE

First among these is the habit of allowing ourselves to be bound not only by the truths of the Christian religion but by the excesses and extravagances which the Christian movement acquired in its earlier days as a violent reaction against what it still calls paganism. By far the most dangerous of these, because it is a blasphemy against life, and, to put it in Christian terms, an accusation of indecency against God, is the notion that sex, with all its operations, is in itself absolutely an obscene thing, and that an immaculate conception is a miracle. So unwholesome an absurdity could only have gained ground under two conditions: one, a reaction against a society in which sensual luxury had been carried to revolting extremes, and, two, a belief that the world was coming to an end, and that therefore sex was no longer a necessity. Christianity, because it began under these conditions, made sexlessness and Communism the two main practical articles of its propaganda; and it has never quite lost its original bias in these directions. In spite of the putting off of the Second Coming from the lifetime of the apostles to the millennium, and of the great disappointment of the year 1000 A.D., in which multitudes of Christians seriously prepared for the end of the world, the prophet who announces that the end is at hand is still popular. Many of the people who ridicule his demonstrations that the fantastic monsters of the book of Revelation are among us in the persons of our own political contemporaries, and who proceed sanely in all their affairs on the assumption that the world is going to last, really do believe that there will be a Judgment Day, and that it *might* even be in their own time. A thunderstorm, an eclipse, or any very unusual weather will make them apprehensive and uncomfortable.

This explains why, for a long time, the Christian Church refused to have anything to do with marriage. The result was, not the abolition of sex, but its excommunication. And, of course, the consequences of persuading people that matrimony was an unholy state were so grossly carnal, that the Church had to execute a complete right-about-face, and try to make people understand that it was a holy state: so holy indeed that it could not be validly inaugurated without the blessing of the Church. And by this teaching it did something to atone for its earlier blasphemy. But the mischief of chopping and changing your doctrine to meet this or that practical emergency instead of keeping it adjusted to the whole scheme of life, is that you end by having half-a-dozen contradictory doctrines to suit half-a-dozen emergencies. The Church solemnized and sanctified marriage without ever giving up its original Pauline doctrine on the subject. And it soon fell into another confusion. At the point at which it took up marriage and endeavored to make it holy, marriage was, as it still is, largely a survival of the custom of selling women to men. Now in all trades a marked difference is made in price between a new article and a second-hand one. The moment we meet with this difference in value between human beings, we may know that we are in the slave-market, where the conception of our relations to the persons sold is neither religious nor natural nor human nor superhuman, but simply commercial. The Church, when it finally gave its blessing to marriage, did not, in its innocence, fathom these commercial traditions. Consequently it tried to sanctify them too, with grotesque results. The slave-dealer having always asked more money for virginity, the Church, instead of detecting the money-changer and driving him out of the temple, took him for a sentimental and chivalrous lover, and, helped by its only half-discarded doctrine of celibacy, gave virginity a heavenly value to ennoble its commercial pretensions. In short, Mammon, always mighty, put the Church in his pocket, where he keeps it to this day, in spite of the occasional saints and martyrs who contrive from time to time to get their heads and souls free to testify against him.

DIVORCE A SACRAMENTAL DUTY

But Mammon overreached himself when he tried to impose his doctrine of inalienable property on the Church under the guise of indissoluble marriage. For the Church tried to shelter this inhuman doctrine and flat contradiction of the gospel by claiming, and rightly claiming, that marriage is a sacrament. So it is; but that is exactly what makes divorce a duty when marriage has lost the inward and spiritual grace of which the marriage ceremony is the outward and visible sign. In vain do bishops stoop to pick up the discarded arguments of the atheists of fifty years ago by pleading that the words of Jesus were in an obscure Aramaic dialect, and were probably misunderstood, as Jesus, they think, could not have said anything a bishop would disapprove of. Unless they are prepared to add that the statement that those who take the sacrament with their lips but not with their hearts eat and drink their own damnation is also a mistranslation from the Aramaic, they are most solemnly bound to shield marriage from profanation, not merely by permitting divorce, but by making it compulsory in certain cases as the Chinese do.

When spiritual revolt broke out in the sixteenth century, and the Church was reformed in several countries, the Reformation was so largely a rebellion against sacerdotalism that marriage was very nearly excommunicated again: our modern civil marriage, round which so many fierce controversies and political conflicts have raged, would have been thoroughly approved of by Calvin, and hailed with relief by Luther. But the instinctive doctrine that there is something holy and mystic in sex, a doctrine which many of us now easily dissociate from any priestly ceremony, but which in those days seemed to all who felt it to need a ritual affirmation, could not be thrown on the scrap-heap with the sale of Indulgences and the like; and so the Reformation left marriage where it was: a curious mixture of commercial sex slavery, early Christian sex abhorrence, and later Christian sex sanctification.

OTHELLO AND DESDEMONA

How strong was the feeling that a husband or a wife is an article of property, greatly depreciated in value at second-hand, and not to be used or touched by any person but the proprietor, may be learnt from Shakespear. His most infatuated and passionate lovers are Antony and Othello; yet both of them betray the commercial and proprietary instinct the moment they lose their tempers. "I found you" says Antony reproaching Cleopatra, "as a morsel cold upon dead Cæsar's trencher." Othello's worst agony is the thought of "keeping a corner in the thing he loves for others' uses." But this is not what a man feels about the thing he loves, but about the thing he owns. I never understood the full significance of Othello's outburst until I one day heard a lady, in the course of a private discussion as to the feasibility of "group marriage," say with cold disgust that she would as soon think of lending her toothbrush to another woman as her husband. The sense of outraged manhood with which I felt myself and all other husbands thus reduced to the rank of a toilet appliance gave me a very unpleasant taste of what Desdemona might have felt had she overheard Othello's outburst. I was so dumbfounded that I had not the presence of mind to ask the lady whether she insisted on having a doctor, a nurse, a dentist, and even a priest and solicitor all to herself as well. But I had too often heard men speak of women as if they were mere personal conveniences to feel surprised that exactly the same view is held, only more fastidiously, by women.

All these views must be got rid of before we can have any healthy public opinion (on which depends our having a healthy population) on the subject of sex, and consequently of marriage. Whilst the subject is considered shameful and sinful we shall have no systematic instruction in sexual hygiene, because such lectures as are given in Germany, France, and even prudish America (where the great Miltonic tradition in this matter still lives) will be considered a corruption of that youthful innocence which now subsists on nasty stories and whispered traditions handed down from generation to generation of school children: stories and traditions which conceal nothing of sex but its dignity, its honor, its sacredness, its rank as the first necessity of society and the deepest concern of the nation. We shall continue to maintain the White Slave Trade and protect its exploiters by, on the one hand, tolerating the white slave as the necessary breakwater of marriage; and, on the other, trampling on her and degrading her until she has nothing to hope from our Courts; and so, with policemen at every corner, and law triumphant all over Europe, she will still be smuggled and cattle-driven from one end of the civilized world to the other, cheated, beaten, bullied, and hunted into the streets to disgusting overwork, without daring to utter the cry for help that brings, not rescue, but exposure and infamy, yet revenging herself terribly in the end by scattering blindness and sterility, pain and disfigurement, insanity and death among us with the certainty that we are much too pious and genteel to allow such things to be mentioned with a view to saving either her or ourselves from them. And all the time we shall keep enthusiastically investing her trade with every allurement that the art of the novelist, the playwright, the dancer, the milliner, the painter, the limelight man, and the sentimental poet can devize, after which we shall continue to be very much shocked and surprised when the cry of the youth, of the young wife, of the mother, of the infected nurse, and of all the other victims, direct and indirect, arises with its invariable refrain: "Why did nobody warn me?"

WHAT IS TO BECOME OF THE CHILDREN?

I must not reply flippantly, Make them all Wards in Chancery; yet that would be enough to put any sensible person on the track of the reply. One would think, to hear the way in which people sometimes ask the question, that not only does marriage prevent the difficulty from ever arising, but that nothing except divorce can ever raise it. It is true that if you divorce the parents, the children have to be disposed of. But if you hang the parents, or imprison the parents, or take the children out of the custody of the parents because they hold Shelley's opinions, or if the parents die, the same difficulty arises. And as these things have happened again and again, and as we have had plenty of experience of divorce decrees and separation orders, the attempt to use children as an obstacle to divorce is hardly worth arguing with. We shall deal with the children just as we should deal with them if their homes were broken up by any other cause. There is a sense in which children are a real obstacle to divorce: they give parents a common interest which keeps together many a couple who, if childless, would separate. The marriage law is superfluous in such cases. This is shewn by the fact that the proportion of childless divorces is much larger than the proportion of divorces from all causes. But it must not be forgotten that the interest of the children forms one of the most powerful arguments for divorce. An unhappy household is a bad nursery. There is something to be said for the polygynous or polyandrous household as a school for children: children really do suffer from having too few parents: this is why uncles and aunts and tutors and governesses are often so good for children. But it is just the polygamous household which our marriage law allows to be broken up, and which, as we have seen, is not possible as a typical institution in a democratic country where the numbers of the sexes are about equal. Therefore polygyny and polyandry as a means of educating children fall to the ground, and with them, I think, must go the opinion which has been expressed by Gladstone and others, that an extension of divorce, whilst admitting many new grounds for it, might exclude the ground of adultery. There are, however, clearly many things that make some of our domestic interiors little private hells for children (especially when the children are quite content in them) which would justify any intelligent State in breaking up the home and giving the custody of the children either to the parent whose conscience had revolted against the corruption of the children, or to neither.

Which brings me to the point that divorce should no longer be confined to cases in which one of the parties petitions for it. If, for instance, you have a thoroughly rascally couple making a living by infamous means and bringing up their children to their trade, the king's proctor, instead of pursuing his present purely mischievous function of preventing couples from being divorced by proving that they both desire it, might very well intervene and divorce these children from their parents. At present, if the Queen herself were to rescue some unfortunate child from degradation and misery and place her in a respectable home, and some unmentionable pair of blackguards claimed the child and proved that they were its father and mother, the child would be given to them in the name of the sanctity of the home and the holiness of parentage, after perpetrating which crime, the law would calmly send an education officer to take the child out of the parents' hands several hours a day in the still more sacred name of compulsory education. (Of course what would really happen would be that the couple would blackmail the Queen for their consent to the salvation of the child, unless, indeed, a hint from a police inspector convinced them that bad characters cannot always rely on pedantically constitutional treatment when they come into conflict with persons in high station.)

The truth is, not only must the bond between man and wife be made subject to a reasonable consideration of the welfare of the parties concerned and of the community, but the whole family bond as well. The theory that the wife is the property of the husband or the husband of the wife is not a whit less abhorrent and mischievous than the theory that the child is the property of the parent. Parental bondage will go the way of conjugal bondage: indeed the order of reform should rather be put the other way about; for the helplessness of children has already compelled the State to intervene between parent and child more than between husband and wife. If you pay less than £40 a year rent, you will sometimes feel tempted to say to the vaccination officer, the school attendance officer, and the sanitary inspector: "Is this child mine or yours?" The answer is that as the child is a vital part of the nation, the nation cannot afford to leave it at the irresponsible disposal of any individual or couple of individuals as a mere small parcel of private property. The only solid ground that the parent can take is that as the State, in spite of its imposing name, can, when all is said, do nothing with the child except place it in the charge of some human being or another, the parent is no worse a custodian than a stranger. And though this proposition may seem highly questionable at first sight to those who imagine that only parents spoil children, yet those who realize that children are as often spoilt by severity and coldness as by indulgence, and that the notion that natural parents are any worse than adopted parents is probably as complete an illusion as the notion that they are any better, see no serious likelihood that State action will detach children from their parents more than it does at present: nay, it is even likely that the present system of taking the children out of the parents' hands and having the parental duty performed by officials, will, as poverty and ignorance become the exception instead of the rule, give way to the system of simply requiring certain results, beginning with the baby's weight and ending perhaps with some sort of practical arts degree, but leaving parents and children to achieve the results as they best may. Such freedom is, of course, impossible in our present poverty-stricken circumstances. As long as the masses of our people are too poor to be good parents or good anything else except beasts of burden, it is no use requiring much more from them but hewing of wood and drawing of water: whatever is to be done must be done *for* them, mostly, alas! by people whose superiority is merely technical. Until we abolish poverty it is impossible to push rational measures of any kind very far: the wolf at the door will compel us to live in a state of siege and to do everything by a bureaucratic martial law that would be quite unnecessary and indeed intolerable in a prosperous community. But, however we settle the question, we must make the parent justify his custody of the child exactly as we should make a stranger justify it. If a family is not achieving the purposes of a family it should be dissolved just as a marriage should when it, too, is not achieving the purposes of marriage. The notion that there is or ever can be anything magical and inviolable in the legal relations of domesticity, and the curious confusion of ideas which makes some of our bishops imagine that in the phrase "Whom God hath joined," the word God means the district registrar or the Reverend John Smith or William Jones, must be got rid of. Means of breaking up undesirable families are as necessary to the preservation of the family as means of dissolving undesirable marriages are to the preservation of marriage. If our domestic laws are kept so inhuman that they at last provoke a furious general insurrection against them as they already provoke many private ones, we shall in a very literal sense empty the baby out with the bath by abolishing an institution which needs nothing more than a little obvious and easy rationalizing to make it not only harmless but comfortable, honorable, and useful.

THE COST OF DIVORCE

But please do not imagine that the evils of indissoluble marriage can be cured by divorce laws administered on our present plan. The very cheapest undefended divorce, even when conducted by a solicitor for its own sake and that of humanity, costs at least £30 out-of-pocket expenses. To a client on business terms it costs about three times as much. Until divorce is as cheap as marriage, marriage will remain indissoluble for all except the handful of people to whom £100 is a procurable sum. For the enormous majority of us there is no difference in this respect between a hundred and a quadrillion. Divorce is the one thing you may not sue for *in forma pauperis*.

Let me, then, recommend as follows:

1. Make divorce as easy, as cheap, and as private as marriage.

2. Grant divorce at the request of either party, whether the other consents or not; and admit no other ground than the request, which should be made without stating any reasons.

3. Confine the power of dissolving marriage for misconduct to the State acting on the petition of the king's proctor or other suitable functionary, who may, however, be moved by either party to intervene in ordinary request cases, not to prevent the divorce

taking place, but to enforce alimony if it be refused and the case is one which needs it.

4. Make it impossible for marriage to be used as a punishment as it is at present. Send the husband and wife to penal servitude if you disapprove of their conduct and want to punish them; but do not send them back to perpetual wedlock.

5. If, on the other hand, you think a couple perfectly innocent and well conducted, do not condemn them also to perpetual wedlock against their wills, thereby making the treatment of what you consider innocence on both sides the same as the treatment of what you consider guilt on both sides.

6. Place the work of a wife and mother on the same footing as other work: that is, on the footing of labor worthy of its hire; and provide for unemployment in it exactly as for unemployment in shipbuilding or any other recognized bread-winning trade.

7. And take and deal with all the consequences of these acts of justice instead of letting yourself be frightened out of reason and good sense by fear of consequences. We must finally adapt our institutions to human nature. In the long run our present plan of trying to force human nature into a mould of existing abuses, superstitions, and corrupt interests, produces the explosive forces that wreck civilization.

8. Never forget that if you leave your law to judges and your religion to bishops you will presently find yourself without either law or religion. If you doubt this, ask any decent judge or bishop. Do *not* ask somebody who does not know what a judge is, or what a bishop is, or what the law is, or what religion is. In other words, do not ask your newspaper. Journalists are too poorly paid in this country to know anything that is fit for publication.

CONCLUSIONS

To sum up, we have to depend on the solution of the problem of unemployment, probably on the principles laid down in the Minority Report of the Royal Commission on the Poor Law, to make the sexual relations between men and women decent and honorable by making women economically independent of men, and (in the younger son section of the upper classes) men economically independent of women. We also have to bring ourselves into line with the rest of Protestant civilization by providing means for dissolving all unhappy, improper, and inconvenient marriages. And, as it is our cautious custom to lag behind the rest of the world to see how their experiments in reform turn out before venturing ourselves, and then take advantage of their experience to get ahead of them, we should recognize that the ancient system of specifying grounds for divorce, such as adultery, cruelty, drunkenness, felony, insanity, vagrancy, neglect to provide for wife and children, desertion, public defamation, violent temper, religious heterodoxy, contagious disease, outrages, indignities, personal abuse, "mental anguish," conduct rendering life burdensome and so forth (all these are examples from some code actually in force at present), is a mistake, because the only effect of compelling people to plead and prove misconduct is that cases are manufactured and clean linen purposely smirched and washed in public, to the great distress and disgrace of innocent children and relatives, whilst the grounds have at the same time to be made so general that any sort of human conduct may be brought within them by a little special pleading and a little mental reservation on the part of witnesses examined on oath. When

it comes to "conduct rendering life burdensome," it
is clear that no marriage is any longer indissoluble;
and the sensible thing to do then is to grant divorce
whenever it is desired, without asking why.

On a fine morning in the spring of 1908 the Norman
kitchen in the Palace of the Bishop of Chelsea looks very
spacious and clean and handsome and healthy.

The Bishop is lucky enough to have a XII century
palace. The palace itself has been lucky enough to escape
being carved up into XV century Gothic, or shaved into
XVIII century ashlar, or "restored" by a XIX century
builder and a Victorian architect with a deep sense of the
umbrella-like gentlemanliness of XIV century vaulting.
The present occupant, A. Chelsea, unofficially Alfred
Bridgenorth, appreciates Norman work. He has, by
adroit complaints of the discomfort of the place, induced
the Ecclesiastical Commissioners to give him some money
to spend on it; and with this he has got rid of the wall
papers, the paint, the partitions, the exquisitely planed
and moulded casings with which the Victorian cabinet-
makers enclosed and hid the huge black beams of hewn
oak, and of all the other expedients of his predecessors
to make themselves feel at home and respectable in a
Norman fortress. It is a house built to last for ever. The
walls and beams are big enough to carry the tower of
Babel, as if the builders, anticipating our modern ideas
and instinctively defying them, had resolved to shew how
much material they could lavish on a house built for the
glory of God, instead of keeping a competitive eye on the
advantage of sending in the lowest tender, and scientifically
calculating how little material would be enough to prevent
the whole affair from tumbling down by its own weight.

The kitchen is the Bishop's favorite room. This is not
at all because he is a man of humble mind; but because
the kitchen is one of the finest rooms in the house. The
Bishop has neither the income nor the appetite to have his
cooking done there. The windows, high up in the wall,
look north and south. The north window is the largest;

and if we look into the kitchen through it we see facing us the south wall with small Norman windows and an open door near the corner to the left. Through this door we have a glimpse of the garden, and of a garden chair in the sunshine. In the right-hand corner is an entrance to a vaulted circular chamber with a winding stair leading up through a tower to the upper floors of the palace. In the wall to our right is the immense fireplace, with its huge spit like a baby crane, and a collection of old iron and brass instruments which pass as the original furniture of the fire, though as a matter of fact they have been picked up from time to time by the Bishop at secondhand shops. In the near end of the left-hand wall a small Norman door gives access to the Bishop's study, formerly a scullery. Farther along, a great oak chest stands against the wall. Across the middle of the kitchen is a big timber table surrounded by eleven stout rush-bottomed chairs: four on the far side, three on the near side, and two at each end. There is a big chair with railed back and sides on the hearth. On the floor is a drugget of thick fibre matting. The only other piece of furniture is a clock with a wooden dial about as large as the bottom of a washtub, the weights, chains, and pendulums being of corresponding magnitude; but the Bishop has long since abandoned the attempt to keep it going. It hangs above the oak chest.

The kitchen is occupied at present by the Bishop's lady, Mrs Bridgenorth, who is talking to Mr William Collins, the greengrocer. He is in evening dress, though it is early forenoon. Mrs Bridgenorth is a quiet happy-looking woman of fifty or thereabouts, placid, gentle, and humorous, with delicate features and fine grey hair with many white threads. She is dressed as for some festivity; but she is taking things easily as she sits in the big chair by the hearth, reading The Times.

Collins is an elderly man with a rather youthful waist. His muttonchop whiskers have a coquettish touch of Dundreary at their lower ends. He is an affable man, with those perfect manners which can be acquired only in keeping a shop for the sale of necessaries of life to ladies whose social position is so unquestionable that they are not anxious about it. He is a reassuring man, with a vigilant grey eye, and the power of saying anything he likes to you without offence, because his tone always implies that he does it with your kind permission. Withal by no means servile: rather gallant and compassionate, but never without a conscientious recognition, on public grounds, of social distinctions. He is at the oak chest counting a pile of napkins.

Mrs Bridgenorth reads placidly: Collins counts: a blackbird sings in the garden. Mrs Bridgenorth puts The Times down in her lap and considers Collins for a moment.

MRS BRIDGENORTH. Do you never feel nervous on these occasions, Collins?

COLLINS. Lord bless you, no, maam. It would be a joke, after marrying five of your daughters, if I was to get nervous over marrying the last of them.

MRS BRIDGENORTH. I have always said you were a wonderful man, Collins.

COLLINS [*almost blushing*] Oh, maam!

MRS BRIDGENORTH. Yes. I never could arrange anything—a wedding or even a dinner—without some hitch or other.

COLLINS. Why should you give yourself the trouble, maam? Send for the greengrocer, maam: thats the secret of easy housekeeping. Bless you, it's his business. It pays him and you, let alone the pleasure in a house like this [*Mrs Bridgenorth bows in acknowledge-ment of the compliment*]. They joke about the green-grocer, just as they joke about the mother-in-law. But they cant get on without both.

MRS BRIDGENORTH. What a bond between us Collins!

COLLINS. Bless you, maam, theres all sorts of bonds between all sorts of people. You are a very affable lady, maam, for a Bishop's lady. I have known Bishops' ladies that would fairly provoke you to up and cheek them; but nobody would ever forget himself and his place with you, maam.

MRS BRIDGENORTH. Collins: you are a flatterer. You will superintend the breakfast yourself as usual, of course, wont you?

COLLINS. Yes, yes, bless you maam, of course. I always do. Them fashionable caterers send down such people as I never did set eyes on. Dukes you would take them for. You see the relatives shaking hands with them and asking them about the family—actually ladies saying "Where have we met before?" and all sorts of confusion. Thats my secret in business, maam. You can always spot me as the greengrocer. It's a fortune to me in these days, when you cant hardly tell who anyone is or isnt. [*He goes out through the tower, and immediately returns for a moment to announce*] The General, maam.

Mrs Bridgenorth rises to receive her brother-in-law, who enters resplendent in full-dress uniform, with many medals and orders. General Bridgenorth is a well set up man of fifty, with large brave nostrils, an iron mouth, faithful dog's eyes, and much natural simplicity and dignity of character. He is ignorant, stupid, and preju-diced, having been carefully trained to be so; and it is not always possible to be patient with him when his unques-tionably good intentions become actively mischievous;

*but one blames society, not himself, for this. He would be
no worse a man than Collins, had he enjoyed Collins's
social opportunities. He comes to the hearth, where Mrs
Bridgenorth is standing with her back to the fireplace.*

MRS BRIDGENORTH. Good morning, Boxer. [*They
shake hands*]. Another niece to give away. This is the
last of them.

THE GENERAL [*very gloomily*] Yes, Alice. Nothing for
the old warrior uncle to do but give away brides to
luckier men than himself. Has—[*he chokes*] has your
sister come yet?

MRS BRIDGENORTH. Why do you always call Lesbia
my sister? Dont you know that it annoys her more
than any of the rest of your tricks?

THE GENERAL. Tricks! Ha! Well, I'll try to break
myself of it; but I think she might bear with me in a
little thing like that. She knows that her name sticks
in my throat. Better call her your sister than try to
call her L—[*he almost breaks down*] L—well, call her
by her name and make a fool of myself by crying. [*He
sits down at the near end of the table*].

MRS BRIDGENORTH [*going to him and rallying him*]
Oh come, Boxer! Really, really! We are no longer boys
and girls. You cant keep up a broken heart all your
life. It must be nearly twenty years since she refused
you. And you know that it's not because she dislikes
you, but only that she's not a marrying woman.

THE GENERAL. It's no use. I love her still. And I cant
help telling her so whenever we meet, though I know
it makes her avoid me. [*He all but weeps*].

MRS BRIDGENORTH. What does she say when you
tell her?

THE GENERAL. Only that she wonders when I am
going to grow out of it. I know now that I shall never
grow out of it.

MRS BRIDGENORTH. Perhaps you would if you married her. I believe youre better as you are, Boxer.

THE GENERAL. I'm a miserable man. I'm really sorry to be a ridiculous old bore, Alice; but when I come to this house for a wedding—to these scenes—to—to—recollections of the past—always to give the bride to somebody else, and never to have my bride given to me—[*he rises abruptly*] May I go into the garden and smoke it off?

MRS BRIDGENORTH. Do, Boxer.

Collins returns with the wedding cake.

MRS BRIDGENORTH. Oh, heres the cake. I believe it's the same one we had for Florence's wedding.

THE GENERAL. I cant bear it [*he hurries out through the garden door*].

COLLINS [*putting the cake on the table*] Well, look at that, maam! Aint it odd that after all the weddings he's given away at, the General cant stand the sight of a wedding cake yet. It always seems to give him the same shock.

MRS BRIDGENORTH. Well, it's his last shock. You have married the whole family now, Collins. [*She takes up The Times again and resumes her seat*].

COLLINS. Except your sister, maam. A fine character of a lady, maam, is Miss Grantham. I have an ambition to arrange her wedding breakfast.

MRS BRIDGENORTH. She wont marry, Collins.

COLLINS. Bless you, maam, they all say that. You and me said it, I'll lay. I did, anyhow.

MRS BRIDGENORTH. No: marriage came natural to me. I should have thought it did to you too.

COLLINS [*pensive*] No, maam: it didnt come natural. My wife had to break me into it. It came natural to her: she's what you might call a regular old hen. Always wants to have her family within sight of her.

Wouldnt go to bed unless she knew they was all safe at home and the door locked, and the lights out. Always wants her luggage in the carriage with her. Always goes and makes the engine driver promise her to be careful. She's a born wife and mother, maam. Thats why my children all ran away from home.

MRS BRIDGENORTH. Did you ever feel inclined to run away, Collins?

COLLINS. Oh yes maam, yes: very often. But when it came to the point I couldnt bear to hurt her feelings. She's a sensitive, affectionate, anxious soul; and she was never brought up to know what freedom is to some people. You see, family life is all the life she knows: she's like a bird born in a cage, that would die if you let it loose in the woods. When I thought how little it was to a man of my easy temper to put up with her, and how deep it would hurt her to think it was because I didnt care for her, I always put off running away til next time; and so in the end I never ran away at all. I daresay it was good for me to be took such care of; but it cut me off from all my old friends something dreadful, maam: especially the women, maam. She never gave them a chance: she didnt indeed. She never understood that married people should take holidays from one another if they are to keep at all fresh. Not that I ever got tired of her, maam; but my! how I used to get tired of home life sometimes. I used to catch myself envying my brother George: I positively did, maam.

MRS BRIDGENORTH. George was a bachelor then, I suppose?

COLLINS. Bless you, no, maam. He married a very fine figure of a woman; but she was that changeable and what you might call susceptible, you would not believe. She didnt seem to have any control over herself when she fell in love. She would mope for a couple of days, crying about nothing; and then she would up and say—no matter who was there to hear her—"I must go to him, George"; and away she would go from her home and her husband without with-your-leave or by-your-leave.

MRS BRIDGENORTH. But do you mean that she did this more than once? That she came back?

COLLINS. Bless you, maam, she done it five times to my own knowledge; and then George gave up telling us about it, he got so used to it.

MRS BRIDGENORTH. But did he always take her back?

COLLINS. Well, what could he do, maam? Three times out of four the men would bring her back the same evening and no harm done. Other times theyd run away from her. What could any man with a heart do but comfort her when she came back crying at the way they dodged her when she threw herself at their heads, pretending they was too noble to accept the sacrifice she was making. George told her again and again that if she'd only stay at home and hold off a bit theyd be at her feet all day long. She got sensible at last and took his advice. George always liked change of company.

MRS BRIDGENORTH. What an odious woman, Collins! Dont you think so?

COLLINS [judicially] Well, many ladies with a domestic turn thought so and said so, maam. But I will say for Mrs George that the variety of experience made her wonderful interesting. Thats where the flighty ones score off the steady ones, maam. Look at my old woman! She's never known any man but me; and she cant properly know me, because she dont know other men to compare me with. Of course she knows her

[114]

parents in—well, in the way one does know one's parents: not knowing half their lives as you might say, or ever thinking that they was ever young; and she knew her children as children, and never thought of them as independent human beings til they ran away and nigh broke her heart for a week or two. But Mrs George she came to know a lot about men of all sorts and ages; for the older she got the younger she liked em; and it certainly made her interesting, and gave her a lot of sense. I have often taken her advice on things when my own poor old woman wouldnt have been a bit of use to me.

MRS BRIDGENORTH. I hope you dont tell your wife that you go elsewhere for advice.

COLLINS. Lord bless you, maam, I'm that fond of my old Matilda that I never tell her anything at all for fear of hurting her feelings. You see, she's such an out-and-out wife and mother that she's hardly a responsible human being out of her house, except when she's marketing.

MRS BRIDGENORTH. Does she approve of Mrs George?

COLLINS. Oh, Mrs George gets round her. Mrs George can get round anybody if she wants to. And then Mrs George is very particular about religion. And she's a clairvoyant.

MRS BRIDGENORTH [surprised] A clairvoyant!

COLLINS [calm] Oh yes, maam, yes. All you have to do is to mesmerize her a bit; and off she goes into a trance, and says the most wonderful things! not things about herself, but as if it was the whole human race giving you a bit of its mind. Oh, wonderful, maam, I assure you. You couldnt think of a game that Mrs George isnt up to.

Lesbia Grantham comes in through the tower. She is

a tall, handsome, slender lady in her prime: that is, between 35 and 55. She has what is called a well-bred air, dressing very carefully to produce that effect without the least regard for the latest fashions, sure of herself, very terrifying to the young and shy, fastidious to the ends of her long finger-tips, and tolerant and amused rather than sympathetic.

LESBIA. Good morning, dear big sister.

MRS BRIDGENORTH. Good morning, dear little sister. [*They kiss*].

LESBIA. Good morning, Collins. How well you are looking! And how young! [*She turns the middle chair away from the table and sits down*].

COLLINS. Thats only my professional habit at a wedding, Miss. You should see me at a political dinner. I look nigh seventy. [*Looking at his watch*] Time's getting along, maam. May I send up word from you to Miss Edith to hurry a bit with her dressing?

MRS BRIDGENORTH. Do, Collins.

Collins goes out through the tower, taking the cake with him.

LESBIA. Dear old Collins! Has he told you any stories this morning?

MRS BRIDGENORTH. Yes. You were just late for a particularly thrilling invention of his.

LESBIA. About Mrs George?

MRS BRIDGENORTH. Yes. He says she's a clairvoyant.

LESBIA. I wonder whether he really invented Mrs George, or stole her out of some book.

MRS BRIDGENORTH. I wonder!

LESBIA. Wheres the Barmecide?

MRS BRIDGENORTH. In the study, working away at his new book. He thinks no more now of having a daughter married than of having an egg for breakfast.

The General, soothed by smoking, comes in from the garden.

THE GENERAL [*with resolute bonhomie*] Ah, Lesbia! How do you do? [*They shake hands; and he takes the chair on her right*].

Mrs Bridgenorth goes out through the tower.

LESBIA. How are you, Boxer? You almost look as gorgeous as the wedding cake.

THE GENERAL. I make a point of appearing in uniform whenever I take part in any ceremony, as a lesson to the subalterns. It is not the custom in England; but it ought to be.

LESBIA. You look very fine, Boxer. What a frightful lot of bravery all these medals must represent!

THE GENERAL. No, Lesbia. They represent despair and cowardice. I won all the early ones by trying to get killed. You know why.

LESBIA. But you had a charmed life?

THE GENERAL. Yes, a charmed life. Bayonets bent on my buckles. Bullets passed through me and left no trace: thats the worst of modern bullets: Ive never been hit by a dum-dum. When I was only a company officer I had at least the right to expose myself to death in the field. Now I'm a General even that resource is cut off. [*Persuasively drawing his chair nearer to her*] Listen to me, Lesbia. For the tenth and last time—

LESBIA [*interrupting*] On Florence's wedding morning, two years ago, you said "For the ninth and last time."

THE GENERAL. We are two years older, Lesbia. I'm fifty: you are—

LESBIA. Yes, I know. It's no use, Boxer. When will you be old enough to take no for an answer?

[117]

THE GENERAL. Never, Lesbia, never. You have never given me a real reason for refusing me yet. I once thought it was somebody else. There were lots of fellows after you; but now theyve all given it up and married. [*Bending still nearer to her*] Lesbia: tell me your secret. Why—

LESBIA [*sniffing disgustedly*] Oh! Youve been smoking. [*She rises and goes to the chair on the hearth*] Keep away, you wretch.

THE GENERAL. But for that pipe, I could not have faced you without breaking down. It has soothed me and nerved me.

LESBIA [*sitting down with The Times in her hand*] Well, it has nerved me to tell you why I'm going to be an old maid.

THE GENERAL [*impulsively approaching her*] Dont say that, Lesbia. It's not natural: it's not right: it's—

LESBIA [*fanning him off*] No: no closer, Boxer, please. [*He retreats, discouraged*]. It may not be natural; but it happens all the same. Youll find plenty of women like me, if you care to look for them: women with lots of character and good looks and money and offers, who wont and dont get married. Cant you guess why?

THE GENERAL. I can understand when there is another.

LESBIA. Yes; but there isnt another. Besides, do you suppose I think, at my time of life, that the difference between one decent sort of man and another is worth bothering about?

THE GENERAL. The heart has its preferences, Lesbia. One image and one only, gets indelibly—

LESBIA. Yes. Excuse my interrupting you so often; but your sentiments are so correct that I always know what you are going to say before you finish. You see, Boxer, everybody is not like you. You are a sentimental noodle: you dont see women as they really are. You dont see me as I really am. Now I do see men as they really are. I see you as you really are.

THE GENERAL [*murmuring*] No: dont say that, Lesbia.

LESBIA. I'm a regular old maid. I'm very particular about my belongings. I like to have my own house, and to have it to myself. I have a very keen sense of beauty and fitness and cleanliness and order. I am proud of my independence and jealous for it. I have a sufficiently well-stocked mind to be very good company for myself if I have plenty of books and music. The one thing I never could stand is a great lout of a man smoking all over my house and going to sleep in his chair after dinner, and untidying everything. Ugh!

THE GENERAL. But love—

LESBIA. Oh, love! Have you no imagination? Do you think I have never been in love with wonderful men? heroes! archangels! princes! sages! even fascinating rascals! and had the strangest adventures with them? Do you know what it is to look at a mere real man after that? a man with his boots in every corner, and the smell of his tobacco in every curtain?

THE GENERAL [*somewhat dazed*] Well but—excuse my mentioning it—dont you want children?

LESBIA. I ought to have children. I should be a good mother to children. I believe it would pay the country very well to pay ME very well to have children. But the country tells me that I cant have a child in my house without a man in it too; so I tell the country that it will have to do without my children. If I am to be a mother, I really cannot have a man bothering me to be a wife at the same time.

THE GENERAL. My dear Lesbia: you know I dont

wish to be impertinent; but these are not correct views for an English lady to express.

LESBIA. That is why I dont express them, except to gentlemen who wont take any other answer. The difficulty, you see, is that I really am an English lady, and am particularly proud of being one.

THE GENERAL. I'm sure of that, Lesbia: quite sure of it. I never meant—

LESBIA [*rising impatiently*] Oh, my dear Boxer, do please try to think of something else than whether you have offended me, and whether you are doing the correct thing as an English gentleman. You are fault-less, and very dull. [*She shakes her shoulders intoler-antly and walks across to the other side of the kitchen*].

THE GENERAL [*moodily*] Ha! thats whats the matter with me. Not clever. A poor silly soldier man.

LESBIA. The whole matter is very simple. As I say, I am an English lady, by which I mean that I have been trained to do without what I cant have on honorable terms, no matter what it is.

THE GENERAL. I really dont understand you, Lesbia.

LESBIA [*turning on him*] Then why on earth do you want to marry a woman you dont understand?

THE GENERAL. I dont know. I suppose I love you.

LESBIA. Well, Boxer, you can love me as much as you like, provided you look happy about it and dont bore me. But you cant marry me; and thats all about it.

THE GENERAL. It's so frightfully difficult to argue the matter fairly with you without wounding your delic-acy by overstepping the bounds of good taste. But surely there are calls of nature—

LESBIA. Dont be ridiculous, Boxer.

THE GENERAL. Well how am I to express it? Hang it all, Lesbia, dont you want a husband?

LESBIA. No. I want children; and I want to devote

myself entirely to my children, and not to their father. The law will not allow me to do that; so I have made up my mind to have neither husband nor children.

THE GENERAL. But, great Heavens, the natural appetites—

LESBIA. As I have said before, an English lady is not the slave of her appetites. That is what an English gentleman seems incapable of understanding. [*She sits down at the end of the table, near the study door*].

THE GENERAL [*huffily*] Oh well, if you refuse, you refuse. I shall not ask you again. I'm sorry I returned to the subject. [*He retires to the hearth and plants himself there, wounded and lofty*].

LESBIA. Dont be cross, Boxer.

THE GENERAL. I'm not cross, only wounded, Lesbia. And when you talk like that, I dont feel convinced: I only feel utterly at a loss.

LESBIA. Well, you know our family rule. When at a loss consult the greengrocer. [*Opportunely Collins comes in through the tower*]. Here he is.

COLLINS. Sorry to be so much in and out, Miss. I thought Mrs Bridgenorth was here. The table is ready now for the breakfast, if she would like to see it.

LESBIA. If you are satisfied, Collins, I am sure she will be.

THE GENERAL. By the way, Collins: I thought theyd made you an alderman.

COLLINS. So they have, General.

THE GENERAL. Then wheres your gown?

COLLINS. I dont wear it in private life, General.

THE GENERAL. Why? Are you ashamed of it?

COLLINS. No, General. To tell you the truth, I take a pride in it. I cant help it.

THE GENERAL. Attention, Collins. Come here.

[*Collins comes to him*]. Do you see my uniform—all my medals ?

COLLINS. Yes, General. They strike the eye, as it were.

THE GENERAL. They are meant to. Very well. Now you know, dont you, that your services to the community as a greengrocer are as important and as dignified as mine as a soldier ?

COLLINS. I'm sure it's very honorable of you to say so, General.

THE GENERAL [*emphatically*] You know also, dont you, that any man who can see anything ridiculous, or unmanly, or unbecoming in your work or in your civic robes is not a gentleman, but a jumping, bounding, snorting cad ?

COLLINS. Well, strictly between ourselves, that is my opinion, General.

THE GENERAL. Then why not dignify my niece's wedding by wearing your robes ?

COLLINS. A bargain's a bargain, General. Mrs Bridgenorth sent for the greengrocer, not for the alderman. It's just as unpleasant to get more than you bargain for as to get less.

THE GENERAL. I'm sure she will agree with me. I attach importance to this as an affirmation of solidarity in the service of the community. The Bishop's apron, my uniform, your robes: the Church, the Army, and the Municipality.

COLLINS [*retiring*] Very well, General. [*He turns dubiously to Lesbia on his way to the tower*]. I wonder what my wife will say, Miss ?

THE GENERAL. What! Is your wife ashamed of your robes ?

COLLINS. No, sir, not ashamed of them. But she grudged the money for them; and she will be afraid of my sleeves getting into the gravy.

Mrs Bridgenorth, her placidity quite upset, comes in with a letter; hurries past Collins; and comes between Lesbia and the General.

MRS BRIDGENORTH. Lesbia: Boxer: heres a pretty mess!

Collins goes out discreetly.

THE GENERAL. Whats the matter?

MRS BRIDGENORTH. Reginald's in London, and wants to come to the wedding.

THE GENERAL [*stupended*] Well, dash my buttons!

LESBIA. Oh, all right, let him come.

THE GENERAL. Let him come! Why, the decree has not been made absolute yet. Is he to walk in here to Edith's wedding, reeking from the Divorce Court?

MRS BRIDGENORTH [*vexedly sitting down in the middle chair*] It's too bad. No: I cant forgive him, Lesbia, really. A man of Reginald's age, with a young wife—the best of girls, and as pretty as she can be—to go off with a common woman from the streets! Ugh!

LESBIA. You must make allowances. What can you expect? Reginald was always weak. He was brought up to be weak. The family property was all mortgaged when he inherited it. He had to struggle along in constant money difficulties, hustled by his solicitors, morally bullied by the Barmecide, and physically bullied by Boxer, while they two were fighting their own way and getting well trained. You know very well he couldnt afford to marry until the mortgages were cleared and he was over fifty. And then of course he made a fool of himself marrying a child like Leo.

THE GENERAL. But to hit her! Absolutely to hit her! He knocked her down—knocked her flat down on a flowerbed in the presence of his gardener. He! the head of the family! the man that stands before the Barmecide and myself as Bridgenorth of Bridgenorth!

[123]

to beat his wife and go off with a low woman and be divorced for it in the face of all England! in the face of my uniform and Alfred's apron! I can never forget what I felt: it was only the King's personal request—virtually a command—that stopped me from resigning my commission. I'd cut Reginald dead if I met him in the street.

MRS BRIDGENORTH. Besides, Leo's coming. Theyd meet. It's impossible, Lesbia.

LESBIA. Oh, I forgot that. That settles it. He mustnt come.

THE GENERAL. Of course he mustnt. You tell him that if he enters this house, I'll leave it; and so will every decent man and woman in it.

COLLINS [*returning for a moment to announce*] Mr Reginald, maam. [*He withdraws when Reginald enters*].

THE GENERAL [*beside himself*] Well, dash my buttons!!

Reginald is just the man Lesbia had described. He is hardened and tough physically, and hasty and boyish in his manner and speech, belonging as he does to the large class of English gentlemen of property (solicitor-managed) who have never developed intellectually since their schooldays. He is a muddled, rebellious, hasty, untidy, forgetful, always late sort of man, who very evidently needs the care of a capable woman, and has never been lucky or attractive enough to get it. All the same, a likeable man, from whom nobody apprehends any malice nor expects any achievement. In everything but years he is younger than his brother the General.

REGINALD [*coming forward between the General and Mrs Bridgenorth*] Alice: it's no use. I cant stay away from Edith's wedding. Good morning, Lesbia. How are you, Boxer ? [*He offers the General his hand*].

THE GENERAL [*with crushing stiffness*] I was just

telling Alice, sir, that if you entered this house, I should leave it.

REGINALD. Well, dont let me detain you, old chap. When you start calling people Sir, youre not particularly good company.

LESBIA. Dont you two begin to quarrel. That wont improve the situation.

MRS BRIDGENORTH. I think you might have waited until you got my answer, Rejjy.

REGINALD. It's so jolly easy to say No in a letter. Wont you let me stay?

MRS BRIDGENORTH. How can I? Leo's coming.

REGINALD, Well, she wont mind.

THE GENERAL. Wont mind!!!!!

LESBIA. Dont talk nonsense, Rejjy; and be off with you.

THE GENERAL [*with biting sarcasm*] At school you had a theory that women liked being knocked down, I remember.

REGINALD. You're a nice, chivalrous, brotherly sort of swine, you are.

THE GENERAL. Mr Bridgenorth: are you going to leave this house or am I?

REGINALD. You are, I hope. [*He emphasizes his intention to stay by sitting down*].

THE GENERAL. Alice: will you allow me to be driven from Edith's wedding by this—

LESBIA [*warningly*] Boxer!

THE GENERAL.—by this Respondent? Is Edith to be given away by him?

MRS BRIDGENORTH. Certainly not. Reginald: you were not asked to come; and I have asked you to go. You know how fond I am of Leo; and you know what she would feel if she came in and found you here.

COLLINS [*again appearing in the tower*] Mrs Reginald, maam.

LESBIA.

MRS BRIDGENORTH.

THE GENERAL.

} No, no. Ask her to—

Oh how unfortunate!

Well, dash my buttons!

[*All three clamoring together*].

It is too late: Leo is already in the kitchen. Collins goes out, mutely abandoning a situation which he deplores but has been unable to save.

Leo is very pretty, very youthful, very restless, and consequently very charming to people who are touched by youth and beauty, as well as to those who regard young women as more or less appetizing lollipops, and dont regard old women at all. Coldly studied, Leo's restlessness is much less lovable than the kittenishness which comes from a rich and fresh vitality. She is a born fusser about herself and everybody else for whom she feels responsible; and her vanity causes her to exaggerate her responsibilities officiously. All her fussing is about little things; but she often calls them by big names, such as Art, the Divine Spark, the world, motherhood, good breeding, the Universe, the Creator, or anything else that happens to strike her imagination as sounding intellectually important. She has more than common imagination and no more than common conception and penetration; so that she is always on the high horse about words and always in the perambulator about things. Considering herself clever, thoughtful, and superior to ordinary weaknesses and prejudices, she recklessly attaches herself to clever men on that understanding, with the result that they are at first delighted, then exasperated, and finally bored. When marrying Reginald she told her friends that there was a great deal in him which needed bringing out. If she were a middle-aged man she would be the terror of his club. Being a pretty young woman, she is forgiven everything, proving that "Tout comprendre, c'est tout pardonner" is an error, the fact being that the secret of forgiving everything is to understand nothing.

She runs in fussily, full of her own importance, and swoops on Lesbia, who is much less disposed to spoil her than Mrs Bridgenorth is. But Leo affects a special intimacy with Lesbia, as of two thinkers among the Philistines.

LEO [*to Lesbia, kissing her*] Good morning. [*Coming to Mrs Bridgenorth*] How do, Alice? [*Passing on towards the hearth*] Why so gloomy, General? [*Reginald rises between her and the General*] Oh, Rejjy! What will the King's Proctor say?

REGINALD. Damn the King's Proctor!

LEO. Naughty. Well, I suppose I must kiss you; but dont any of you tell. [*She kisses him. They can hardly believe their eyes*]. Have you kept all your promises?

REGINALD. Oh, dont begin bothering about those—

LEO [*insisting*] Have? You? Kept? Your? Promises? Have you rubbed your head with the lotion every night?

REGINALD. Yes, yes. Nearly every night.

LEO. Nearly! I know what that means. Have you worn your liver pad?

THE GENERAL [*solemnly*] Leo: forgiveness is one of the most beautiful traits in a woman's nature; but there are things that should not be forgiven to a man. When a man knocks a woman down [*Leo gives a little shriek of laughter and collapses on a chair next Mrs Bridgenorth, on her left*]—

REGINALD [*sardonically*] The man that would raise his hand to a woman, save in the way of kindness, is unworthy the name of Bridgenorth. [*He sits down at the end of the table nearest the hearth*].

[127]

THE GENERAL [*much huffed*] Oh, well, if Leo does not mind, of course I have no more to say. But I think you might, out of consideration for the family, beat your wife in private and not in the presence of the gardener.

REGINALD [*out of patience*] Whats the good of beating your wife unless theres a witness to prove it afterwards? You dont suppose a man beats his wife for the fun of it, do you? How could she have got her divorce if I hadnt beaten her? Nice state of things, that!

THE GENERAL [*gasping*] Do you mean to tell me that you did it in cold blood? simply to get rid of your wife?

REGINALD. No, I didnt: I did it to get her rid of me. What would you do if you were fool enough to marry a woman thirty years younger than yourself, and then found that she didnt care for you, and was in love with a young fellow with a face like a mushroom?

LEO. He has not. [*Bursting into tears*] And you are most unkind to say I didnt care for you. Nobody could have been fonder of you.

REGINALD. A nice way of shewing your fondness! I had to go out and dig the flower bed all over with my own hands to soften it. I had to pick all the stones out of it. And then she complained that I hadnt done it properly, because she got a worm down her neck. I had to go to Brighton with a poor creature who took a fancy to me on the way down, and got conscientious scruples about committing perjury after dinner. I had to put her down in the hotel book as Mrs Reginald Bridgenorth: Leo's name! Do you know what that feels like to a decent man? Do you know what a decent man feels about his wife's name? How would you like to go into a hotel before all the waiters and people with—with that on your arm? Not that it was the poor girl's fault, of course; only she started crying because I couldnt stand her touching me; and now she keeps writing to me. And then I'm held up in the public court for cruelty and adultery, and turned away from Edith's wedding by Alice, and lectured by you! a bachelor, and a precious green one at that. What do you know about it?

THE GENERAL. Am I to understand that the whole case was one of collusion?

REGINALD. Of course it was. Half the cases are collusions: what are people to do? [*The General, passing his hand dazedly over his bewildered brow, sinks into the railed chair*]. And what do you take me for, that you should have the cheek to pretend to believe all that rot about my knocking Leo about and leaving her for—for a—a—Ugh! you should have seen her.

THE GENERAL. This is perfectly astonishing to me. Why did you do it. Why did Leo allow it?

REGINALD. Youd better ask her.

LEO [*still in tears*] I'm sure I never thought it would be so horrid for Rejjy. I offered honorably to do it myself, and let him divorce me; but he wouldnt. And he said himself that it was the only way to do it—that it was the law that he should do it that way. I never saw that hateful creature until that day in Court. If he had only shewn her to me before, I should never have allowed it.

MRS BRIDGENORTH. You did all this for Leo's sake, Rejjy?

REGINALD [*with an unbearable sense of injury*] I shouldnt mind a bit if it were for Leo's sake. But to have to do it to make room for that mushroom-faced serpent—!

[129]

THE GENERAL [*jumping up*] What right had he to be made room for? Are you in your senses? What right?

REGINALD. The right of being a young man, suitable to a young woman. I had no right at my age to marry Leo: she knew no more about life than a child.

LEO. I knew a great deal more about it than a great baby like you. I'm sure I dont know how youll get on with no one to take care of you: I often lie awake at night thinking about it. And now youve made me thoroughly miserable.

REGINALD. Serve you right! [*She weeps*]. There: dont get into a tantrum, Leo.

LESBIA. May one ask who is the mushroom-faced serpent?

LEO. He isnt.

REGINALD. Sinjon Hotchkiss, of course.

MRS BRIDGENORTH. Sinjon Hotchkiss! Why, he's coming to the wedding!

REGINALD. What! In that case I'm off [*he makes for the tower*].

LEO		[*seizing him*] No you shant. You promised to be nice to him.
THE GENERAL	[*all four rushing after him and capturing him on the threshold*]	No, dont go, old chap. Not from Edith's wedding.
MRS BRIDGE-NORTH		Oh, do stay, Rejjy. I shall really be hurt if you desert us.
LESBIA		Better stay, Reginald. You must meet sooner or later.

REGINALD. A moment ago, when I wanted to stay,

you were all shoving me out of the house. Now that I want to go, you wont let me.

MRS BRIDGENORTH. I shall send a note to Mr Hotchkiss not to come.

LEO [*weeping again*] Oh, Alice! [*She comes back to her chair, heartbroken*].

REGINALD [*out of patience*] Oh well, let her have her way. Let her have her mushroom. Let him come. Let them all come.

He crosses the kitchen to the oak chest and sits sulkily on it. Mrs Bridgenorth shrugs her shoulders and sits at the table in Reginald's neighborhood listening in placid helplessness. Lesbia, out of patience with Leo's tears, goes into the garden and sits near the door, snuffing up the open air in her relief from the domestic stuffiness of Reginald's affairs.

LEO. It's so cruel of you to go on pretending that I dont care for you, Rejjy.

REGINALD [*bitterly*] She explained to me that it was only that she had exhausted my conversation.

THE GENERAL [*coming paternally to Leo*] My dear girl: all the conversation in the world has been exhausted long ago. Heaven knows I have exhausted the conversation of the British Army these thirty years; but I dont leave it on that account.

LEO. It's not that Ive exhausted it; but he will keep on repeating it when I want to read or go to sleep. And Sinjon amuses me. He's so clever.

THE GENERAL [*stung*] Ha! The old complaint. You all want geniuses to marry. This demand for clever men is ridiculous. Somebody must marry the plain, honest, stupid fellows. Have you thought of that?

LEO. But there are such lots of stupid women to marry. Why do they want to marry us? Besides, Rejjy knows that I'm quite fond of him. I like him because he wants me; and I like Sinjon because I want him. I feel that I have a duty to Rejjy.

THE GENERAL. Precisely: you have.

LEO. And, of course, Sinjon has the same duty to me.

THE GENERAL. Tut, tut!

LEO. Oh, how silly the law is! Why cant I marry them both?

THE GENERAL [shocked] Leo!

LEO. Well, I love them both. I should like to marry a lot of men. I should like to have Rejjy for every day, and Sinjon for concerts and theatres and going out in the evenings, and some great austere saint for about once a year at the end of the season, and some perfectly blithering idiot of a boy to be quite wicked with. I so seldom feel wicked; and, when I do, it's such a pity to waste it merely because it's too silly to confess to a real grown-up man.

REGINALD. This is the kind of thing, you know— [Helplessly] Well, there it is!

THE GENERAL [decisively] Alice: this is a job for the Barmecide. He's a Bishop: it's his duty to talk to Leo. I can stand a good deal; but when it comes to flat polygamy and polyandry, we ought to do something.

MRS BRIDGENORTH [going to the study door] Do come here a moment, Alfred. We're in a difficulty.

THE BISHOP [within] Ask Collins. I'm busy.

MRS BRIDGENORTH. Collins wont do. It's something very serious. Do come just a moment, dear. [When she hears him coming she takes a chair at the nearest end of the table].

The Bishop comes out of his study. He is still a slim active man, spare of flesh, and younger by temperament than his brothers. He has a delicate skin, fine hands, a salient nose with chin to match, a short beard which accentuates his sharp chin by bristling forward, clever, *humorous eyes, not without a glint of mischief in them, ready bright speech, and the ways of a successful man who is always interested in himself and generally rather well pleased with himself. When Lesbia hears his voice she turns her chair towards him, and presently rises and stands in the doorway listening to the conversation.*

THE BISHOP [*going to Leo*] Good morning, my dear. Hullo! Youve brought Reginald with you. Thats very nice of you. Have you reconciled them, Boxer?

THE GENERAL. Reconciled them! Why, man, the whole divorce was a put-up job. She wants to marry some fellow named Hotchkiss.

REGINALD. A fellow with a face like—

LEO. You shant, Rejjy. He has a very fine face.

MRS BRIDGENORTH. And now she says she wants to marry both of them, and a lot of other people as well.

LEO. I didnt say I wanted to marry them: I only said I should like to marry them.

THE BISHOP. Quite a nice distinction, Leo.

LEO. Just occasionally, you know.

THE BISHOP [*sitting down cosily beside her*] Quite so. Sometimes a poet, sometimes a Bishop, sometimes a fairy prince, sometimes somebody quite indescribable, and sometimes nobody at all.

LEO. Yes: thats just it. How did you know?

THE BISHOP. Oh, I should say most imaginative and cultivated young women feel like that. I wouldnt give a rap for one who didnt. Shakespear pointed out long ago that a woman wanted a Sunday husband as well as a weekday one. But, as usual, he didnt follow up the idea.

THE GENERAL [*aghast*] Am I to understand—

THE BISHOP [*cutting him short*] Now, Boxer, am I the Bishop or are you?

THE GENERAL [*sulkily*] You.

THE BISHOP. Then dont ask me are you to understand. "Yours not to reason why: yours but to do and die"—

THE GENERAL. Oh, very well: go on. I'm not clever. Only a silly soldier man. Ha! Go on. [*He throws himself into the railed chair, as one prepared for the worst*].

MRS BRIDGENORTH. Alfred: dont tease Boxer.

THE BISHOP. If we are going to discuss ethical questions we must begin by giving the devil fair play. Boxer never does. England never does. We always assume that the devil is guilty: and we wont allow him to prove his innocence, because it would be against public morals if he succeeded. We used to do the same with prisoners accused of high treason. And the consequence is that we overreach ourselves; and the devil gets the better of us after all. Perhaps thats what most of us intend him to do.

THE GENERAL. Alfred: we asked you here to preach to Leo. You are preaching at me instead. I am not conscious of having said or done anything that calls for that unsolicited attention.

THE BISHOP. But poor little Leo has only told the simple truth; whilst you, Boxer, are striking moral attitudes.

THE GENERAL. I suppose thats an epigram. I dont understand epigrams. I'm only a silly soldier man. Ha! But I can put a plain question. Is Leo to be encouraged to be a polygamist?

THE BISHOP. Remember the British Empire, Boxer. Youre a British General, you know.

THE GENERAL. What has that to do with polygamy?

THE BISHOP. Well, the great majority of our fellow-subjects are polygamists. I cant as a British Bishop insult them by speaking disrespectfully of polygamy.

It's a very interesting question. Many very interesting men have been polygamists: Solomon, Mahomet, and our friend the Duke of—of—hm! I never can remember his name.

THE GENERAL. It would become you better, Alfred, to send that silly girl back to her husband and her duty than to talk clever and mock at your religion. "What God hath joined together let no man put asunder." Remember that.

THE BISHOP. Dont be afraid, Boxer. What God hath joined together no man ever shall put asunder: God will take care of that. [*To Leo*] By the way, who was it that joined you and Reginald, my dear?

LEO. It was that awful little curate that afterwards drank, and travelled first class with a third-class ticket, and then tried to go on the stage. But they wouldnt have him. He called himself Egerton Fotheringay.

THE BISHOP. Well, whom Egerton Fotheringay hath joined, let Sir Gorell Barnes put asunder by all means.

THE GENERAL. I may be a silly soldier man; but I call this blasphemy.

THE BISHOP [*gravely*] Better for me to take the name of Mr Egerton Fotheringay in earnest than for you to take a higher name in vain.

LESBIA. Cant you three brothers ever meet without quarrelling?

THE BISHOP [*mildly*] This is not quarrelling, Lesbia: it's only English family life. Good morning.

LEO. You know, Bishop, it's very dear of you to take my part; but I'm not sure that I'm not a little shocked.

THE BISHOP. Then I think Ive been a little more successful than Boxer in getting you into a proper frame of mind.

THE GENERAL [*snorting*] Ha!

LEO. Not a bit; for now I'm going to shock you worse than ever. I think Solomon was an old beast.

THE BISHOP. Precisely what you ought to think of him, my dear. Dont apologize.

THE GENERAL [*more shocked*] Well, but hang it! Solomon was in the Bible. And, after all, Solomon was Solomon.

LEO. And I stick to it: I still want to have a lot of interesting men to know quite intimately—to say everything I think of to them, and have them say everything they think of to me.

THE BISHOP. So you shall, my dear, if you are lucky. But you know you neednt marry them all. Think of all the buttons you would have to sew on. Besides, nothing is more dreadful than a husband who keeps telling you everything he thinks, and always wants to know what you think.

LEO [*struck by this*] Well, thats very true of Rejjy: in fact, thats why I had to divorce him.

THE BISHOP [*condoling*] Yes: he repeats himself dreadfully, doesnt he?

REGINALD. Look here, Alfred. If I have my faults, let her find them out for herself without your help.

THE BISHOP. She has found them all out already, Reginald.

LEO [*a little huffily*] After all, there are worse men than Reginald. I daresay he's not so clever as you; but still he's not such a fool as you seem to think him!

THE BISHOP. Quite right, dear: stand up for your husband. I hope you will always stand up for all your husbands. [*He rises and goes to the hearth, where he stands complacently with his back to the fireplace, beaming at them all as at a roomful of children*].

LEO. Please dont talk as if I wanted to marry a whole regiment. For me there can never be more than two. I shall never love anybody but Rejjy and Sinjon.

REGINALD. A man with a face like a—

LEO. I wont have it, Rejjy. It's disgusting.

THE BISHOP. You see, my dear, youll exhaust Sin-jon's conversation too in a week or so. A man is like a phonograph with half-a-dozen records. You soon get tired of them all; and yet you have to sit at table whilst he reels them off to every new visitor. In the end you have to be content with his common humanity; and when you come down to that, you find out about men what a great English poet of my acquaintance used to say about women: that they all taste alike. Marry whom you please: at the end of a month he'll be Reginald over again. It wasnt worth changing: indeed it wasnt.

LEO. Then it's a mistake to get married.

THE BISHOP. It is, my dear; but it's a much bigger mistake not to get married.

THE GENERAL [*rising*] Ha! You hear that, Lesbia? [*He joins her at the garden door*].

LESBIA. Thats only an epigram, Boxer.

THE GENERAL. Sound sense, Lesbia. When a man talks rot, thats epigram: when he talks sense, then I agree with him.

REGINALD [*coming off the oak chest and looking at his watch*] It's getting late. Wheres Edith? Hasnt she got into her veil and orange blossoms yet?

MRS BRIDGENORTH. Do go and hurry her, Lesbia.

LESBIA [*going out through the tower*] Come with me, Leo.

LEO [*following Lesbia out*] Yes, certainly.

The Bishop goes over to his wife and sits down, taking her hand and kissing it by way of beginning a conversation with her.

THE BISHOP. Alice: Ive had another letter from the mysterious lady who cant spell. I like that woman's

letters. Theres an intensity of passion in them that
fascinates me.

MRS BRIDGENORTH. Do you mean Incognita Appassionata?

THE BISHOP. Yes.

THE GENERAL [*turning abruptly: he has been looking
out into the garden*] Do you mean to say that women
write love-letters to you?

THE BISHOP. Of course.

THE GENERAL. They never do to me.

THE BISHOP. The Army doesnt attract women: the
Church does.

REGINALD. Do you consider it right to let them?
They may be married women, you know.

THE BISHOP. They always are. This one is. [*To Mrs
Bridgenorth*] Dont you think her letters are quite the
best love-letters I get? [*To the two men*] Poor Alice
has to read my love-letters aloud to me at breakfast,
when theyre worth it.

MRS BRIDGENORTH. There really is something fascinating about Incognita. She never gives her address.
Thats a good sign.

THE GENERAL. Mf! No assignations, you mean?

THE BISHOP. Oh yes: she began the correspondence
by making a very curious but very natural assignation. She wants me to meet her in heaven. I hope I
shall.

THE GENERAL. Well, I must say I hope not, Alfred. I
hope not.

MRS BRIDGENORTH. She says she is happily married,
and that love is a necessary of life to her, but that she
must have, high above all her lovers—

THE BISHOP. She has several apparently—

MRS BRIDGENORTH.—some great man who will
never know her, never touch her, as she is on earth,

[138]

but whom she can meet in heaven when she has risen above all the everyday vulgarities of earthly love.

THE BISHOP [*rising*] Excellent. Very good for her; and no trouble to me. Everybody ought to have one of these idealizations, like Dante's Beatrice. [*He clasps his hands behind him, and strolls to the hearth and back, singing*].

Lesbia appears in the tower, rather perturbed.

LESBIA. Alice: will you come upstairs? Edith is not dressed.

MRS BRIDGENORTH [*rising*] Not dressed! Does she know what hour it is?

LESBIA. She has locked herself into her room, reading.

The Bishop's song ceases: he stops dead in his stroll.

THE GENERAL. Reading!

THE BISHOP. What is she reading?

LESBIA. Some pamphlet that came by the eleven o'clock post. She wont come out. She wont open the door. And she says she doesnt know whether she's going to be married or not til she's finished the pamphlet. Did you ever hear such a thing? Do come and speak to her.

MRS BRIDGENORTH. Alfred: you had better go.

THE BISHOP. Try Collins.

LESBIA. Weve tried Collins already. He got all that Ive told you out of her through the keyhole. Come, Alice [*She vanishes. Mrs Bridgenorth hurries after her*].

THE BISHOP. This means a delay. I shall go back to my work [*he makes for the study door*].

REGINALD. What are you working at now?

THE BISHOP [*stopping*] A chapter in my history of marriage. I'm just at the Roman business, you know.

THE GENERAL [*coming from the garden door to the chair Mrs Bridgenorth has just left, and sitting down*] Not more Ritualism, I hope, Alfred?

THE BISHOP. Oh no. I mean ancient Rome. [*He seats himself on the edge of the table*]. I've just come to the period when the propertied classes refused to get married and went in for marriage settlements instead. A few of the oldest families stuck to the marriage tradition so as to keep up the supply of vestal virgins, who had to be legitimate; but nobody else dreamt of getting married. It's all very interesting, because we're coming to that here in England; except that as we dont require any vestal virgins, nobody will get married at all, except the poor, perhaps.

THE GENERAL. You take it devilishly coolly. Reginald: do you think the Barmecide's quite sane?

REGINALD. No worse than ever he was.

THE GENERAL [*to the Bishop*] Do you mean to say you believe such a thing will ever happen in England as that respectable people will give up being married?

THE BISHOP. In England especially they will. In other countries the introduction of reasonable divorce laws will save the situation; but in England we always let an institution strain itself until it breaks. Ive told our last four Prime Ministers that if they didnt make our marriage laws reasonable there would be a strike against marriage, and that it would begin among the propertied classes, where no Government would dare to interfere with it.

REGINALD. What did they say to that?

THE BISHOP. The usual thing. Quite agreed with me, but were sure that they were the only sensible men in the world and that the least hint of marriage reform would lose them the next election. And then lost it all the same: on cordite, on drink, on Chinese labor in South Africa, on all sorts of trumpery.

REGINALD [*lurching across the kitchen towards the hearth with his hands in his pockets*] It's no use: they

wont listen to our sort. [*Turning on them*] Of course
they have to make you a Bishop and Boxer a General,
because, after all, their blessed rabble of snobs and
cads and half-starved shopkeepers cant do government work; and the bounders and week-enders are
too lazy and vulgar. Theyd simply rot without us; but
what do they ever do for us? what attention do they
ever pay to what we say and what we want? I take it
that we Bridgenorths are a pretty typical English
family of the sort that has always set things straight
and stuck up for the right to think and believe according to our conscience. But nowadays we are expected
to dress and eat as the week-end bounders do, and to
think and believe as the converted cannibals of Central
Africa do, and to lie down and let every snob and every
cad and ever halfpenny journalist walk over us. Why,
theres not a newspaper in England today that represents what I call solid Bridgenorth opinion and
tradition. Half of them read as if they were published
at the nearest mothers' meeting, and the other half at
the nearest motor garage. Do you call these chaps
gentlemen? Do you call them Englishmen? I dont.
[*He throws himself disgustedly into the nearest chair*].

THE GENERAL [*excited by Reginald's eloquence*] Do
you see my uniform? What did Collins say? It strikes
the eye. It was meant to. I put it on expressly to give
the modern army bounder a smack in the eye. Somebody has to set a right example by beginning. Well,
let it be a Bridgenorth. I believe in family blood and
tradition, by George.

THE BISHOP [*musing*] I wonder who will begin the
stand against marriage. It must come some day. I was
married myself before I'd thought about it; and even
if I had thought about it I was too much in love with
Alice to let anything stand in the way. But, you know,

Ive seen one of our daughters after another—Ethel,
Jane, Fanny, and Christina and Florence—go out at
that door in their veils and orange blossoms; and Ive
always wondered whether theyd have gone quietly if
theyd known what they were doing. Ive a horrible
misgiving about that pamphlet. All progress means
war with Society. Heaven forbid that Edith should be
one of the combatants!

*St John Hotchkiss comes into the tower ushered by
Collins. He is a very smart young gentleman of twenty-
nine or thereabouts, correct in dress to the last thread of
his collar, but too much preoccupied with his ideas to be
embarrassed by any concern as to his appearance. He
talks about himself with energetic gaiety. He talks to
other people with a sweet forbearance (implying a
kindly consideration for their stupidity) which infuri-
ates those whom he does not succeed in amusing. They
either lose their tempers with him or try in vain to snub
him.*

COLLINS [*announcing*] Mr Hotchkiss. [*He withdraws*].

HOTCHKISS [*clapping Reginald gaily on the shoulder as
he passes him*] Tootle loo, Rejjy.

REGINALD [*curtly, without rising or turning his head*]
Morning.

HOTCHKISS. Good morning, Bishop.

THE BISHOP [*coming off the table*] What on earth are
you doing here, Sinjon? You belong to the bridegroom's party: youve no business here until after the
ceremony.

HOTCHKISS. Yes, I know: thats just it. May I have a
word with you in private? Rejjy or any of the family
wont matter; but—[*he glances at the General, who has
risen rather stiffly, as he strongly disapproves of the
part played by Hotchkiss in Reginald's domestic affairs*].

THE BISHOP. All right, Sinjon. This is our brother,

General Bridgenorth. [*He goes to the hearth and posts himself there, with his hands clasped behind him*].

HOTCHKISS. Oh, good! [*He turns to the General, and takes out a card-case*]. As you are in the service, allow me to introduce myself. Read my card, please. [*He presents his card to the astonished General*].

THE GENERAL [*reading*] "Mr St John Hotchkiss, the Celebrated Coward, late Lieutenant in the 165th Fusiliers."

REGINALD [*with a chuckle*] He was sent back from South Africa because he funked an order to attack, and spoiled his commanding officer's plan.

THE GENERAL [*very gravely*] I remember the case now. I had forgotten the name. I'll not refuse your acquaintance, Mr Hotchkiss; partly because youre my brother's guest, and partly because Ive seen too much active service not to know that every man's nerve plays him false at one time or another, and that some very honorable men should never go into action at all, because theyre not built that way. But if I were you I should not use that visiting card. No doubt it's an honorable trait in your character that you dont wish any man to give you his hand in ignorance of your disgrace; but you had better allow us to forget. We wish to forget. It isnt your disgrace alone: it's a disgrace to the army and to all of us. Pardon my plain speaking.

HOTCHKISS [*sunnily*] My dear General, I dont know what fear means in the military sense of the word. Ive fought seven duels with the sabre in Italy and Austria, and one with pistols in France, without turning a hair. There was no other way in which I could vindicate my motives in refusing to make that attack at Smutsfontein. I dont pretend to be a brave man. I'm afraid of wasps. I'm afraid of cats. In spite of the voice of reason, I'm afraid of ghosts; and twice Ive fled across Europe from false alarms of cholera. But afraid to fight I am not. [*He turns gaily to Reginald and slaps him on the shoulder*]. Eh, Rejjy ? [*Reginald grunts*].

THE GENERAL. Then why did you not do your duty at Smutsfontein ?

HOTCHKISS. I did my duty—my higher duty. If I had made that attack, my commanding officer's plan would have been successful, and he would have been promoted. Now I happen to think that the British Army should be commanded by gentlemen, and by gentlemen alone. This man was not a gentleman. I sacrificed my military career—I faced disgrace and social ostracism—rather than give that man his chance.

THE GENERAL [*generously indignant*] Your commanding officer, sir, was my friend Major Billiter.

HOTCHKISS. Precisely. What a name !

THE GENERAL. And pray, sir, on what ground do you dare allege that Major Billiter is not a gentleman ?

HOTCHKISS. By an infallible sign: one of those trifles that stamp a man. He eats rice pudding with a spoon.

THE GENERAL [*very angry*] Confound you, *I* eat rice pudding with a spoon. Now !

HOTCHKISS. Oh, so do I, frequently. But there are ways of doing these things. Billiter's way was unmistakeable.

THE GENERAL. Well, *I*'ll tell you something now. When I thought you were only a coward, I pitied you, and would have done what I could to help you back to your place in Society—

HOTCHKISS [*interrupting him*] Thank you: I havnt lost it. My motives have been fully appreciated. I was made an honorary member of two of the smartest clubs in London when the truth came out.

THE GENERAL. Well, sir, those clubs consist of snobs; and you are a jumping, bounding, prancing, snorting snob yourself.

THE BISHOP [*amused but hospitably remonstrant*] My dear Boxer!

HOTCHKISS [*delighted*] How kind of you to say so, General! Youre quite right: I am a snob. Why not? The whole strength of England lies in the fact that the enormous majority of the English people are snobs. They insult poverty. They despise vulgarity. They love nobility. They admire exclusiveness. They will not obey a man risen from the ranks. They never trust one of their own class. I agree with them. I share their instincts. In my undergraduate days I was a Republican—a Socialist. I tried hard to feel toward a common man as I do towards a duke. I couldnt. Neither can you. Well, why should we be ashamed of this aspiration towards what is above us? Why dont I say that an honest man's the noblest work of God? Because I dont think so. If he's not a gentleman, I dont care whether he's honest or not: I shouldnt let his son marry my daughter. And thats the test, mind. Thats the test. You feel as I do. You are a snob in fact: I am a snob, not only in fact, but on principle. I shall go down in history, not as the first snob, but as the first avowed champion of English snobbery, and its first martyr in the army. The navy boasts two such martyrs in Captains Kirby and Wade, who were shot for refusing to fight under Admiral Benbow, a promoted cabin boy. I have always envied them their glory.

THE GENERAL. As a British General, sir, I have to inform you that if any officer under my command violated the sacred equality of our profession by putting a single jot of his duty or his risk on the shoulders of the humblest drummer boy, I'd shoot him with my own hand.

HOTCHKISS. That sentiment is not your equality, General, but your superiority. Ask the Bishop. [*He seats himself on the edge of the table*].

THE BISHOP. I cant support you, Sinjon. My profession also compels me to turn my back on snobbery. You see, I have to do such a terribly democratic thing to every child that is brought to me. Without distinction of class I have to confer on it a rank so high and awful that all the grades in Debrett and Burke seem like the medals they give children in Infant Schools in comparison. I'm not allowed to make any class distinction. They are all soldiers and servants, not officers and masters.

HOTCHKISS. Ah, youre quoting the Baptism service. Thats not a bit real, you know. If I may say so, you would both feel so much more at peace with yourselves if you would acknowledge and confess your real convictions. You know you dont really think a Bishop the equal of a curate, or a lieutenant in a line regiment the equal of a general.

THE BISHOP. Of course I do. I was a curate myself.

THE GENERAL. And I was a lieutenant in a line regiment.

REGINALD. And I was nothing. But we're all our own and one-another's equals, arnt we? So perhaps when youve quite done talking about yourselves, we shall get to whatever business Sinjon came about.

HOTCHKISS [*coming off the table hastily*] Oh! true, my dear fellow. I beg a thousand pardons. It's about the wedding!

THE GENERAL. What about the wedding?

HOTCHKISS. Well, we cant get our man up to the scratch. Cecil has locked himself in his room and wont see or speak to anyone. I went up to his room and banged at the door. I told him I should look through the keyhole if he didnt answer. I looked through the keyhole. He was sitting on his bed, reading a book. [*Reginald rises in consternation. The General recoils*]. I told him not to be an ass, and so forth. He said he was not going to budge until he had finished the book. I asked him did he know what time it was, and whether he happened to recollect that he had a rather important appointment to marry Edith. He said the sooner I stopped interrupting him, the sooner he'd be ready. Then he stuffed his fingers in his ears; turned over on his elbows; and buried himself in his beastly book. I couldnt get another word out of him: so I thought I'd better come here and warn you.

REGINALD. This looks to me like a practical joke. Theyve arranged it between them.

THE BISHOP. No. Edith has no sense of humor. And Ive never seen a man in a jocular mood on his wedding morning.

Collins appears in the tower, ushering in the bridegroom, a young gentleman with good looks of the serious kind, somewhat careworn by an exacting conscience and just now distracted by insoluble problems of conduct.

COLLINS [*announcing*] Mr Cecil Sykes. [*He retires*].

HOTCHKISS. Look here, Cecil: this is all wrong. Youve no business here until after the wedding. Hang it, man! youre the bridegroom.

SYKES [*coming to the Bishop, and addressing him with dogged desperation*] Ive come here to say this. When I proposed to Edith I was in utter ignorance of what I was letting myself in for legally. Having given my word, I will stand to it. You have me at your mercy: marry me if you insist. But take notice that I protest. [*He sits down distractedly in the railed chair*].

THE GENERAL. ⎱
REGINALD. ⎰ [*Both highly incensed*] ⎰ What the devil do you mean by this ? What the— Confound your impertinence, what do you—

HOTCHKISS. ⎱ Easy, Rejjy. Easy, old man. Steady, steady, steady. [*Reginald subsides into his chair. Hotchkiss sits on his right, appeasing him*].

THE BISHOP. ⎰ No, please, Rej. Control yourself, Boxer, I beg you.

THE GENERAL. I tell you I cant control myself. Ive been controlling myself for the last half-hour until I feel like bursting. [*He sits down furiously at the end of the table next the study*].

SYKES [*pointing to the simmering Reginald and the boiling General*] Thats just it, Bishop. Edith is her uncles' niece. She cant control herself any more than they can. And she's a Bishop's daughter. That means that she's engaged in social work of all sorts: organizing shop assistants and sweated work girls and all that. When her blood boils about it (and it boils at least once a week) she doesnt care what she says.

REGINALD. Well: you knew that when you proposed to her.

SYKES. Yes; but I didnt know that when we were married I should be legally responsible if she libelled anybody, though all her property is protected against me as if I were the lowest thief and cadger. This morning somebody sent me Belfort Bax's essays on Men's Wrongs; and they have been a perfect eye-opener to me. Bishop: I'm not thinking of myself: I would face anything for Edith. But my mother and sisters are wholly dependent on my property. I'd rather have to cut off an inch from my right arm than a hundred a year from my mother's income. I owe everything to her care of me.

Edith, in dressing-jacket and petticoat, comes in through the tower, swiftly and determinedly, pamphlet in hand, principles up in arms, more of a bishop than her father, yet as much a gentlewoman as her mother. She is the typical spoilt child of a clerical household: almost as terrible a product as the typical spoilt child of a Bohemian household: that is, all her childish affectations of conscientious scruple and religious impulse have been applauded and deferred to until she has become an ethical snob of the first water. Her father's sense of humor and her mother's placid balance have done something to save her humanity; but her impetuous temper and energetic will, unrestrained by any touch of humor or scepticism, carry everything before them. Imperious and dogmatic, she takes command of the party at once.

EDITH [*standing behind Cecil's chair*] Cecil: I heard your voice. I must speak to you very particularly. Papa: go away. Go away everybody.

THE BISHOP [*crossing to the study door*] I think there can be no doubt that Edith wishes us to retire. Come. [*He stands in the doorway, waiting for them to follow*].

SYKES. Thats it, you see. It's just this outspokenness that makes my position hard, much as I admire her for it.

EDITH. Do you want me to flatter and be untruthful?

SYKES. No, not exactly that.

EDITH. Does anybody want me to flatter and be untruthful?

HOTCHKISS. Well, since you ask me, I do. Surely it's the very first qualification for tolerable social intercourse.

THE GENERAL [*markedly*] I hope you will always tell me the truth, my darling, at all events.

EDITH [*complacently coming to the fireplace*] You can depend on me for that, Uncle Boxer.

HOTCHKISS. Are you sure you have any adequate idea of what the truth about a military man really is?

REGINALD [*aggressively*] Whats the truth about you I wonder?

HOTCHKISS. Oh, quite unfit for publication in its entirety. If Miss Bridgenorth begins telling it, I shall have to leave the room.

REGINALD. I'm not at all surprised to hear it. [*Rising*] But whats it got to do with our business here today? Is it you thats going to be married or is it Edith?

HOTCHKISS. I'm so sorry. I get so interested in myself that I thrust myself into the front of every discussion in the most insufferable way. [*Reginald, with an exclamation of disgust, crosses the kitchen towards the study door*]. But, my dear Rejjy, are you quite sure that Miss Bridgenorth is going to be married? Are you, Miss Bridgenorth?

Before Edith has time to answer her mother returns with Leo and Lesbia.

LEO. Yes, here she is, of course. I told you I heard her dash downstairs. [*She comes to the end of the table next the fireplace*].

MRS BRIDGENORTH [*transfixed in the middle of the kitchen*] And Cecil!!!

LESBIA. And Sinjon!

THE BISHOP. Edith wishes to speak to Cecil. [*Mrs Bridgenorth comes to him. Lesbia goes into the garden, as before*]. Let us go into my study.

LEO. But she must come and dress. Look at the hour!

MRS BRIDGENORTH. Come, Leo dear. [*Leo follows her reluctantly. They are about to go into the study with the Bishop*].

HOTCHKISS. Do you know, Miss Bridgenorth, I

should most awfully like to hear what you have to say to poor Cecil.

REGINALD [*scandalized*] Well!

EDITH. Who is poor Cecil, pray?

HOTCHKISS. One always calls a man that on his wedding morning: I dont know why. I'm his best man, you know. Dont you think it gives me a certain right to be present in Cecil's interest?

THE GENERAL [*gravely*] There is such a thing as delicacy, Mr Hotchkiss.

HOTCHKISS. There is such a thing as curiosity, General.

THE GENERAL [*furious*] Delicacy is thrown away here, Alfred. Edith: you had better take Sykes into the study.

The group at the study door breaks up. The General flings himself into the last chair on the long side of the table, near the garden door. Leo sits at the end, next him, and Mrs Bridgenorth next Leo. Reginald returns to the oak chest, to be near Leo; and the Bishop goes to his wife and stands by her.

HOTCHKISS [*to Edith*] Of course I'll go if you wish me to. But Cecil's objection to go through with it was so entirely on public grounds—

EDITH [*with quick suspicion*] His objection?

SYKES. Sinjon: you have no right to say that. I expressly said that I'm ready to go through with it.

EDITH. Cecil: do you mean to say that you have been raising difficulties about our marriage?

SYKES. I raise no difficulty. But I do beg you to be careful what you say about people. You must remember, my dear, that when we are married I shall be responsible for everything you say. Only last week you said on a public platform that Slattox and Chinnery were scoundrels. They could have got a thousand

[151]

pounds damages apiece from me for that if we'd been married at the time.

EDITH [*austerely*] I never said anything of the sort. I never stoop to mere vituperation: what would my girls say of me if I did? I chose my words most carefully. I said they were tyrants, liars, and thieves; and so they are. Slattox is even worse.

HOTCHKISS. I'm afraid that would be at least five thousand pounds.

SYKES. If it were only myself, I shouldnt care. But my mother and sisters! Ive no right to sacrifice them.

EDITH. You neednt be alarmed. I'm not going to be married.

ALL THE REST. Not!

SYKES [*in consternation*] Edith! Are you throwing me over?

EDITH. How can I? you have been beforehand with me.

SYKES. On my honor, no. All I said was that I didnt know the law when I asked you to be my wife.

EDITH. And you wouldnt have asked me if you had. Is that it?

SYKES. No. I should have asked you for my sake to be a little more careful—not to ruin me uselessly.

EDITH. You think the truth useless?

HOTCHKISS. Much worse than useless, I assure you. Frequently most mischievous.

EDITH. Sinjon: hold your tongue. You are a chatter-box and a fool!

MRS BRIDGENORTH ⎱ [*shocked*] ⎰Edith!
THE BISHOP ⎰ ⎱My love!

HOTCHKISS [*mildly*] I shall not take an action, Cecil.

EDITH [*to Hotchkiss*] Sorry; but you are old enough to know better. [*To the others*] And now since there is to be no wedding, we had better get back to our work.

Mamma: will you tell Collins to cut up the wedding cake into thirty-three pieces for the club girls. My not being married is no reason why they should be disappointed. [*She turns to go*].

HOTCHKISS [*gallantly*] If youll allow me to take Cecil's place, Miss Bridgenorth—

LEO. Sinjon!

HOTCHKISS. Oh, I forgot. I beg your pardon. [*To Edith, apologetically*] A prior engagement.

EDITH. What! You and Leo! I thought so. Well, hadnt you two better get married at once? I dont approve of long engagements. The breakfast's ready: the cake's ready: everything's ready. I'll lend Leo my veil and things.

THE BISHOP. I'm afraid they must wait until the decree is made absolute, my dear. And the license is not transferable.

EDITH. Oh well, it cant be helped. Is there anything else before I go off to the Club?

SYKES. You dont seem much disappointed, Edith. I cant help saying that much.

EDITH. And you cant help looking enormously relieved, Cecil. We shant be any worse friends, shall we?

SYKES [*distractedly*] Of course not. Still—I'm perfectly ready—at least—if it were not for my mother— Oh, I dont know what to do. Ive been so fond of you; and when the worry of the wedding was over I should have been so fond of you again—

EDITH [*petting him*] Come, come! dont make a scene, dear. Youre quite right. I dont think a woman doing public work ought to get married unless her husband feels about it as she does. I dont blame you at all for throwing me over.

REGINALD [*bouncing off the chest, and passing behind*

the General to the other end of the table] No: dash it! I'm not going to stand this. Why is the man always to be put in the wrong? Be honest, Edith. Why werent you dressed? Were you going to throw him over? If you were, take your fair share of the blame; and dont put it all on him.

HOTCHKISS [*sweetly*] Would it not be better—

REGINALD [*violently*] Now look here, Hotchkiss. Who asked you to cut in? Is your name Edith? Am I your uncle?

HOTCHKISS. I wish you were: I should like to have an uncle Reginald.

REGINALD. Yah! Sykes: are you ready to marry Edith or are you not?

SYKES. Ive already said that I'm quite ready. A promise is a promise.

REGINALD. We dont want to know whether a promise is a promise or not. Cant you answer yes or no without spoiling it and setting Hotchkiss here grinning like a Cheshire cat? If she puts on her veil and goes to Church, will you marry her?

SYKES. Certainly. Yes.

REGINALD. Thats all right. Now, Edie, put on your veil and off with you to Church. The bridegroom's waiting. [*He sits down at the table*].

EDITH. Is it understood that Slattox and Chinnery are liars and thieves, and that I hope by next Wednesday to have in my hands conclusive evidence that Slattox is something much worse?

SYKES. I made no conditions as to that when I proposed to you; and now I cant go back. I hope Providence will spare my poor mother. I say again I'm ready to marry you.

EDITH. Then I think you shew great weakness of character; and instead of taking advantage of it I shall

set you a better example. I want to know is this true.
[*She produces a pamphlet and takes it to the Bishop;
then sits down between Hotchkiss and her mother*].

THE BISHOP [*reading the title*] DO YOU KNOW WHAT
YOU ARE GOING TO DO? BY A WOMAN WHO HAS
DONE IT. May I ask my dear, what she did?

EDITH. She got married. When she had three children
—the eldest only four years old—her husband committed a murder, and then attempted to commit
suicide, but only succeeded in disfiguring himself.
Instead of hanging him, they sent him to penal servitude for life, for the sake, they said, of his wife and
infant children. And she could not get a divorce from
that horrible murderer. They would not even keep
him imprisoned for life. For twenty years she had to
live singly, bringing up her children by her own work,
and knowing that just when they were grown up and
beginning life, this dreadful creature would be let out
to disgrace them all, and prevent the two girls getting
decently married, and drive the son out of the country
perhaps. Is that really the law? Am I to understand
that if Cecil commits a murder, or forges, or steals, or
becomes an atheist, I cant get divorced from him?

THE BISHOP. Yes, my dear. That is so. You must
take him for better for worse.

EDITH. Then I most certainly refuse to enter into any
such wicked contract. What sort of servants? what
sort of friends? what sort of Prime Ministers should
we have if we took them for better for worse for all
their lives? We should simply encourage them in every
sort of wickedness. Surely my husband's conduct is of
more importance to me than Mr Balfour's or Mr
Asquith's. If I had known the law I would never
have consented. I dont believe any woman would if
she realized what she was doing.

SYKES. But I'm not going to commit murder.

EDITH. How do you know? Ive sometimes wanted to murder Slattox. Have you never wanted to murder somebody, Uncle Rejjy?

REGINALD [*at Hotchkiss, with intense expression*] Yes.

LEO. Rejjy!

REGINALD. I said yes; and I mean yes. There was one night, Hotchkiss, when I jolly nearly shot you and Leo and finished up with myself; and thats the truth.

LEO [*suddenly whimpering*] Oh Rejjy [*she runs to him and kisses him*].

REGINALD [*wrathfully*] Be off. [*She returns weeping to her seat*].

MRS BRIDGENORTH [*petting Leo, but speaking to the company at large*] But isnt all this great nonsense? What likelihood is there of any of us committing a crime?

HOTCHKISS. Oh yes, I assure you. I went into the matter once very carefully; and I found that things I have actually done—things that everybody does, I imagine—would expose me, if I were found out and prosecuted, to ten years penal servitude, two years hard labor, and the loss of all civil rights. Not counting that I'm a private trustee, and, like all private trustees, a fraudulent one. Otherwise, the widow for whom I am trustee would starve occasionally, and the children get no education. And I'm probably as honest as any here.

THE GENERAL [*outraged*] Do you imply that I have been guilty of conduct that would expose me to penal servitude?

HOTCHKISS. I should think it quite likely. But of course I dont know.

MRS BRIDGENORTH. But bless me! marriage is not a

question of law, is it? Have you children no affection for one another? Surely thats enough?

HOTCHKISS. If it's enough, why get married?

MRS BRIDGENORTH. Stuff, Sinjon! Of course people must get married. [*Uneasily*] Alfred: why dont you say something? Surely youre not going to let this go on?

THE GENERAL. Ive been waiting for the last twenty minutes, Alfred, in amazement! in stupefaction! to hear you put a stop to all this. We look to you: it's your place, your office, your duty. Exert your authority at once.

THE BISHOP. You must give the devil fair play, Boxer. Until you have heard and weighed his case you have no right to condemn him. I'm sorry you have been kept waiting twenty minutes; but I myself have waited twenty years for this to happen. Ive often wrestled with the temptation to pray that it might not happen in my own household. Perhaps it was a presentiment that it might become a part of our old Bridgenorth burden that made me warn our Governments so earnestly that unless the law of marriage were first made human, it could never become divine.

MRS BRIDGENORTH. Oh, do be sensible about this. People must get married. What would you have said if Cecil's parents had not been married?

THE BISHOP. They were not, my dear.

HOTCHKISS.		Hallo!
REGINALD.		What d'ye mean?
THE GENERAL.		Eh?
LEO.		Not married!
MRS BRIDGENORTH.		What!

SYKES [*rising in amazement*] What on earth do you mean, Bishop? My parents were married.

HOTCHKISS. You cant remember, Cecil.

SYKES. Well, I never asked my mother to shew me her marriage lines, if thats what you mean. What man ever has? I never suspected—I never knew—Are you joking? Or have we all gone mad?

THE BISHOP. Dont be alarmed, Cecil. Let me explain. Your parents were not Anglicans. You were not, I think, Anglican yourself, until your second year at Oxford. They were Positivists. They went through the Positivist ceremony at Newton Hall in Fetter Lane after entering into the civil contract before the Registrar of the West Strand District. I ask you, as an Anglican Catholic, was that a marriage?

SYKES [*overwhelmed*] Great Heavens, no! a thousand times, no. I never thought of that. I'm a child of sin. [*He collapses into the railed chair*].

THE BISHOP. Oh, come, come! You are no more a child of sin than any Jew, or Mahometan, or Nonconformist, or anyone else born outside the Church. But you see how it affects my view of the situation. To me there is only one marriage that is holy: the Church's sacrament of marriage. Outside that, I can recognize no distinction between one civil contract and another. There was a time when all marriages were made in Heaven. But because the Church was unwise and would not make its ordinances reasonable, its power over men and women was taken away from it; and marriages gave place to contracts at a registry office. And now that our Governments refuse to make these contracts reasonable, those whom we in our blindness drove out of the Church will be driven out of the registry office; and we shall have the history of Ancient Rome repeated. We shall be joined by our solicitors for seven, fourteen, or twenty-one years—or perhaps months. Deeds of partnership will replace the old vows.

THE GENERAL. Would you, a Bishop, approve of such partnerships?

THE BISHOP. Do you think that I, a Bishop, approve of the Deceased Wife's Sister Act? That did not prevent its becoming law.

THE GENERAL. But when the Government sounded you as to whether youd marry a man to his deceased wife's sister you very naturally and properly told them youd see them damned first.

THE BISHOP [*horrified*] No, no, really, Boxer! You must not—

THE GENERAL [*impatiently*] Oh, of course I dont mean that you used those words. But that was the meaning and the spirit of it.

THE BISHOP. Not the spirit, Boxer, I protest. But never mind that. The point is that State marriage is already divorced from Church marriage. The relations between Leo and Rejjy and Sinjon are perfectly legal; but do you expect me, as a Bishop, to approve of them?

THE GENERAL. I dont defend Reginald. He should have kicked you out of the house, Mr Hotchkiss.

REGINALD [*rising*] How could I kick him out of the house? He's stronger than me: he could have kicked me out if it came to that. He did kick me out: what else was it but kicking out, to take my wife's affections from me and establish himself in my place? [*He comes to the hearth*].

HOTCHKISS. I protest, Reginald, I said all that a man could to prevent the smash.

REGINALD. Oh, I know you did: I dont blame you: people dont do these things to one another: they happen and they cant be helped. What was I to do? I was old: she was young. I was dull: he was brilliant. I had a face like a walnut: he had a face like a mushroom. I was as glad to have him in the house as she was: he amused me. And we were a couple of fools: he gave us good advice—told us what to do when we didnt know. She found out that I wasnt any use to her and he was; so she nabbed him and gave me the chuck.

LEO. If you dont stop talking in that disgraceful way about our married life, I'll leave the room and never speak to you again.

REGINALD. Youre not going to speak to me again, anyhow, are you? Do you suppose I'm going to visit you when you marry him?

HOTCHKISS. I hope so. Surely youre not going to be vindictive, Rejjy. Besides, youll have all the advantages I formerly enjoyed. Youll be the visitor, the relief, the new face, the fresh news, the hopeless attachment: *I* shall only be the husband.

REGINALD [*savagely*] Will you tell me this, any of you? how is it that we always get talking about Hotchkiss when our business is about Edith? [*He fumes up the kitchen to the tower and back to his chair*].

MRS BRIDGENORTH. Will somebody tell me how the world is to get on if nobody is to get married?

SYKES. Will somebody tell me what an honorable man and a sincere Anglican is to propose to a woman whom he loves and who loves him and wont marry him?

LEO. Will somebody tell me how I'm to arrange to take care of Rejjy when I'm married to Sinjon. Rejjy must not be allowed to marry anyone else, especially that odious nasty creature that told all those wicked lies about him in Court.

HOTCHKISS. Let us draw up the first English partnership deed.

LEO. For shame, Sinjon!

THE BISHOP. Somebody must begin, my dear. Ive a

very strong suspicion that when it is drawn up it will be so much worse than the existing law that you will all prefer getting married. We shall therefore be doing the greatest possible service to morality by just trying how the new system would work.

LESBIA [*suddenly reminding them of her forgotten presence as she stands thoughtfully in the garden doorway*] Ive been thinking.

THE BISHOP [*to Hotchkiss*] Nothing like making people think: is there, Sinjon?

LESBIA [*coming to the table, on the General's left*] A woman has no right to refuse motherhood. That is clear, after the statistics given in The Times by Mr Sidney Webb.

THE GENERAL. Mr Webb has nothing to do with it. It is the Voice of Nature.

LESBIA. But if she is an English lady it is her right and her duty to stand out for honorable conditions. If we can agree on the conditions, I am willing to enter into an alliance with Boxer.

The General staggers to his feet, momentarily stupent and speechless.

EDITH [*rising*] And I with Cecil.

LEO [*rising*] And I with Rejjy and St John.

THE GENERAL [*aghast*] An alliance! Do you mean a—a—a—

REGINALD. She only means bigamy, as I understand her.

THE GENERAL. Alfred: how long more are you going to stand there and countenance this lunacy? Is it a horrible dream or am I awake? In the name of common sense and sanity, let us get back to real life—

Collins comes in through the tower, in alderman's robes. The ladies who are standing sit down hastily, and look as unconcerned as possible.

COLLINS. Sorry to hurry you, my lord; but the Church has been full this hour past; and the organist has played all the wedding music in Lohengrin three times over.

THE GENERAL. The very man we want. Alfred: I'm not equal to this crisis. You are not equal to it. The Army has failed. The Church has failed. I shall put aside all idle social distinctions and appeal to the Municipality.

MRS BRIDGENORTH. Do, Boxer. He is sure to get us out of this difficulty.

Collins, a little puzzled, comes forward affably to Hotchkiss's left.

HOTCHKISS [*rising, impressed by the aldermanic gown*] Ive not had the pleasure. Will you introduce me?

COLLINS [*confidentially*] All right, sir. Only the greengrocer, sir, in charge of the wedding breakfast. Mr Alderman Collins, sir, when I'm in my gown.

HOTCHKISS [*staggered*] Very pleased indeed [*he sits down again*].

THE BISHOP. Personally I value the counsel of my old friend, Mr Alderman Collins, very highly. If Edith and Cecil will allow him—

EDITH. Collins has known me from my childhood: I'm sure he will agree with me.

COLLINS. Yes, miss: you may depend on me for that. Might I ask what the difficulty is?

EDITH. Simply this. Do you expect me to get married in the existing state of the law?

SYKES [*rising and coming to Collins's left elbow*] I put it to you as a sensible man: is it any worse for her than for me?

REGINALD [*leaving his place and thrusting himself between Collins and Sykes, who returns to his chair*] Thats not the point. Let this be understood, Mr

Collins. It's not the man who is backing out: it's the woman. [*He posts himself on the hearth*].

LESBIA. We do not admit that, Collins. The women are perfectly ready to make a reasonable arrangement.

LEO. With both men.

THE GENERAL. The case is now before you, Mr Collins. And I put it to you as one man to another: did you ever hear such crazy nonsense?

MRS BRIDGENORTH. The world must go on, mustnt it, Collins?

COLLINS [*snatching at this, the first intelligible proposition he has heard*] Oh, the world will go on, maam: dont you be afraid of that. It aint so easy to stop it as the earnest kind of people think.

EDITH. I knew you would agree with me, Collins. Thank you.

HOTCHKISS. Have you the least idea of what they are talking about, Mr Alderman?

COLLINS. Oh, thats all right, sir. The particulars dont matter. I never read the report of a Committee: after all, what can they say that you dont know? You pick it up as they go on talking. [*He goes to the corner of the table and speaks across it to the company*]. Well, my Lord and Miss Edith and Madam and Gentlemen, it's like this. Marriage is tolerable enough in its way if youre easygoing and dont expect too much from it. But it doesnt bear thinking about. The great thing is to get the young people tied up before they know what theyre letting themselves in for. Theres Miss Lesbia now. She waited til she started thinking about it; and then it was all over. If you once start arguing, Miss Edith and Mr Sykes, youll never get married. Go and get married first: youll have plenty of arguing afterwards, miss, believe me.

HOTCHKISS. Your warning comes too late. Theyve started arguing already.

THE GENERAL. But you dont take in the full—well, I
dont wish to exaggerate; but the only word I can find
is the full horror of the situation. These ladies not
only refuse our honorable offers, but as I understand
it—and I'm sure I beg your pardon most heartily,
if I'm wrong, as I hope I am—they actually call on us
to enter into—I'm sorry to use the expression; but
what can I say?—into ALLIANCES with them under
contracts to be drawn up by our confounded solicitors.

COLLINS. Dear me, General: thats something new
when the parties belong to the same class.

THE BISHOP. Not new, Collins. The Romans did it.

COLLINS. Yes: they would, them Romans. When
youre in Rome do as the Romans do, is an old saying.
But we're not in Rome at present, my lord.

THE BISHOP. We have got into many of their ways.
What do you think of the contract system, Collins?

COLLINS. Well, my lord, when theres a question of a
contract, I always say, shew it to me on paper. If it's
to be talk, let it be talk; but if it's to be a contract,
down with it in black and white; and then we shall
know what we're about.

HOTCHKISS. Quite right, Mr Alderman. Let us draft
it at once. May I go into the study for writing materials, Bishop?

THE BISHOP. Do, Sinjon.

Hotchkiss goes into the library.

COLLINS. If I might point out a difficulty, my lord—

THE BISHOP. Certainly. [*He goes to the fourth chair
from the General's left, but before sitting down, court-
eously points to the chair at the end of the table next the
hearth*]. Wont you sit down, Mr Alderman? [*Collins,
very appreciative of the Bishop's distinguished consideration, sits down. The Bishop then takes his seat*].

COLLINS. We are at present six men to four ladies.
Thats not fair.

REGINALD. Not fair to the men, you mean.

LEO. Oh! Rejjy has said something clever! Can I be mistaken in him?

Hotchkiss comes back with a blotter and some paper. He takes the vacant place in the middle of the table between Lesbia and the Bishop.

COLLINS. I tell you the truth, my lord and ladies and gentlemen: I dont trust my judgment on this subject. Theres a certain lady that I always consult on delicate points like this. She has a very exceptional experience, and a wonderful temperament and instinct in affairs of the heart.

HOTCHKISS. Excuse me, Mr Alderman: I'm a snob, and I warn you that theres no use consulting anyone who will not advise us frankly on class lines. Marriage is good enough for the lower classes: they have facilities for desertion that are denied to us. What is the social position of this lady?

COLLINS. The highest in the borough, sir. She is the Mayoress. But you need not stand in awe of her, sir. She is my sister-in-law. [*To the Bishop*] Ive often spoken of her to your lady, my lord. [*To Mrs Bridgenorth*] Mrs George, maam.

MRS BRIDGENORTH [*startled*] Do you mean to say, Collins, that Mrs George is a real person?

COLLINS [*equally startled*] Didnt you believe in her, maam?

MRS BRIDGENORTH. Never for a moment.

THE BISHOP. We always thought that Mrs George was too good to be true. I still dont believe in her, Collins. You must produce her if you are to convince me.

COLLINS [*overwhelmed*] Well, I'm so taken aback by this that—Well I never!!! Why! she's at the church this moment, waiting to see the wedding.

THE BISHOP. Then produce her. [*Collins shakes his*

head]. Come, Collins! confess. Theres no such person.

COLLINS. There is, my lord: there is, I assure you. You ask George. It's true *I* cant produce her; but you can, my lord.

THE BISHOP. I!

COLLINS. Yes, my lord, you. For some reason that I never could make out, she has forbidden me to talk about you, or to let her meet you. Ive asked her to come here of a wedding morning to help with the flowers or the like; and she has always refused. But if you order her to come as her Bishop, she'll come. She has some very strange fancies, has Mrs George. Send your ring to her, my lord—the official ring—send it by some very stylish gentleman—perhaps Mr Hotchkiss here would be good enough to take it—and she'll come.

THE BISHOP [*taking off his ring and handing it to Hotchkiss*] Oblige me by undertaking the mission.

HOTCHKISS. But how am I to know the lady?

COLLINS. She has gone to the church in state, sir, and will be attended by a Beadle with a mace. He will point her out to you; and he will take the front seat of the carriage on the way back.

HOTCHKISS. No, by heavens! Forgive me, Bishop; but you are asking too much. I ran away from the Boers because I was a snob. I run away from the Beadle for the same reason. I absolutely decline the mission.

THE GENERAL [*rising impressively*] Be good enough to give me that ring, Mr Hotchkiss.

HOTCHKISS. With pleasure. [*He hands it to him*].

THE GENERAL. I shall have great pleasure, Mr Alderman, in waiting on the Mayoress with the Bishop's orders; and I shall be proud to return with municipal honors. [*He stalks out gallantly, Collins rising for a moment to bow to him with marked dignity*].

REGINALD. Boxer is rather a fine old josser in his way.

HOTCHKISS. His uniform gives him an unfair advantage. He will take all the attention off the Beadle.

COLLINS. I think it would be as well, my lord, to go on with the contract while we're waiting. The truth is, we shall none of us have much of a look-in when Mrs George comes; so we had better finish the writing part of the business before she arrives.

HOTCHKISS. I think I have the preliminaries down all right. [*Reading*] 'Memorandum of Agreement made this day of blank blank between blank blank of blank blank in the County of blank, Esquire, hereinafter called the Gentleman, of the one part, and blank blank of blank in the County of blank, hereinafter called the Lady, of the other part, whereby it is declared and agreed as follows.'

LEO [*rising*] You might remember your manners, Sinjon. The lady comes first. [*She goes behind him and stoops to look at the draft over his shoulder*].

HOTCHKISS. To be sure. I beg your pardon. [*He alters the draft*].

LEO. And you have got only one lady and one gentleman. There ought to be two gentlemen.

COLLINS. Oh, thats a mere matter of form, maam. Any number of ladies or gentlemen can be put in.

LEO. Not any number of ladies. Only one lady. Besides, that creature wasnt a lady.

REGINALD. You shut your head, Leo. This is a general sort of contract for everybody: it's not your contract.

LEO. Then what use is it to me?

HOTCHKISS. You will get some hints from it for your own contract.

[167]

EDITH. I hope there will be no hinting. Let us have the plain straightforward truth and nothing but the truth.

COLLINS. Yes, yes, miss: it will be all right. Theres nothing underhand, I assure you. It's a model agreement, as it were.

EDITH [*unconvinced*] I hope so.

HOTCHKISS. What is the first clause in an agreement, usually? You know, Mr Alderman.

COLLINS [*at a loss*] Well, sir, the Town Clerk always sees to that. Ive got out of the habit of thinking for myself in these little matters. Perhaps his lordship knows.

THE BISHOP. I'm sorry to say I dont. But Soames will know. Alice: where is Soames?

HOTCHKISS. He's in there [*pointing to the study*].

THE BISHOP [*to his wife*] Coax him to join us, my love. [*Mrs Bridgenorth goes into the study*]. Soames is my chaplain, Mr Collins. The great difficulty about Bishops in the Church of England today is that the affairs of the diocese make it necessary that a Bishop should be before everything a man of business, capable of sticking to his desk for sixteen hours a day. But the result of having Bishops of this sort is that the spiritual interests of the Church, and its influence on the souls and imaginations of the people, very soon begin to go rapidly to the devil—

EDITH [*shocked*] Papa!

THE BISHOP. I am speaking technically, not in Boxer's manner. Indeed the Bishops themselves went so far in that direction that they gained a reputation for being spiritually the stupidest men in the country and commercially the sharpest. I found a way out of this difficulty. Soames was my solicitor. I found that Soames, though a very capable man of business, had a romantic secret history. His father was an eminent Nonconformist divine who habitually spoke of the Church of England as The Scarlet Woman. Soames became secretly converted to Anglicanism at the age of fifteen. He longed to take holy orders, but didnt dare to, because his father had a weak heart and habitually threatened to drop dead if anybody hurt his feelings. You may have noticed that people with weak hearts are the tyrants of English family life. So poor Soames had to become a solicitor. When his father died—by a curious stroke of poetic justice he died of scarlet fever, and was found to have had a perfectly sound heart—I ordained Soames and made him my chaplain. He is now quite happy. He is a celibate; fasts strictly on Fridays and throughout Lent; wears a cassock and biretta; and has more legal business to do than ever he had in his old office in Ely Place. And he sets me free for the spiritual and scholarly pursuits proper to a Bishop.

MRS BRIDGENORTH [*coming back from the study with a knitting basket*] Here he is. [*She resumes her seat, and knits*].

Soames comes in in cassock and biretta. He salutes the company by blessing them with two fingers.

HOTCHKISS. Take my place, Mr Soames. [*He gives up his chair to him, and retires to the oak chest, on which he seats himself*].

THE BISHOP. No longer Mr Soames, Sinjon. Father Anthony.

SOAMES [*taking his seat*] I was christened Oliver Cromwell Soames. My father had no right to do it. I have taken the name of Anthony. When you become parents, young gentlemen, be very careful not to label a helpless child with views which it may come to hold in abhorrence.

THE BISHOP. Has Alice explained to you the nature of the document we are drafting?

SOAMES. She has indeed.

LESBIA. That sounds as if you disapproved.

SOAMES. It is not for me to approve or disapprove. I do the work that comes to my hand from my ecclesiastical superior.

THE BISHOP. Dont be uncharitable, Anthony. You must give us your best advice.

SOAMES. My advice to you all is to do your duty by taking the Christian vows of celibacy and poverty. The Church was founded to put an end to marriage and to put an end to property.

MRS BRIDGENORTH. But how could the world go on, Anthony?

SOAMES. Do your duty and see. Doing your duty is your business: keeping the world going is in higher hands.

LESBIA. Anthony: youre impossible.

SOAMES [*taking up his pen*] You wont take my advice. I didnt expect you would. Well, I await your instructions.

REGINALD. We got stuck on the first clause. What should we begin with?

SOAMES. It is usual to begin with the term of the contract.

EDITH. What does that mean?

SOAMES. The term of years for which it is to hold good.

LEO. But this is a marriage contract.

SOAMES. Is the marriage to be for a year, a week, or a day?

REGINALD. Come, I say, Anthony! Youre worse than any of us. A day!

SOAMES. Off the path is off the path. An inch or a mile: what does it matter?

LEO. If the marriage is not to be for ever, I'll have nothing to do with it. I call it immoral to have a marriage for a term of years. If the people dont like it they can get divorced.

REGINALD. It ought to be for just as long as the two people like. Thats what I say.

COLLINS. They may not agree on the point, sir. It's often fast with one and loose with the other.

LESBIA. I should say for as long as the man behaves himself.

THE BISHOP. Suppose the woman doesnt behave herself?

MRS BRIDGENORTH. The woman may have lost all her chances of a good marriage with anybody else. She should not be cast adrift.

REGINALD. So may the man! What about his home?

LEO. The wife ought to keep an eye on him, and see that he is comfortable and takes care of himself properly. The other man wont want her all the time.

LESBIA. There may not be another man.

LEO. Then why on earth should she leave him?

LESBIA. Because she wants to.

LEO. Oh, if people are going to be let do what they want to, then I call it simple immorality. [She goes indignantly to the oak chest, and perches herself on it close beside Hotchkiss].

REGINALD [watching them sourly] You do it yourself, dont you?

LEO. Oh, thats quite different. Dont make foolish witticisms, Rejjy.

THE BISHOP. We dont seem to be getting on. What do you say, Mr Alderman?

COLLINS. Well my lord, you see people do persist in talking as if marriages was all of one sort. But theres almost as many different sorts of marriages as theres different sorts of people. Theres the young things that marry for love, not knowing what theyre doing, and the old things that marry for money and comfort and companionship. Theres the people that marry for children. Theres the people that dont intend to have children and that arnt fit to have them. Theres the people that marry because theyre so much run after by the other sex that they have to put a stop to it somehow. Theres the people that want to try a new experience, and the people that want to have done with experiences. How are you to please them all? Why, youll want half a dozen different sorts of contract.

THE BISHOP. Well, if so, let us draw them all up. Let us face it.

REGINALD. Why should we be held together whether we like it or not? Thats the question thats at the bottom of it all.

MRS BRIDGENORTH. Because of the children, Rejjy.

COLLINS. But even then, maam, why should we be held together when thats all over—when the girls are married and the boys out in the world and in business for themselves? When thats done with, the real work of the marriage is done with. If the two like to stay together, let them stay together. But if not, let them part, as old people in the workhouses do. Theyve had enough of one another. Theyve found one another out. Why should they be tied together to sit there grudging and hating and spiting one another like so many do? Put it twenty years from the birth of the youngest child.

SOAMES. How if there be no children?

COLLINS. Let em take one another on liking.

MRS BRIDGENORTH. Collins!

LEO. You wicked old man!

[172]

THE BISHOP [*remonstrating*] My dear, my dear!

LESBIA. And what is a woman to live on, pray, when she is no longer liked, as you call it?

SOAMES [*with sardonic formality*] It is proposed that the term of the agreement be twenty years from the birth of the youngest child when there are children. Any amendment?

LEO. I protest. It must be for life. It would not be a marriage at all if it were not for life.

SOAMES. Mrs Reginald Bridgenorth proposes life. Any seconder?

LEO. Dont be soulless, Anthony.

LESBIA. I have a very important amendment. If there are any children, the man must be cleared completely out of the house for two years on each occasion. At such times he is superfluous, importunate, and ridiculous.

COLLINS. But where is he to go, miss?

LESBIA. He can go where he likes as long as he does not bother the mother.

REGINALD. And is she to be left lonely—

LESBIA. Lonely! With her child. The poor woman would be only too glad to have a moment to herself. Dont be absurd, Rejjy.

REGINALD. The father is to be a wandering wretched outcast, living at his club, and seeing nobody but his friends' wives!

LESBIA [*ironically*] Poor fellow!

HOTCHKISS. The friends' wives are perhaps the solution of the problem. You see, their husbands will also be outcasts; and the poor ladies will occasionally pine for male society.

LESBIA. There is no reason why a mother should not have male society. What she clearly should not have is a husband.

SOAMES. Anything else, Miss Grantham?

LESBIA. Yes: I must have my own separate house, or my own separate part of a house. Boxer smokes: I cant endure tobacco. Boxer believes that an open window means death from cold and exposure to the night air: I must have fresh air always. We can be friends; but we cant live together; and that must be put in the agreement.

EDITH. Ive no objection to smoking; and as to opening the windows, Cecil will of course have to do what is best for his health.

THE BISHOP. Who is to be the judge of that, my dear? You or he?

EDITH. Neither of us. We must do what the doctor orders.

REGINALD. Doctor be—!

LEO [admonitorily] Rejjy!

REGINALD [to Soames] You take my tip, Anthony. Put a clause into that agreement that the doctor is to have no say in the job. It's bad enough for the two people to be married to one another without their both being married to the doctor as well.

LESBIA. That reminds me of something very important. Boxer believes in vaccination: I do not. There must be a clause that I am to decide on such questions as I think best.

LEO [to the Bishop] Baptism is nearly as important as vaccination: isnt it?

THE BISHOP. It used to be considered so, my dear.

LEO. Well, Sinjon scoffs at it: he says that godfathers are ridiculous. I must be allowed to decide.

REGINALD. Theyll be his children as well as yours, you know.

LEO. Dont be indelicate, Rejjy.

EDITH. You are forgetting the very important matter of money.

COLLINS. Ah! Money! Now we're coming to it!

EDITH. When I'm married I shall have practically no money except what I shall earn.

THE BISHOP. I'm sorry, Cecil. A Bishop's daughter is a poor man's daughter.

SYKES. But surely you dont imagine that I'm going to let Edith work when we're married. I'm not a rich man; but Ive enough to spare her that; and when my mother dies—

EDITH. What nonsense! Of course I shall work when I'm married. I shall keep your house.

SYKES. Oh, that!

REGINALD. You call that work?

EDITH. Dont you? Leo used to do it for nothing; so no doubt you thought it wasnt work at all. Does your present housekeeper do it for nothing?

REGINALD. But it will be part of your duty as a wife.

EDITH. Not under this contract. I'll not have it so. If I'm to keep the house, I shall expect Cecil to pay me at least as well as he would pay a hired housekeeper. I'll not go begging to him every time I want a new dress or a cab fare, as so many women have to do.

SYKES. You know very well I would grudge you nothing, Edie.

EDITH. Then dont grudge me my self-respect and independence. I insist on it in fairness to you, Cecil, because in this way there will be a fund belonging solely to me; and if Slattox takes an action against you for anything I say, you can pay the damages and stop the interest out of my salary.

SOAMES. You forget that under this contract he will not be liable, because you will not be his wife in law.

EDITH. Nonsense! Of course I shall be his wife.

COLLINS [*his curiosity roused*] Is Slattox taking an action against you, miss? Slattox is on the Council with me. Could I settle it?

EDITH. He has not taken an action; but Cecil says he will.

COLLINS. What for, miss, if I may ask?

EDITH. Slattox is a liar and a thief; and it is my duty to expose him.

COLLINS. You surprise me, miss. Of course Slattox is in a manner of speaking a liar. If I may say so without offence, we're all liars, if it was only to spare one another's feelings. But I shouldnt call Slattox a thief. He's not all that he should be, perhaps; but he pays his way.

EDITH. If that is only your nice way of saying that Slattox is entirely unfit to have two hundred girls in his power as absolute slaves, then I shall say that too about him at the very next public meeting I address. He steals their wages under pretence of fining them. He steals their food under pretence of buying it for them. He lies when he denies having done it. And he does other things, as you evidently know, Collins. Therefore I give you notice that I shall expose him before all England without the least regard to the consequences to myself.

SYKES. Or to me?

EDITH. I take equal risks. Suppose you felt it to be your duty to shoot Slattox, what would become of me and the children? I'm sure I dont want anybody to be shot: not even Slattox; but if the public never will take any notice of even the most crying evil until somebody is shot, what are people to do but shoot somebody?

SOAMES [*inexorably*] I'm waiting for my instructions as to the term of the agreement.

REGINALD [*impatiently, leaving the hearth and going behind Soames*] It's no good talking all over the shop like this. We shall be here all day. I propose that the agreement holds good until the parties are divorced.

SOAMES. They cant be divorced. They will not be married.

REGINALD. But if they cant be divorced, then this will be worse than marriage.

MRS BRIDGENORTH. Of course it will. Do stop this nonsense. Why, who are the children to belong to?

LESBIA. We have already settled that they are to belong to the mother.

REGINALD. No: I'm dashed if you have. I'll fight for the ownership of my own children tooth and nail; and so will a good many other fellows, I can tell you.

EDITH. It seems to me that they should be divided between the parents. If Cecil wishes any of the children to be his exclusively, he should pay me a certain sum for the risk and trouble of bringing them into the world: say a thousand pounds apiece. The interest on this could go towards the support of the child as long as we live together. But the principal would be my property. In that way, if Cecil took the child away from me, I should at least be paid for what it had cost me.

MRS BRIDGENORTH [*putting down her knitting in amazement*] Edith! Who ever heard of such a thing!!

EDITH. Well, how else do you propose to settle it?

THE BISHOP. There is such a thing as a favorite child. What about the youngest child—the Benjamin —the child of its parents' matured strength and charity, always better treated and better loved than the unfortunate eldest children of their youthful ignorance and wilfulness? Which parent is to own the youngest child, payment or no payment?

COLLINS. Theres a third party, my lord. Theres the child itself. My wife is so fond of her children that they cant call their lives their own. They all run away from home to escape from her. A child hasnt a grown-up person's appetite for affection. A little of it goes a long way with them; and they like a good imitation of it better than the real thing, as every nurse knows.

SOAMES. Are you sure that any of us, young or old, like the real thing as well as we like an artistic imitation of it? Is not the real thing accursed? Are not the best beloved always the good actors rather than the true sufferers? Is not love always falsified in novels and plays to make it endurable? I have noticed in myself a great delight in pictures of the Saints and of Our Lady; but when I fall under that most terrible curse of the priest's lot, the curse of Joseph pursued by the wife of Potiphar, I am invariably repelled and terrified.

HOTCHKISS. Are you now speaking as a saint, Father Anthony, or as a solicitor?

SOAMES. There is no difference. There is not one Christian rule for solicitors and another for saints. Their hearts are alike; and their way of salvation is along the same road.

THE BISHOP. But "few there be that find it." Can you find it for us, Anthony?

SOAMES. It lies broad before you. It is the way to destruction that is narrow and tortuous. Marriage is an abomination which the Church was founded to cast out and replace by the communion of saints. I learnt that from every marriage settlement I drew up as a solicitor no less than from inspired revelation. You have set yourselves here to put your sin before you in black and white; and you cant agree upon or endure one article of it.

SYKES. It's certainly rather odd that the whole thing seems to fall to pieces the moment you touch it.

THE BISHOP. You see, when you give the devil fair play he loses his case. He has not been able to produce even the first clause of a working agreement; so I'm afraid we cant wait for him any longer.

LESBIA. Then the community will have to do without my children.

EDITH. And Cecil will have to do without me.

LEO [*getting off the chest*] And I positively will not marry Sinjon if he is not clever enough to make some provision for my looking after Rejjy. [*She leaves Hotchkiss, and goes back to her chair at the end of the table behind Mrs Bridgenorth*].

MRS BRIDGENORTH. And the world will come to an end with this generation, I suppose.

COLLINS. Cant nothing be done, my lord?

THE BISHOP. You can make divorce reasonable and decent: that is all.

LESBIA. Thank you for nothing. If you will only make marriage reasonable and decent, you can do as you like about divorce. I have not stated my deepest objection to marriage; and I dont intend to. There are certain rights I will not give any person over me.

REGINALD. Well, I think it jolly hard that a man should support his wife for years, and lose the chance of getting a really good wife, and then have her refuse to be a wife to him.

LESBIA. I'm not going to discuss it with you, Rejjy. If your sense of personal honor doesnt make you understand, nothing will.

SOAMES [*implacably*] I'm still awaiting my instructions.

They look at one another, each waiting for one of the others to suggest something. Silence.

REGINALD [*blankly*] I suppose, after all, marriage is better than—well, than the usual alternative.

SOAMES [*turning fiercely on him*] What right have you to say so? You know that the sins that are wasting and maddening this unhappy nation are those committed in wedlock.

COLLINS. Well, the single ones cant afford to indulge their affections the same as married people.

SOAMES. Away with it all, I say. You have your Master's commandments. Obey them.

HOTCHKISS [*rising and leaning on the back of the chair left vacant by the General*] I really must point out to you, Father Anthony, that the early Christian rules of life were not made to last, because the early Christians did not believe that the world itself was going to last. Now we know that we shall have to go through with it. We have found that there are millions of years behind us; and we know that there are millions before us. Mrs Bridgenorth's question remains unanswered. How is the world to go on? You say that that is not our business—that it is the business of Providence. But the modern Christian view is that we are here to do the business of Providence and nothing else. The question is, how? Am I not to use my reason to find out why? Isnt that what my reason is for? Well, all my reason tells me at present is that you are an impracticable lunatic.

SOAMES. Does that help?

HOTCHKISS. No.

SOAMES. Then pray for light.

HOTCHKISS. No: I am a snob, not a beggar. [*He sits down in the General's chair*].

COLLINS. We dont seem to be getting on, do we? Miss Edith: you and Mr Sykes had better go off to church and settle the right and wrong of it afterwards. Itll ease your minds, believe me: I speak from experience. You will burn your boats, as one might say.

SOAMES. We should never burn our boats. It is death in life.

COLLINS. Well, Father, I will say for you that you have views of your own and are not afraid to out with them. But some of us are of a more cheerful disposition. On the Borough Council now, you would be in a minority of one. You must take human nature as it is.

SOAMES. Upon what compulsion must I? I'll take divine nature as it is. I'll not hold a candle to the devil.

THE BISHOP. Thats a very unchristian way of treating the devil.

REGINALD. Well, we dont seem to be getting any further, do we?

THE BISHOP. Will you give it up and get married, Edith?

EDITH. No. What I propose seems to me quite reasonable.

THE BISHOP. And you, Lesbia?

LESBIA. Never.

MRS BRIDGENORTH. Never is a long word, Lesbia. Dont say it.

LESBIA [with a flash of temper] Dont pity me, Alice, please. As I said before, I am an English lady, quite prepared to do without anything I cant have on honorable conditions.

SOAMES [after a silence of utter deadlock] I am still awaiting my instructions.

REGINALD. Well, we dont seem to be getting along, do we?

LEO [out of patience] You said that before, Rejjy. Do not repeat yourself.

REGINALD. Oh, bother! [He goes to the garden door and looks out gloomily].

SOAMES [rising with the paper in his hands] Psha! [He tears it in pieces]. So much for your contract!

[181]

THE VOICE OF THE BEADLE. By your leave there, gentlemen. Make way for the Mayoress. Way for the worshipful the Mayoress, my lords and gentlemen. [*He comes in through the tower, in cocked hat and gold-braided overcoat, bearing the borough mace, and posts himself at the entrance*]. By your leave, gentlemen, way for the worshipful Mayoress.

COLLINS [*moving back towards the wall*] Mrs George, my lord.

Mrs George is every inch a Mayoress in point of stylish dressing; and she does it very well indeed. There is nothing quiet about Mrs George: she is not afraid of colors, and knows how to make the most of them. Not at all a lady in Lesbia's use of the term as a class label, she proclaims herself to the first glance as the triumphant, pampered, wilful, intensely alive woman who has always been rich among poor people. In a historical museum she would explain Edward the Fourth's taste for shopkeepers' wives. Her age, which is certainly 40, and might be 50, is carried off by her vitality, her resilient figure, and her confident carriage. So far, a remarkably well-preserved woman. But her beauty is wrecked, like an ageless landscape ravaged by long and fierce war. Her eyes are alive, arresting and haunting; and there is still a turn of delicate beauty and pride in her indomitable chin; but her cheeks are wasted and lined, her mouth writhen and piteous. The whole face is a battle-field of the passions, quite deplorable until she speaks, when an alert sense of fun rejuvenates her in a moment, and makes her company irresistible.

All rise except Soames, who sits down. Leo joins Reginald at the garden door. Mrs Bridgenorth hurries to the tower to receive her guest, and gets as far as Soames's chair when Mrs George appears. Hotchkiss, apparently recognizing her, recoils in consternation to the study door at the furthest corner of the room from her.

MRS GEORGE [*coming straight to the Bishop with the ring in her hand*] Here is your ring, my lord; and here am I. It's your doing, remember: not mine.

THE BISHOP. Good of you to come.

MRS BRIDGENORTH. How do you do, Mrs Collins?

MRS GEORGE [*going to her past the Bishop, and gazing intently at her*] Are you his wife?

MRS BRIDGENORTH. The Bishop's wife? Yes.

MRS GEORGE. What a destiny! And you look like any other woman!

MRS BRIDGENORTH [*introducing Lesbia*] My sister, Miss Grantham.

MRS GEORGE. So strangely mixed up with the story of the General's life?

THE BISHOP. You know the story of his life, then.

MRS GEORGE. Not all. We reached the house before he brought it up to the present day. But enough to know the part played in it by Miss Grantham.

MRS BRIDGENORTH [*introducing Leo*] Mrs Reginald Bridgenorth.

REGINALD. The late Mrs Reginald Bridgenorth.

LEO. Hold your tongue, Rejjy. At least have the decency to wait until the decree is made absolute.

MRS GEORGE [*to Leo*] Well, youve more time to get married again than he has, havnt you?

MRS BRIDGENORTH [*introducing Hotchkiss*] Mr St John Hotchkiss.

Hotchkiss, still far aloof by the study door, bows.

MRS GEORGE. What! That! [*She makes a half tour of the kitchen and ends right in front of him*]. Young man: do you remember coming into my shop and telling me that my husband's coals were out of place in your cellar, as Nature evidently intended them for the roof?

HOTCHKISS. I remember that deplorable impertinence with shame and confusion. You were kind enough to answer that Mr Collins was looking out for a clever young man to write advertisements, and that I could take the job if I liked.

MRS GEORGE. It's still open. [*She turns to Edith*].

MRS BRIDGENORTH. My daughter Edith. [*She comes towards the study door to make the introduction*].

MRS GEORGE. The bride! [*Looking at Edith's dressing-jacket*] Youre not going to get married like that, are you?

THE BISHOP [*coming round the table to Edith's left*] Thats just what we are discussing. Will you be so good as to join us and allow us the benefit of your wisdom and experience?

MRS GEORGE. Do you want the Beadle as well? He's a married man.

They all turn involuntarily and contemplate the Beadle, who sustains their gaze with dignity.

THE BISHOP. We think there are already too many men to be quite fair to the women.

MRS GEORGE. Right, my lord. [*She goes back to the tower and addresses the Beadle*] Take away that bauble, Joseph. Wait for me wherever you find yourself most comfortable in the neighborhood. [*The Beadle withdraws. She notices Collins for the first time*]. Hullo, Bill: youve got em all on too. Go and hunt up a drink for Joseph: theres a dear. [*Collins goes out. She looks at Soames's cassock and biretta*]. What! Another uniform! Are you the sexton? [*He rises*].

THE BISHOP. My chaplain, Father Anthony.

MRS GEORGE. Oh Lord! [*To Soames, coaxingly*] You dont mind, do you?

SOAMES. I mind nothing but my duties.

THE BISHOP. You know everybody now, I think.

MRS GEORGE [*turning to the railed chair*] Who's this?

THE BISHOP. Oh, I beg your pardon, Cecil. Mr Sykes. The bridegroom.

MRS GEORGE [*to Sykes*] Adorned for the sacrifice, arnt you?

SYKES. It seems doubtful whether there is going to be any sacrifice.

MRS GEORGE. Well, I want to talk to the women first. Shall we go upstairs and look at the presents and dresses?

MRS BRIDGENORTH. If you wish, certainly.

REGINALD. But the men want to hear what you have to say too.

MRS GEORGE. I'll talk to them afterwards: one by one.

HOTCHKISS [*to himself*] Great Heavens!

MRS BRIDGENORTH. This way, Mrs Collins. [*She leads the way out through the tower, followed by Mrs George, Lesbia, Leo, and Edith*].

THE BISHOP. Shall we try to get through the last batch of letters whilst they are away, Soames?

SOAMES. Yes, certainly. [*To Hotchkiss, who is in his way*] Excuse me.

The Bishop and Soames go into the study, disturbing Hotchkiss, who, plunged in a strange reverie, has forgotten where he is. Awakened by Soames, he stares distractedly; then, with sudden resolution, goes swiftly to the middle of the kitchen.

HOTCHKISS. Cecil. Rejjy. [*Startled by his urgency, they hurry to him*]. I'm frightfully sorry to desert on this day; but I must bolt. This time it really is pure cowardice. I cant help it.

REGINALD. What are you afraid of?

HOTCHKISS. I dont know. Listen to me. I was a young fool living by myself in London. I ordered my first ton of coals from that woman's husband. At that time I did not know that it is not true economy to buy the lowest priced article: I thought all coals were alike, and tried the thirteen shilling kind because it seemed cheap. It proved unexpectedly inferior to the family Silkstone; and in the irritation into which the first scuttle threw me, I called at the shop and made an idiot of myself as she described.

SYKES. Well, suppose you did! Laugh at it, man.

HOTCHKISS. At that, yes. But there was something worse. Judge of my horror when, calling on the coal merchant to make a trifling complaint at finding my grate acting as a battery of quick-firing guns, and being confronted by his vulgar wife, I felt in her presence an extraordinary sensation of unrest, of emotion, of unsatisfied need. I'll not disgust you with details of the madness and folly that followed that meeting. But it went as far as this: that I actually found myself prowling past the shop at night under a sort of desperate necessity to be near some place where she had been. A hideous temptation to kiss the doorstep because her foot had pressed it made me realize how mad I was. I tore myself away from London by a supreme effort; but I was on the point of returning like a needle to the lodestone when the outbreak of the war saved me. On the field of battle the infatuation wore off. The Billiter affair made a new man of me: I felt that I had left the follies and puerilities of the old days behind me for ever. But half-an-hour ago—when the Bishop sent off that ring—a sudden grip at the base of my heart filled me with a nameless terror—me, the fearless! I recognized its cause when she walked into the room. Cecil: this woman is a harpy, a siren, a mermaid, a vampire. There is only one chance for me: flight, instant precipitate flight. Make my excuses. Forget me. Farewell. [*He makes for the door and is confronted by Mrs George entering*]. Too late: I'm lost. [*He turns back and throws himself desperately into the chair nearest the study door: that being the furthest away from her*].

MRS GEORGE [*coming to the hearth and addressing Reginald*] Mr Bridgenorth: will you oblige me by leaving me with this young man. I want to talk to him like a mother, on your business.

REGINALD. Do, maam. He needs it badly. Come along, Sykes. [*He goes into the study*].

SYKES [*looks irresolutely at Hotchkiss*]—?

HOTCHKISS. Too late, you cant save me now, Cecil. Go.

Sykes goes into the study. Mrs George strolls across to Hotchkiss and contemplates him curiously.

HOTCHKISS. Useless to prolong this agony. [*Rising*] Fatal woman—if woman you are indeed and not a fiend in human form—

MRS GEORGE. Is this out of a book? Or is it your usual society small talk?

HOTCHKISS [*recklessly*] Jibes are useless: the force that is sweeping me away will not spare you. I must know the worst at once. What was your father?

MRS GEORGE. A licensed victualler who married his barmaid. You would call him a publican, most likely.

HOTCHKISS. Then you are a woman totally beneath me. Do you deny it? Do you set up any sort of pretence to be my equal in rank, in age, or in culture?

MRS GEORGE. Have you eaten anything that has disagreed with you?

HOTCHKISS [*witheringly*] Inferior!

MRS GEORGE. Thank you. Anything else?

HOTCHKISS. This. I love you. My intentions are not honorable. [*She shews no dismay*]. Scream. Ring the bell. Have me turned out of the house.

MRS GEORGE [*with sudden depth of feeling*] Oh, if you could restore to this wasted exhausted heart one ray of the passion that once welled up at the glance—at the touch of a lover! It's you who would scream, then, young man. Do you see this face, once fresh and rosy like your own, now scarred and riven by a hundred burnt-out fires?

HOTCHKISS [*wildly*] Slate fires. Thirteen shillings a ton. Fires that shoot out destructive meteors, blinding and burning, sending men into the streets to make fools of themselves.

MRS GEORGE. You seem to have got it pretty bad, Sinjon.

HOTCHKISS. Dont dare call me Sinjon.

MRS GEORGE. My name is Zenobia Alexandrina. You may call me Polly for short.

HOTCHKISS. Your name is Ashtoreth—Durga—there is no name yet invented malign enough for you.

MRS GEORGE [*sitting down comfortably*] Come! Do you really think youre better suited to that young saucebox than her husband? You enjoyed her company when you were only the friend of the family—when there was the husband there to shew off against and to take all the responsibility. Are you sure youll enjoy it as much when you are the husband? She isnt clever, you know. She's only silly-clever.

HOTCHKISS [*uneasily leaning against the table and holding on to it to control his nervous movements*] Need you tell me? fiend that you are!

MRS GEORGE. You amused the husband, didnt you?

HOTCHKISS. He has more real sense of humor than she. He's better bred. That was not my fault.

MRS GEORGE. My husband has a sense of humor too.

HOTCHKISS. The coal merchant—I mean the slate merchant.

MRS GEORGE [*appreciatively*] He would just love to hear you talk. He's been dull lately for want of a change of company and a bit of fresh fun.

HOTCHKISS [*flinging a chair opposite her and sitting down with an overdone attempt at studied insolence*] And pray what is your wretched husband's vulgar conviviality to me?

MRS GEORGE. You love me?

HOTCHKISS. I loathe you.

MRS GEORGE. It's the same thing.

HOTCHKISS. Then I'm lost.

MRS GEORGE. You may come and see me if you promise to amuse George.

HOTCHKISS. I'll insult him, sneer at him, wipe my boots on him.

MRS GEORGE. No you wont, dear boy. Youll be a perfect gentleman.

HOTCHKISS [*beaten; appealing to her mercy*] Zenobia—

MRS GEORGE. Polly, please.

HOTCHKISS. Mrs Collins—

MRS GEORGE. Sir?

HOTCHKISS. Something stronger than my reason and common sense is holding my hands and tearing me along. I make no attempt to deny that it can drag me where you please and make me do what you like. But at least let me know your soul as you seem to know mine. Do you love this absurd coal merchant.

MRS GEORGE. Call him George.

HOTCHKISS. Do you love your Jorjy Porjy?

MRS GEORGE. Oh, I dont know that I love him. He's my husband, you know. But if I got anxious about George's health, and I thought it would nourish him, I would fry you with onions for his breakfast and think nothing of it. George and I are good friends. George belongs to me. Other men may come and go; but George goes on for ever.

HOTCHKISS. Yes: a husband soon becomes nothing

but a habit. Listen: I suppose this detestable fascination you have for me is love.

MRS GEORGE. Any sort of feeling for a woman is called love nowadays.

HOTCHKISS. Do you love me?

MRS GEORGE [*promptly*] My love is not quite so cheap an article as that, my lad. I wouldnt cross the street to have another look at you—not yet. *I'm* not starving for love like the robins in winter, as the good ladies youre accustomed to are. Youll have to be very clever, and very good, and very real, if you are to interest me. If George takes a fancy to you, and you amuse him enough, I'll just tolerate you coming in and out occasionally for—well, say a month. If you can make a friend of me in that time so much the better for you. If you can touch my poor dying heart even for an instant, I'll bless you, and never forget you. You may try—if George takes to you.

HOTCHKISS. I'm to come on liking for the month?

MRS GEORGE. On condition that you drop Mrs Reginald.

HOTCHKISS. But she wont drop me. Do you suppose I ever wanted to marry her? I was a homeless bachelor; and I felt quite happy at their house as their friend. Leo was an amusing little devil; but I liked Reginald much more than I liked her. She didnt understand. One day she came to me and told me that the inevitable had happened. I had tact enough not to ask her what the inevitable was; and I gathered presently that she had told Reginald that their marriage was a mistake and that she loved me and could no longer see me breaking my heart for her in suffering silence. What could I say? What could I do? What can I say now? What can I do now?

MRS GEORGE. Tell her that the habit of falling in love

with other men's wives is growing on you; and that I'm your latest.

HOTCHKISS. What! Throw her over when she has thrown Reginald over me!

MRS GEORGE [*rising*] You wont then? Very well. Sorry we shant meet again: I should have liked to see more of you for George's sake. Goodbye [*she moves away from him towards the hearth*].

HOTCHKISS [*appealing*] Zenobia—

MRS GEORGE. I thought I had made a difficult conquest. Now I see you are only one of those poor petticoat-hunting creatures that any woman can pick up. Not for me, thank you. [*Inexorable, she turns towards the tower to go*].

HOTCHKISS [*following*] Dont be an ass, Polly.

MRS GEORGE [*stopping*] Thats better.

HOTCHKISS. Cant you see that I maynt throw Leo over just because I should be only too glad to. It would be dishonorable.

MRS GEORGE. Will you be happy if you marry her?

HOTCHKISS. No, great heavens, NO!

MRS GEORGE. Will she be happy when she finds you out?

HOTCHKISS. She's incapable of happiness. But she's not incapable of the pleasure of holding a man against his will.

MRS GEORGE. Right, young man. You will tell her, please, that you love me: before everybody, mind, the very next time you see her.

HOTCHKISS. But—

MRS GEORGE. Those are my orders, Sinjon. I cant have you marry another woman until George is tired of you.

HOTCHKISS. Oh, if only I didnt selfishly want to obey you!

The General comes in from the garden. Mrs George goes half way to the garden door to speak to him. Hotchkiss posts himself on the hearth.

MRS GEORGE. Where have you been all this time?

THE GENERAL. I'm afraid my nerves were a little upset by our conversation. I just went into the garden and had a smoke. I'm all right now [*he strolls down to the study door and presently takes a chair at that end of the big table*].

MRS GEORGE. A smoke! Why, you said she couldnt bear it.

THE GENERAL. Good heavens! I forgot! It's such a natural thing to do, somehow.

Lesbia comes in through the tower.

MRS GEORGE. He's been smoking again.

LESBIA. So my nose tells me. [*She goes to the end of the table nearest the hearth, and sits down*].

THE GENERAL. Lesbia: I'm very sorry. But if I gave it up, I should become so melancholy and irritable that you would be the first to implore me to take to it again.

MRS GEORGE. Thats true. Women drive their husbands into all sorts of wickedness to keep them in good humor. Sinjon: be off with you: this doesnt concern you.

LESBIA. Please dont disturb yourself, Sinjon. Boxer's broken heart has been worn on his sleeve too long for any pretence of privacy.

THE GENERAL. You are cruel, Lesbia: devilishly cruel. [*He sits down, wounded*].

LESBIA. You are vulgar, Boxer.

HOTCHKISS. In what way? I ask, as an expert in vulgarity.

LESBIA. In two ways. First, he talks as if the only thing of any importance in life was which particular woman he shall marry. Second, he has no self-control.

THE GENERAL. Women are not all the same to me, Lesbia.

MRS GEORGE. Why should they be, pray? Women are all different: it's the men who are all the same. Besides, what does Miss Grantham know about either men or women? She's got too much self-control.

LESBIA [*widening her eyes and lifting her chin haughtily*] And pray how does that prevent me from knowing as much about men and women as people who have no self-control?

MRS GEORGE. Because it frightens people into behaving themselves before you; and then how can you tell what they really are? Look at me! I was a spoilt child. My brothers and sisters were well brought up, like all children of respectable publicans. So should I have been if I hadnt been the youngest: ten years younger than my youngest brother. My parents were tired of doing their duty by their children by that time; and they spoilt me for all they were worth. I never knew what it was to want money or anything that money could buy. When I wanted my own way, I had nothing to do but scream for it til I got it. When I was annoyed *I* didnt control myself: I scratched and called names. Did you ever, after you were grown up, pull a grown-up woman's hair? Did you ever bite a grown-up man? Did you ever call both of them every name you could lay your tongue to?

LESBIA [*shivering with disgust*] No.

MRS GEORGE. Well, I did. I know what a woman is like when her hair's pulled. I know what a man is like when he's bit. I know what theyre both like when you tell them what you really feel about them. And thats how I know more of the world than you.

LESBIA. The Chinese know what a man is like when he is cut into a thousand pieces, or boiled in oil. That sort of knowledge is of no use to me. I'm afraid we shall never get on with one another, Mrs George. I live like a fencer, always on guard. I like to be confronted with people who are always on guard. I hate sloppy people, slovenly people, people who cant sit up straight, sentimental people!

MRS GEORGE. Oh, sentimental your grandmother! You dont learn to hold your own in the world by standing on guard, but by attacking, and getting well hammered yourself.

LESBIA. I'm not a prize-fighter, Mrs Collins. If I cant get a thing without the indignity of fighting for it, I do without it.

MRS GEORGE. Do you? Does it strike you that if we were all as clever as you at doing without, there wouldnt be much to live for, would there?

THE GENERAL. I'm afraid, Lesbia, the things you do without are the things you dont want.

LESBIA [*surprised at his wit*] Thats not bad for the silly soldier man. Yes, Boxer: the truth is, I dont want you enough to make the very unreasonable sacrifices required by marriage. And yet that is exactly why I ought to be married. Just because I have the qualities my country wants most I shall go barren to my grave; whilst the women who have neither the strength to resist marriage nor the intelligence to understand its infinite dishonor will make the England of the future. [*She rises and walks towards the study*].

THE GENERAL [*as she is about to pass him*] Well, I shall not ask you again, Lesbia.

LESBIA. Thank you, Boxer. [*She passes on to the study door*].

MRS GEORGE. Youre quite done with him, are you?

[194]

LESBIA. As far as marriage is concerned, yes. The field is clear for you, Mrs George. [*She goes into the study*].

The General buries his face in his hands. Mrs George comes round the table to him.

MRS GEORGE [*sympathetically*] She's a nice woman, that. And a sort of beauty about her too, different from anyone else.

THE GENERAL [*overwhelmed*] Oh Mrs Collins, thank you, thank you a thousand times. [*He rises effusively*]. You have thawed the long-frozen springs (*he kisses her hand*), forgive me; and thank you: bless you—[*he again takes refuge in the garden, choked with emotion*].

MRS GEORGE [*looking after him triumphantly*] Just caught the dear old warrior on the bounce, eh?

HOTCHKISS. Unfaithful to me already!

MRS GEORGE. I'm not your property, young man: dont you think it. [*She goes over to him and faces him*]. You understand that? [*He suddenly snatches her into his arms and kisses her*]. Oh! You dare do that again, you young blackguard; and I'll jab one of these chairs in your face [*she seizes one and holds it in readiness*]. Now you shall not see me for another month.

HOTCHKISS [*deliberately*] I shall pay my first visit to your husband this afternoon.

MRS GEORGE. Youll see what he'll say to you when I tell him what youve just done.

HOTCHKISS. What can he say? What dare he say?

MRS GEORGE. Suppose he kicks you out of the house?

HOTCHKISS. How can he? Ive fought seven duels with sabres. Ive muscles of iron. Nothing hurts me: not even broken bones. Fighting is absolutely uninteresting to me because it doesnt frighten me or amuse me; and I always win. Your husband is in all these respects an average man, probably. He will be horribly afraid of me; and if under the stimulus of your presence, and for your sake, and because it is the right thing to do among vulgar people, he were to attack me, I should simply defeat him and humiliate him [*he gradually gets his hands on the chair and takes it from her, as his words go home phrase by phrase*]. Sooner than expose him to that, you would suffer a thousand stolen kisses, wouldnt you?

MRS GEORGE [*in utter consternation*] You young viper!

HOTCHKISS. Ha ha! You are in my power. That is one of the oversights of your code of honor for husbands: the man who can bully them can insult their wives with impunity. Tell him if you dare. If I choose to take ten kisses, how will you prevent me?

MRS GEORGE. You come within reach of me and I'll not leave a hair on your head.

HOTCHKISS [*catching her wrists dexterously*] Ive got your hands.

MRS GEORGE. Youve not got my teeth. Let go; or I'll bite. I will, I tell you. Let go.

HOTCHKISS. Bite away: I shall taste quite as nice as George.

MRS GEORGE. You beast. Let me go. Do you call yourself a gentleman, to use your brute strength against a woman?

HOTCHKISS. You are stronger than me in every way but this. Do you think I will give up my one advantage? Promise youll receive me when I call this afternoon.

MRS GEORGE. After what youve just done? Not if it was to save my life.

HOTCHKISS. I'll amuse George.

MRS GEORGE. He wont be in.

HOTCHKISS [*taken aback*] Do you mean that we should be alone?

MRS GEORGE [*snatching away her hands triumphantly as his grasp relaxes*] Aha! Thats cooled you, has it?

HOTCHKISS [*anxiously*] When will George be at home?

MRS GEORGE. It wont matter to you whether he's at home or not. The door will be slammed in your face whenever you call.

HOTCHKISS. No servant in London is strong enough to close a door that I mean to keep open. You cant escape me. If you persist, I'll go into the coal trade; make George's acquaintance on the coal exchange; and coax him to take me home with him to make your acquaintance.

MRS GEORGE. We have no use for you, young man: neither George nor I [*she sails away from him and sits down at the end of the table near the study door*].

HOTCHKISS [*following her and taking the next chair round the corner of the table*] Yes you have. George cant fight for you: I can.

MRS GEORGE [*turning to face him*] You bully. You low bully.

HOTCHKISS. You have courage and fascination: I have courage and a pair of fists. We're both bullies, Polly.

MRS GEORGE. You have a mischievous tongue. Thats enough to keep you out of my house.

HOTCHKISS. It must be rather a house of cards. A word from me to George—just the right word, said in the right way—and down comes your house.

MRS GEORGE. Thats why I'll die sooner than let you into it.

HOTCHKISS. Then as surely as you live, I enter the coal trade tomorrow. George's taste for amusing company will deliver him into my hands. Before a month passes your home will be at my mercy.

MRS GEORGE [*rising, at bay*] Do you think I'll let myself be driven into a trap like this?

HOTCHKISS. You are in it already. Marriage is a trap. You are married. Any man who has the power to spoil your marriage has the power to spoil your life. I have that power over you.

MRS GEORGE [*desperate*] You mean it?

HOTCHKISS. I do.

MRS GEORGE [*resolutely*] Well, spoil my marriage and be—

HOTCHKISS [*springing up*] Polly!

MRS GEORGE. Sooner than be your slave I'd face any unhappiness.

HOTCHKISS. What! Even for George?

MRS GEORGE. There must be honor between me and George, happiness or no happiness. Do your worst.

HOTCHKISS [*admiring her*] Are you really game, Polly? Dare you defy me?

MRS GEORGE. If you ask me another question I shant be able to keep my hands off you [*she dashes distractedly past him to the other end of the table, her fingers crisping*].

HOTCHKISS. That settles it. Polly: I adore you: we were born for one another. As I happen to be a gentleman, I'll never do anything to annoy or injure you except that I reserve the right to give you a black eye if you bite me; but youll never get rid of me now to the end of your life.

MRS GEORGE. I shall get rid of you if the beadle has to brain you with the mace for it [*she makes for the tower*].

HOTCHKISS [*running between the table and the oak chest and across to the tower to cut her off*] You shant.

MRS GEORGE [*panting*] Shant I though?

HOTCHKISS. No you shant. I have one card left to play that youve forgotten. Why were you so unlike yourself when you spoke to the Bishop?

MRS GEORGE [*agitated beyond measure*] Stop. Not that. You shall respect that if you respect nothing else. I forbid you. [*He kneels at her feet*]. What are you doing? Get up: dont be a fool.

HOTCHKISS. Polly: I ask you on my knees to let me make George's acquaintance in his home this afternoon; and I shall remain on my knees til the Bishop comes in and sees us. What will he think of you then?

MRS GEORGE [*beside herself*] Wheres the poker?

She rushes to the fireplace; seizes the poker; and makes for Hotchkiss, who flies to the study door. The Bishop enters just then and finds himself between them, narrowly escaping a blow from the poker.

THE BISHOP. Dont hit him, Mrs Collins. He is my guest.

Mrs George throws down the poker; collapses into the nearest chair; and bursts into tears. The Bishop goes to her and pats her consolingly on the shoulder. She shudders all through at his touch.

THE BISHOP. Come! you are in the house of your friends. Can we help you?

MRS GEORGE [*to Hotchkiss, pointing to the study*] Go in there, you. Youre not wanted here.

HOTCHKISS. You understand, Bishop, that Mrs Collins is not to blame for this scene. I'm afraid Ive been rather irritating.

THE BISHOP. I can quite believe it, Sinjon.

Hotchkiss goes into the study.

THE BISHOP [*turning to Mrs George with great kindness of manner*] I'm sorry you have been worried [*he sits down on her left*]. Never mind him. A little pluck, a little gaiety of heart, a little prayer; and youll be laughing at him.

MRS GEORGE. Never fear. I have all that. It was as much my fault as his; and I should have put him in his place with a clip of that poker on the side of his head if you hadnt come in.

THE BISHOP. You might have put him in his coffin that way, Mrs Collins. And I should have been very sorry; because we are all fond of Sinjon.

MRS GEORGE. Yes: it's your duty to rebuke me. But do you think I dont know?

THE BISHOP. I dont rebuke you. Who am I that I should rebuke you? Besides, I know there are discussions in which the poker is the only possible argument.

MRS GEORGE. My lord: be earnest with me. I'm a very funny woman, I daresay; but I come from the same workshop as you. I heard you say that yourself years ago.

THE BISHOP. Quite so; but then I'm a very funny Bishop. Since we are both funny people, let us not forget that humor is a divine attribute.

MRS GEORGE. I know nothing about divine attributes or whatever you call them; but I can feel when I am being belittled. It was from you that I learnt first to respect myself. It was through you that I came to be able to walk safely through many wild and wilful paths. Dont go back on your own teaching.

THE BISHOP. I'm not a teacher: only a fellow-traveller of whom you asked the way. I pointed ahead—ahead of myself as well as of you.

MRS GEORGE [rising and standing over him almost threatingly] As I'm a living woman this day, if I find you out to be a fraud, I'll kill myself.

THE BISHOP. What! Kill yourself for finding out something! For becoming a wiser and therefore a better woman! What a bad reason!

MRS GEORGE. I have sometimes thought of killing you, and then killing myself.

THE BISHOP. Why on earth should you kill yourself—
not to mention me?

MRS GEORGE. So that we might keep our assignation
in Heaven.

THE BISHOP [*rising and facing her, breathless*] Mrs
Collins! You are Incognita Appassionata!

MRS GEORGE. You read my letters, then? [*With a
sigh of grateful relief, she sits down quietly, and says*]
Thank you.

THE BISHOP [*remorsefully*] And I have broken the
spell by making you come here [*sitting down again*].
Can you ever forgive me?

MRS GEORGE. You couldnt know that it was only the
coal merchant's wife, could you?

THE BISHOP. Why do you say only the coal merchant's wife?

MRS GEORGE. Many people would laugh at it.

THE BISHOP. Poor people! It's so hard to know the
right place to laugh, isnt it?

MRS GEORGE. I didnt mean to make you think the
letters were from a fine lady. I wrote on cheap paper;
and I never could spell.

THE BISHOP. Neither could I. So that told me
nothing.

MRS GEORGE. One thing I should like you to know.

THE BISHOP. Yes?

MRS GEORGE. We didnt cheat your friend. They were
as good as we could do at thirteen shillings a ton.

THE BISHOP. Thats important. Thank you for telling
me.

MRS GEORGE. I have something else to say; but will
you please ask somebody to come and stay here while
we talk? [*He rises and turns to the study door*]. Not a
woman if you dont mind. [*He nods understandingly
and passes on*]. Not a man either.

THE BISHOP [*stopping*] Not a man and not a woman!
We have no children left, Mrs Collins. They are all
grown up and married.

MRS GEORGE. That other clergyman would do.

THE BISHOP. What! The sexton?

MRS GEORGE. Yes. He didnt mind my calling him
that, did he? It was only my ignorance.

THE BISHOP. Not at all. [*He opens the study door and
calls*] Soames! Anthony! [*To Mrs George*] Call him
Father: he likes it. [*Soames appears at the study door*].
Mrs Collins wishes you to join us, Anthony.

> *Soames looks puzzled.*

MRS GEORGE. You dont mind, Dad, do you? [*As this
greeting visibly gives him a shock that hardly bears out
the Bishop's advice, she says anxiously*] That was what
you told me to call him, wasnt it?

SOAMES. I am called Father Anthony, Mrs Collins.
But it does not matter what you call me. [*He comes in,
and walks past her to the hearth*].

THE BISHOP. Mrs Collins has something to say to me
that she wants you to hear.

SOAMES. I am listening.

THE BISHOP [*going back to his seat next her*] Now.

MRS GEORGE. My lord: you should never have
married.

SOAMES. This woman is inspired. Listen to her, my
lord.

THE BISHOP [*taken aback by the directness of the
attack*] I married because I was so much in love with
Alice that all the difficulties and doubts and dangers
of marriage seemed to me the merest moonshine.

MRS GEORGE. Yes: it's mean to let poor young things
in for so much while theyre in that state. Would you
marry now that you know better if you were a
widower?

THE BISHOP. I'm old now. It wouldnt matter.

MRS GEORGE. But would you if it did matter?

THE BISHOP. I think I should marry again lest anyone should imagine I had found marriage unhappy
with Alice.

SOAMES [*sternly*] Are you fonder of your wife than of
your salvation?

THE BISHOP. Oh, very much. When you meet a man
who is very particular about his salvation, look out
for a woman who is very particular about her character; and marry them to one another: theyll make a
perfect pair. I advise you to fall in love, Anthony.

SOAMES [*with horror*] I!!

THE BISHOP. Yes, you! think of what it would do for
you. For her sake you would come to care unselfishly
and diligently for money instead of being selfishly and
lazily indifferent to it. For her sake you would come
to care in the same way for preferment. For her sake
you would come to care for your health, your appearance, the good opinion of your fellow creatures, and all
the really important things that make men work and
strive instead of mooning and nursing their salvation.

SOAMES. In one word, for the sake of one deadly sin I
should come to care for all the others.

THE BISHOP. Saint Anthony! Tempt him, Mrs
Collins: tempt him.

MRS GEORGE [*rising and looking strangely before her*]
Take care, my lord: you still have the power to make
me obey your commands. And do you, Mr Sexton,
beware of an empty heart.

THE BISHOP. Yes. Nature abhors a vacuum, Anthony.
I would not dare go about with an empty heart; why,
the first girl I met would fly into it by mere atmos-
pheric pressure. Alice keeps them out now. Mrs
Collins knows.

MRS GEORGE [*a faint convulsion passing like a wave over her*] I know more than either of you. One of you has not yet exhausted his first love: the other has not yet reached it. But I—I—[*she reels and is again convulsed*].

THE BISHOP [*saving her from falling*] Whats the matter? Are you ill, Mrs Collins? [*He gets her back into her chair*]. Soames: theres a glass of water in the study—quick. [*Soames hurries to the study door*].

MRS GEORGE. No. [*Soames stops*]. Dont call. Dont bring anyone. Cant you hear anything?

THE BISHOP. Nothing unusual. [*He sits by her, watching her with intense surprise and interest*].

MRS GEORGE. No music?

SOAMES. No. [*He steals to the end of the table and sits on her right, equally interested*].

MRS GEORGE. Do you see nothing—not a great light?

THE BISHOP. We are still walking in darkness.

MRS GEORGE. Put your hand on my forehead: the hand with the ring. [*He does so. Her eyes close*].

SOAMES [*inspired to prophesy*] There was a certain woman, the wife of a coal merchant, which had been a great sinner—

The Bishop, startled, takes his hand away. Mrs George's eyes open vividly as she interrupts Soames.

MRS GEORGE. You prophesy falsely, Anthony: never in all my life have I done anything that was not ordained for me. [*More quietly*] Ive been myself. Ive not been afraid of myself. And at last I have escaped from myself, and am become a voice for them that are afraid to speak, and a cry for the hearts that break in silence.

SOAMES [*whispering*] Is she inspired?

THE BISHOP. Marvellous. Hush.

MRS GEORGE. I have earned the right to speak. I have

dared: I have gone through: I have not fallen withered in the fire: I have come at last out beyond, to the back of Godspeed.

THE BISHOP. And what do you see there, at the back of Godspeed?

SOAMES [*hungrily*] Give us your message.

MRS GEORGE [*with intensely sad reproach*] When you loved me I gave you the whole sun and stars to play with. I gave you eternity in a single moment, strength of the mountains in one clasp of your arms, and the volume of all the seas in one impulse of your souls. A moment only; but was it not enough? Were you not paid then for all the rest of your struggle on earth? Must I mend your clothes and sweep your floors as well? Was it not enough? I paid the price without bargaining: I bore the children without flinching: was that a reason for heaping fresh burdens on me? I carried the child in my arms: must I carry the father too? When I opened the gates of paradise, were you blind? was it nothing to you? When all the stars sang in your ears and all the winds swept you into the heart of heaven, were you deaf? were you dull? was I no more to you than a bone to a dog? Was it not enough? We spent eternity together; and you ask me for a little lifetime more. We possessed all the universe together; and you ask me to give you my scanty wages as well. I have given you the greatest of all things; and you ask me to give you little things. I gave you your own soul: you ask me for my body as a plaything. Was it not enough? Was it not enough?

SOAMES. Do you understand this, my lord?

THE BISHOP. I have that advantage over you, Anthony, thanks to Alice. [*He takes Mrs George's hand*]. Your hand is very cold. Can you come down to earth? Do you remember who I am, and who you are?

MRS GEORGE. It was enough for me. I did not ask to meet you—to touch you—[*the Bishop quickly releases her hand*]. When you spoke to my soul years ago from your pulpit, you opened the doors of my salvation to me; and now they stand open for ever. It was enough. I have asked you for nothing since: I ask you for nothing now. I have lived: it is enough. I have had my wages; and I am ready for my work. I thank you and bless you and leave you. You are happier in that than I am; for when I do for men what you did for me, I have no thanks, and no blessing: I am their prey; and there is no rest from their loving and no mercy from their loathing.

THE BISHOP. You must take us as we are, Mrs Collins.

SOAMES. No. Take us as we are capable of becoming.

MRS GEORGE. Take me as I am: I ask no more. [*She turns her head to the study door and cries*] Yes: come in, come in.

    Hotchkiss comes softly in from the study.

HOTCHKISS. Will you be so kind as to tell me whether I am dreaming? In there I have heard Mrs Collins saying the strangest things, and not a syllable from you two.

SOAMES. My lord: is this possession by the devil?

THE BISHOP. Or the ecstasy of a saint?

HOTCHKISS. Or the convulsion of the pythoness on the tripod?

THE BISHOP. May not the three be one?

MRS GEORGE [*troubled*] You are paining and tiring me with idle questions. You are dragging me back to myself. You are tormenting me with your evil dreams of saints and devils and—what was it?—[*striving to fathom it*] the pythoness—the pythoness—[*giving it up*] I dont understand. I am a woman: a human creature like yourselves. Will you not take me as I am?

SOAMES. Yes; but shall we take you and burn you?

THE BISHOP. Or take you and canonize you?

HOTCHKISS [*gaily*] Or take you as a matter of course? [*Swiftly to the Bishop*] We must get her out of this: it's dangerous. [*Aloud to her*] May I suggest that you shall be Anthony's devil and the Bishop's saint and my adored Polly? [*Slipping behind her, he picks up her hand from her lap and kisses it over her shoulder*].

MRS GEORGE [*waking*] What was that? Who kissed my hand? [*To the Bishop, eagerly*] Was it you? [*He shakes his head. She is mortified*]. I beg your pardon.

THE BISHOP. Not at all. I'm not repudiating that honor. Allow me [*he kisses her hand*].

MRS GEORGE. Thank you for that. It was not the sexton, was it?

SOAMES. I!

HOTCHKISS. It was I, Polly, your ever faithful.

MRS GEORGE [*turning and seeing him*] Let me catch you doing it again: thats all. How do you come there? I sent you away. [*With great energy, becoming quite herself again*] What the goodness gracious has been happening?

HOTCHKISS. As far as I can make out, you have been having a very charming and eloquent sort of fit.

MRS GEORGE [*delighted*] What! My second sight! [*To the Bishop*] Oh, how I have prayed that it might come to me if ever I met you! And now it has come. How stunning! You may believe every word I said: I cant remember it now; but it was something that was just bursting to be said; and so it laid hold of me and said itself. Thats how it is, you see.

   Edith and Cecil Sykes come in through the tower. She

*has her hat on. Leo follows. They have evidently been
out together. Sykes, with an unnatural air, half foolish,
half rakish, as if he had lost all his self-respect and were
determined not to let it prey on his spirits, throws himself into a chair at the end of the table near the hearth,
and thrusts his hands into his pockets, like Hogarth's
Rake, without waiting for Edith to sit down. She sits in
the railed chair. Leo takes the chair nearest the tower on
the long side of the table, brooding, with closed lips.*

THE BISHOP. Have you been out, my dear?

EDITH. Yes.

THE BISHOP. With Cecil?

EDITH. Yes.

THE BISHOP. Have you come to an understanding?

No reply. Blank silence.

SYKES. You had better tell them, Edie.

EDITH. Tell them yourself.

The General comes in from the garden.

THE GENERAL [*coming forward to the table*] Can anybody oblige me with some tobacco? Ive finished mine;
and my nerves are still far from settled.

THE BISHOP. Wait a moment, Boxer. Cecil has
something important to tell us.

SYKES. Weve done it. Thats all.

HOTCHKISS. Done what, Cecil?

SYKES. Well, what do you suppose?

EDITH. Got married, of course.

THE GENERAL. Married! Who gave you away?

SYKES [*jerking his head towards the tower*] This gentleman did. [*Seeing that they do not understand, he looks
round and sees that there is no one there*]. Oh! I thought
he came in with us. He's gone downstairs, I suppose.
The Beadle.

THE GENERAL. The Beadle! What the devil did he do
that for?

SYKES. Oh, I dont know: I didnt make any bargain with him. [*To Mrs George*] How much ought I to give him, Mrs Collins?

MRS GEORGE. Five shillings. [*To the Bishop*] I want to rest for a moment: there! in your study. I saw it here [*she touches her forehead*].

THE BISHOP [*opening the study door for her*] By all means. Turn my brother out if he disturbs you. Soames: bring the letters out here.

SYKES. He wont be offended at my offering it, will he?

MRS GEORGE. Not he! He touches children with the mace to cure them of ringworm for fourpence apiece. [*She goes into the study. Soames follows her*].

THE GENERAL. Well, Edith, I'm a little disappointed. I must say. However, I'm glad it was done by somebody in a public uniform.

Mrs Bridgenorth and Lesbia come in through the tower. Mrs Bridgenorth makes for the Bishop. He goes to her, and they meet near the oak chest. Lesbia comes between Sykes and Edith.

THE BISHOP. Alice, my love, theyre married.

MRS BRIDGENORTH [*placidly*] Oh, well, thats all right. Better tell Collins.

Soames comes back from the study with his writing materials. He seats himself at the nearest end of the table and goes on with his work. Hotchkiss sits down in the next chair round the table corner, with his back to him.

LESBIA. You have both given in, have you?

EDITH. Not at all. We have provided for everything.

SOAMES. How?

EDITH. Before going to the church, we went to the office of that insurance company—whats its name, Cecil?

SYKES. The British Family Insurance Corporation. It insures you against poor relations and all sorts of family contingencies.

EDITH. It has consented to insure Cecil against libel actions brought against him on my account. It will give us specially low terms because I am a Bishop's daughter.

SYKES. And I have given Edie my solemn word that if I ever commit a crime I'll knock her down before a witness and go off to Brighton with another lady.

LESBIA. Thats what you call providing for everything! [*She goes to the middle of the table on the garden side and sits down*].

LEO. Do make him see that there are no worms before he knocks you down, Edith. Wheres Rejjy?

REGINALD [*coming in from the study*] Here. Whats the matter?

LEO [*springing up and flouncing round to him*] Whats the matter! You may well ask. While Edie and Cecil were at the insurance office I took a taxi and went off to your lodgings; and a nice mess I found everything in. Your clothes are in a disgraceful state. Your liver-pad has been made into a kettle-holder. Youre no more fit to be left to yourself than a one-year-old baby.

REGINALD. Oh, I cant be bothered looking after things like that. I'm all right.

LEO. Youre not: youre a disgrace. You never consider that youre a disgrace to me: you think only of yourself. You must come home with me and be taken proper care of: my conscience will not allow me to let you live like a pig. [*She arranges his necktie*]. You must stay with me until I marry Sinjon; and then we can adopt you or something.

REGINALD [*breaking loose from her and stumping off past Hotchkiss towards the hearth*] No, I'm dashed if I'll be adopted by Sinjon. You can adopt him if you like.

HOTCHKISS [*rising*] I suggest that that would really

be the better plan, Leo. Ive a confession to make to you. I'm not the man you took me for. Your objection to Rejjy was that he had low tastes.

REGINALD [*turning*] Was it? by George!

LEO. I said slovenly habits. I never thought he had really low tastes until I saw that woman in court. How he could have chosen such a creature and let her write to him after—

REGINALD. Is this fair? I never—

HOTCHKISS. Of course you didnt, Rejjy. Dont be silly, Leo. It's I who really have low tastes.

LEO. You!

HOTCHKISS. Ive fallen in love with a coal merchant's wife. I adore her. I would rather have one of her boot-laces than a lock of your hair. [*He folds his arms and stands like a rock*].

REGINALD. You damned scoundrel, how dare you throw my wife over like that before my face? [*He seems on the point of assaulting Hotchkiss when Leo gets between them and draws Reginald away towards the study door*].

LEO. Dont take any notice of him, Rejjy. Go at once and get that odious decree demolished or annulled or whatever it is. Tell Sir Gorell Barnes that I have changed my mind. [*To Hotchkiss*] I might have known that you were too clever to be really a gentleman. [*She takes Reginald away to the oak chest and seats him there. He chuckles. Hotchkiss resumes his seat, brooding*].

THE BISHOP. All the problems appear to be solving themselves.

LESBIA. Except mine.

THE GENERAL. But, my dear Lesbia, you see what has happened here today. [*Coming a little nearer and bending his face towards hers*] Now I put it to you, does it not shew you the folly of not marrying?

LESBIA. No: I cant say it does. And [*rising*] you have been smoking again.

THE GENERAL. You drive me to it, Lesbia. I cant help it.

LESBIA [*standing behind her chair with her hands on the back of it and looking radiant*] Well, I wont scold you today. I feel in particularly good humor just now.

THE GENERAL. May I ask why, Lesbia?

LESBIA [*drawing a large breath*] To think that after all the dangers of the morning I am still unmarried! still independent! still my own mistress! still a glorious strong-minded old maid of old England!

Soames silently springs up and makes a long stretch from his end of the table to shake her hand across it.

THE GENERAL. Do you find any real happiness in being your own mistress? Would it not be more generous—would you not be happier as someone else's mistress—

LESBIA. Boxer!

THE GENERAL [*rising, horrified*] No, no, you must know, my dear Lesbia, that I was not using the word in its improper sense. I am sometimes unfortunate in my choice of expressions; but you know what I mean. I feel sure you would be happier as my wife.

LESBIA. I daresay I should, in a frowsty sort of way. But I prefer my dignity and my independence. I'm afraid I think this rage for happiness rather vulgar.

THE GENERAL. Oh, very well, Lesbia. I shall not ask you again. [*He sits down huffily*].

LESBIA. You will, Boxer; but it will be no use. [*She also sits down again and puts her hand almost affectionately on his*]. Some day I hope to make a friend of you; and then we shall get on very nicely.

THE GENERAL [*starting up again*] Ha! I think you are hard, Lesbia. I shall make a fool of myself if I remain here. Alice: I shall go into the garden for a while.

COLLINS [*appearing in the tower*] I think everything is in order now, maam.

THE GENERAL [*going to him*] Oh, by the way, could you oblige me—[*the rest of the sentence is lost in a whisper*].

COLLINS. Certainly, General. [*He takes out a tobacco pouch and hands it to the General, who takes it and goes into the garden*].

LESBIA. I dont believe theres a man in England who really and truly loves his wife as much as he loves his pipe.

THE BISHOP. By the way, what has happened to the wedding party?

SYKES. I dont know. There wasnt a soul in the church when we were married except the pew opener and the curate who did the job.

EDITH. They had all gone home.

MRS BRIDGENORTH. But the bridesmaids?

COLLINS. Me and the beadle have been all over the place in a couple of taxies, maam; and weve collected them all. They were a good deal disappointed on account of their dresses, and thought it all rather irregular; but theyve agreed to come to the breakfast. The truth is, theyre wild with curiosity to know how it all happened. The organist held on until the organ was nigh worn out, and himself worse than the organ. He asked me particularly to tell you my lord, that he held back Mendelssohn til the very last; but when that was gone he thought he might as well go too. So he played God Save The King and cleared out the church. He's coming to the breakfast to explain.

LEO. Please remember, Collins, that there is no truth whatever in the rumor that I am separated from my husband, or that there is, or ever has been, anything between me and Mr Hotchkiss.

COLLINS. Bless you, maam! one could always see that. [*To Mrs Bridgenorth*] Will you receive here or in the hall, maam?

MRS BRIDGENORTH. In the hall. Alfred: you and Boxer must go there and be ready to keep the first arrivals talking til we come. We have to dress Edith. Come, Lesbia: come, Leo: we must all help. Now, Edith [*Lesbia, Leo, and Edith go out through the tower*]. Collins: we shall want you when Miss Edith's dressed to look over her veil and things and see that theyre all right.

COLLINS. Yes, maam. Anything you would like mentioned about Miss Lesbia, maam?

MRS BRIDGENORTH. No. She wont have the General. I think you may take that as final.

COLLINS. What a pity, maam! A fine lady wasted, maam. [*They shake their heads sadly; and Mrs Bridgenorth goes out through the tower*].

THE BISHOP. I'm going to the hall, Collins, to receive. Rejjy: go and tell Boxer; and come both of you to help with the small talk. Come, Cecil. [*He goes out through the tower, followed by Sykes*].

REGINALD [*to Hotchkiss*] Youve always talked a precious lot about behaving like a gentleman. Well, if you think youve behaved like a gentleman to Leo, youre mistaken. And I shall have to take her part, remember that.

HOTCHKISS. I understand. Your doors are closed to me.

REGINALD [*quickly*] Oh no. Dont be hasty. I think I should like you to drop in after a while, you know. She gets so cross and upset when theres nobody to liven up the house a bit.

HOTCHKISS. I'll do my best.

REGINALD [*relieved*] Righto. You dont mind, old chap, do you?

HOTCHKISS. It's Fate. Ive touched coal; and my hands are black; but theyre clean. So long, Rejjy. [*They shake hands; and Reginald goes into the garden to collect Boxer*].

COLLINS. Excuse me, sir; but do you stay to breakfast? Your name is on one of the covers; and I should like to change it if youre not remaining.

HOTCHKISS. How do I know? Is my destiny any longer in my own hands? Go: ask SHE WHO MUST BE OBEYED.

COLLINS [*awestruck*] Has Mrs George taken a fancy to you, sir?

HOTCHKISS. Would she had! Worse, man, worse: Ive taken a fancy to Mrs George.

COLLINS. Dont despair, sir: if George likes your conversation youll find their house a very pleasant one: livelier than Mr Reginald's was, I daresay.

HOTCHKISS [*calling*] Polly.

COLLINS [*promptly*] Oh, if it's come to Polly already, sir, I should say you were all right.

Mrs George appears at the door of the study.

HOTCHKISS. Your brother-in-law wishes to know whether I'm to stay for the wedding breakfast. Tell him.

MRS GEORGE. He stays, Bill, if he chooses to behave himself.

HOTCHKISS [*to Collins*] May I, as a friend of the family, have the privilege of calling you Bill?

COLLINS. With pleasure, sir, I'm sure, sir.

HOTCHKISS. My own pet name in the bosom of my family is Sonny.

MRS GEORGE. Why didnt you tell me that before? Sonny is just the name I wanted for you. [*She pats his cheek familiarly: he rises abruptly and goes to the hearth, where he throws himself moodily into the railed chair*]. Bill: I'm not going into the hall until there are enough people there to make a proper little court for me. Send the Beadle for me when you think it looks good enough.

COLLINS. Right, maam. [*He goes out through the tower*].

Mrs George, left alone with Hotchkiss and Soames, suddenly puts her hands on Soames's shoulders and bends over him].

MRS GEORGE. The Bishop said I was to tempt you, Anthony.

SOAMES [*without looking round*] Woman: go away.

MRS GEORGE. Anthony:

> "When other lips and other hearts
> Their tale of love shall tell

HOTCHKISS [*sardonically*]

> In language whose excess imparts
> The power they feel so well.

MRS GEORGE.

> Though hollow hearts may wear a mask
> Twould break your own to see,
> In such a moment I but ask
> That youll remember me."

And you will, Anthony. I shall put my spell on you.

SOAMES. Do you think that a man who has sung the Magnificat and adored the Queen of Heaven has any ears for such trash as that or any eyes for such trash as you—saving your poor little soul's presence. Go home to your duties, woman.

MRS GEORGE [*highly approving his fortitude*] Anthony: I adopt you as my father. Thats the talk! Give me a man whose whole life doesnt hang on some scrubby woman in the next street; and I'll never let him go [*she slaps him heartily on the back*].

SOAMES. Thats enough. You have another man to talk to. I'm busy.

MRS GEORGE [*leaving Soames and going a step or two nearer Hotchkiss*] Why arnt you like him, Sonny? Why do you hang on to a scrubby woman in the next street?

HOTCHKISS [*thoughtfully*] I must apologize to Billiter.

MRS GEORGE. Who is Billiter?

HOTCHKISS. A man who eats rice pudding with a spoon. Ive been eating rice pudding with a spoon ever since I saw you first. [*He rises*] We all eat our rice pudding with a spoon, dont we, Soames?

SOAMES. We are members of one another. There is no need to refer to me. In the first place, I'm busy: in the second, youll find it all in the Church Catechism, which contains most of the new discoveries with which the age is bursting. Of course you should apologize to Billiter. He is your equal. He will go to the same heaven if he behaves himself and to the same hell if he doesnt.

MRS GEORGE [*sitting down*] And so will my husband the coal merchant.

HOTCHKISS. If I were your husband's superior here I should be his superior in heaven or hell: equality lies deeper than that. The coal merchant and I are in love with the same woman. That settles the question for me for ever. [*He prowls across the kitchen to the garden door, deep in thought*].

SOAMES. Psha!

MRS GEORGE. You dont believe in women, do you, Anthony? He might as well say that he and George both like fried fish.

HOTCHKISS. I do not like fried fish. Dont be low, Polly.

[217]

SOAMES. Woman: do not presume to accuse me of unbelief. And do you, Hotchkiss, not despise this woman's soul because she speaks of fried fish. Some of the victims of the Miraculous Draught of Fishes were fried. And I eat fried fish every Friday and like it. You are as ingrained a snob as ever.

HOTCHKISS [*impatiently*] My dear Anthony: I find you merely ridiculous as a preacher, because you keep referring me to places and documents and alleged occurrences in which, as a matter of fact, I dont believe. I dont believe in anything but my own will and my own pride and honor. Your fishes and your catechisms and all the rest of it make a charming poem which you call your faith. It fits you to perfection; but it doesnt fit me. I happen, like Napoleon to prefer Mahometanism. [*Mrs George, associating Mahometanism with polygamy, looks at him with a quick suspicion*]. I believe the whole British Empire will adopt a reformed Mahometanism before the end of the century. The character of Mahomet is congenial to me. I admire him, and share his views of life to a considerable extent. That beats you, you see, Soames. Religion is a great force: the only real motive force in the world; but what you fellows dont understand is that you must get at a man through his own religion and not through yours. Instead of facing that fact, you persist in trying to convert all men to your own little sect, so that you can use it against them afterwards. You are all missionaries and proselytizers trying to uproot the native religion from your neighbor's flowerbeds and plant your own in its place. You would rather let a child perish in ignorance than have it taught by a rival sectary. You talk to me of the quintessential equality of coal merchants and British officers; and yet you cant see the quintessential equality of all the religions. Who are you, anyhow, that you should know better than Mahomet or Confucius or any of the other Johnnies who have been on this job since the world existed?

MRS GEORGE [*admiring his eloquence*] George will like you, Sonny. You should hear him talking about the Church.

SOAMES. Very well, then: go to your doom, both of you. There is only one religion for me: that which my soul knows to be true; but even irreligion has one tenet; and that is the sacredness of marriage. You two are on the verge of deadly sin. Do you deny that?

HOTCHKISS. You forget, Anthony: the marriage itself is the deadly sin according to you.

SOAMES. The question is not now what I believe, but what you believe. Take the vows with me; and give up that woman if you have the strength and the light. But if you are still in the grip of this world, at least respect its institutions. Do you believe in marriage or do you not?

HOTCHKISS. My soul is utterly free from any such superstition. I solemnly declare that between this woman, as you impolitely call her, and me, I see no barrier that my conscience bids me respect. I loathe the whole marriage morality of the middle classes with all my instincts. If I were an eighteenth century marquis I could not feel more free with regard to a Parisian citizen's wife than I do with regard to Polly. I despise all this domestic purity business as the lowest depth of narrow, selfish, sensual, wife-grabbing vulgarity.

MRS GEORGE [*rising promptly*] Oh, indeed. Then youre not coming home with me, young man. I'm sorry; for it's refreshing to have met once in my life a man who wasnt frightened by my wedding ring; but I'm

looking out for a friend and not for a French marquis;
so youre not coming home with me.

HOTCHKISS [*inexorably*] Yes, I am.

MRS GEORGE. No.

HOTCHKISS. Yes. Think again. You know your set
pretty well, I suppose, your petty tradesmen's set.
You know all its scandals and hypocrisies, its jealous-
ies and squabbles, its hundreds of divorce cases that
never come into court, as well as its tens that do.

MRS GEORGE. We're not angels. I know a few scandals; but most of us are too dull to be anything but
good.

HOTCHKISS. Then you must have noticed that just
as all murderers, judging by their edifying remarks on
the scaffold, seem to be devout Christians, so all
libertines, both male and female, are invariably people
overflowing with domestic sentimentality and pro-
fessions of respect for the conventions they violate in
secret.

MRS GEORGE. Well, you dont expect them to give
themselves away, do you?

HOTCHKISS. They are people of sentiment, not of
honor. Now, I'm not a man of sentiment, but a man of
honor. I know well what will happen to me when once
I cross the threshold of your husband's house and
break bread with him. This marriage bond which I
despise will bind me as it never seems to bind the
people who believe in it, and whose chief amusement
it is to go to the theatres where it is laughed at.
Soames: youre a Communist, arnt you?

SOAMES. I am a Christian. That obliges me to be a
Communist.

HOTCHKISS. And you believe that many of our
landed estates were stolen from the Church by Henry
the eighth?

SOAMES. I do not merely believe that: I know it as a lawyer.

HOTCHKISS. Would you steal a turnip from one of the landlords of those stolen lands?

SOAMES [*fencing with the question*] They have no right to their lands.

HOTCHKISS. Thats not what I ask you. Would you steal a turnip from one of the fields they have no right to?

SOAMES. I do not like turnips.

HOTCHKISS. As you are a lawyer, answer me.

SOAMES. I admit that I should probably not do so. I should perhaps be wrong not to steal the turnip: I cant defend my reluctance to do so; but I think I should not do so. I know I should not do so.

HOTCHKISS. Neither shall I be able to steal George's wife. I have stretched out my hand for that forbidden fruit before; and I know that my hand will always come back empty. To disbelieve in marriage is easy: to love a married woman is easy; but to betray a comrade, to be disloyal to a host, to break the covenant of bread and salt, is impossible. You may take me home with you, Polly: you have nothing to fear.

MRS GEORGE. And nothing to hope?

HOTCHKISS. Since you put it in that more than kind way, Polly, absolutely nothing.

MRS GEORGE. Hm! Like most men, you think you know everything a woman wants, dont you? But the thing one wants most has nothing to do with marriage at all. Perhaps Anthony here has a glimmering of it. Eh, Anthony?

SOAMES. Christian fellowship?

MRS GEORGE. You call it that, do you?

SOAMES. What do you call it?

COLLINS [*appearing in the tower with the Beadle*] Now, Polly, the hall's full; and theyre waiting for you.

THE BEADLE. Make way there, gentlemen, please. Way for the worshipful the Mayoress. If you please, my lords and gentlemen. By your leave, ladies and gentlemen: way for the Mayoress.

Mrs George takes Hotchkiss's arm, and goes out, preceded by the Beadle.

Soames resumes his writing tranquilly.

Press Cuttings

A topical sketch compiled from
the editorial and correspondence
columns of the daily papers
during the Women's War of 1909

Composition begun c. 27 March 1909; completed 2 May 1909. First published in German translation, as *Zeitungsausschnitte*, in *März* (Berlin), July 1909. First English publication, 1909. First collected in *Translations and Tomfooleries*, 1926. First presented at a "Private Reception" at the Royal Court Theatre, London, on 9 July 1909; repeated on 12 July.

General Mitchener   *Robert Loraine*
Prime Minister Balsquith   *Leon Quartermaine*
Mrs Farrell   *Agnes Thomas*
An Orderly   *Ernest Cosham*
Mrs Rosa Carmina Banger   Alice Beet
Lady Corinthia Fanshawe   *Ethelwyn Jones*

Period—The forenoon of the First of April, three years hence

Scene—*General Mitchener's Office in the War Office*

By direction of the Lord Chamberlain the General and the Prime Minister in this play must in all public performances of it be addressed and described as General Bones and Mr Johnson, and by no means as General Mitchener and Mr Balsquith. The allusions to commoner persons are allowed to stand as they are.

General Mitchener, by the way, is not the late Lord Kitchener, but an earlier and more highly connected commander. Balsquith (Balfour-Asquith) is obviously neither of these statesmen, and cannot in the course of nature be both.

The forenoon of the first of April, three years hence.

General Mitchener is at his writing-table in the War Office, opening letters. On his left is the fireplace, with a fire burning. On his right, against the opposite wall, is a standing desk with an office stool. The door is in the wall behind him, half way between the table and the desk. The table is not quite in the middle of the room; it is nearer to the hearthrug than to the desk. There is a chair at each end of it for persons having business with the General. There is a telephone on the table.

Long silence.

A VOICE FROM THE STREET. Votes for Women!

The General starts convulsively; snatches a revolver from a drawer; and listens in an agony of apprehension. Nothing happens. He puts the revolver back, ashamed; wipes his brow; and resumes his work. He is startled afresh by the entry of an Orderly. This Orderly is an unsoldierly, slovenly, discontented young man.

MITCHENER. Oh, it's only you. Well?

THE ORDERLY. Another one, sir. She's chained herself.

MITCHENER. Chained herself? How? To what? Weve taken away the railings and everything that a chain can be passed through.

THE ORDERLY. We forgot the doorscraper, sir. She lay down on the flags and got the chain through before she started hollerin. She's lying there now; and she downfaces us that youve got the key of the padlock in a letter in a buff envelope, and that youll see her when you open it.

MITCHENER. She's mad. Have the scraper dug up and let her go home with it hanging round her neck.

[226]

THE ORDERLY. There is a buff envelope there, sir.

MITCHENER. Youre all afraid of these women. [*He picks the letter up*] It does seem to have a key in it. [*He opens the letter; takes out a key and a note; and reads*] "Dear Mitch"—Well, I'm dashed!

THE ORDERLY. Yes, sir.

MITCHENER. What do you mean by Yes, sir?

THE ORDERLY. Well, you said you was dashed, sir; and you did look—if youll excuse my saying it, sir— well, you looked it.

MITCHENER [*who has been reading the letter, and is too astonished to attend to the Orderly's reply*] This is a letter from the Prime Minister asking me to release the woman with this key if she padlocks herself, and to have her shewn up and see her at once.

THE ORDERLY [*tremulously*] Dont do it, governor.

MITCHENER [*angrily*] How often have I ordered you not to address me as governor? Remember that you are a soldier and not a vulgar civilian. Remember also that when a man enters the army he leaves fear behind him. Heres the key. Unlock her and shew her up.

THE ORDERLY. Me unlock her! I dursent. Lord knows what she'd do to me.

MITCHENER [*pepperily, rising*] Obey your orders instantly, sir; and dont presume to argue. Even if she kills you, it is your duty to die for your country. Right about face. March.

The Orderly goes out, trembling.

THE VOICE OUTSIDE. Votes for Women! Votes for Women! Votes for Women!

MITCHENER [*mimicking her*] Votes for Women! Votes for Women! Votes for Women! [*In his natural voice*] Votes for children! Votes for babies! Votes for monkeys! [*He posts himself on the hearthrug and awaits the enemy*].

THE ORDERLY [*outside*] In you go. [*He pushes a panting Suffraget into the room*] The person, sir. [*He withdraws*].

The Suffraget takes off her tailor-made skirt and reveals a pair of fashionable trousers.

MITCHENER [*horrified*] Stop, madam. What are you doing? you must not undress in my presence. I protest. Not even your letter from the Prime Minister—

THE SUFFRAGET. My dear Mitchener: I am the Prime Minister. [*He takes off his hat and cloak; throws them on the desk; and confronts the General in the ordinary costume of a Cabinet Minister*].

MITCHENER. Good heavens! Balsquith!

BALSQUITH [*throwing himself into Mitchener's chair*] Yes: it is indeed Balsquith. It has come to this: that the only way the Prime Minister of England can get from Downing Street to the War Office is by assuming this disguise; shrieking "VOTES FOR WOMEN"; and chaining himself to your doorscraper. They were at the corner in force. They cheered me. Bellachristina herself was there. She shook my hand and told me to say I was a vegetarian, as the diet was better in Holloway for vegetarians.

MITCHENER. Why didnt you telephone?

BALSQUITH. They tap the telephone. Every switchboard in London is in their hands, or in those of their young men.

MITCHENER. Where on earth did you get the dress? I hope it's not a French dress!

BALSQUITH. Great heavens, no. We're not allowed even to put on our gloves with French chalk. Everything's labelled "Made in Camberwell."

MITCHENER. As a Tariff Reformer, I must say Quite right. [*Balsquith has a strong controversial impulse and is evidently going to dispute this profession of faith*]. No matter. Dont argue. What have you come for?

BALSQUITH. Sandstone has resigned.

MITCHENER [*amazed*] Old Red resigned!

BALSQUITH. Resigned.

MITCHENER. But how? Why? Oh, impossible! the proclamation of martial law last Tuesday made Sandstone virtually Dictator in the metropolis; and to resign now is flat desertion.

BALSQUITH. Yes, yes, my dear Mitchener: I know all that as well as you do: I argued with him until I was black in the face, and he so red about the neck that if I had gone on he would have burst. He is furious because we have abandoned his plan.

MITCHENER. But you accepted it unconditionally.

BALSQUITH. Yes, before we knew what it was. It was unworkable, you know.

MITCHENER. I dont know. Why is it unworkable?

BALSQUITH. I mean the part about drawing a cordon round Westminster at a distance of two miles, and turning all women out of it.

MITCHENER. A masterpiece of strategy. Let me explain. The Suffragets are a very small body; but they are numerous enough to be troublesome—even dangerous—when they are all concentrated in one place—say in Parliament Square. But by making a two-mile radius and pushing them beyond it, you scatter their attack over a circular line twelve miles long. Just what Wellington would have done.

BALSQUITH. But the women wont go.

MITCHENER. Nonsense: they must go.

BALSQUITH. They wont.

MITCHENER. What does Sandstone say?

BALSQUITH. He says: Shoot them down.

[229]

MITCHENER. Of course.

BALSQUITH. Youre not serious?

MITCHENER. I'm perfectly serious.

BALSQUITH. But you cant shoot them down! Women, you know!

MITCHENER [*straddling confidently*] Yes you can. Strange as it may seem to you as a civilian, Balsquith, if you point a rifle at a woman and fire it, she will drop exactly as a man drops.

BALSQUITH. But suppose your own daughters—Helen and Georgina—

MITCHENER. My daughters would not dream of disobeying the proclamation. [*As an afterthought*] At least Helen wouldnt.

BALSQUITH. But Georgina?

MITCHENER. Georgina would if she knew she'd be shot if she didnt. Thats how the thing would work. Military methods are really the most merciful in the end. You keep sending these misguided women to Holloway and killing them slowly and inhumanly by ruining their health; and it does no good: they go on worse than ever. Shoot a few, promptly and humanely; and there will be an end at once of all resistance and of all the suffering that resistance entails.

BALSQUITH. But public opinion would never stand it.

MITCHENER [*walking about and laying down the law*] Theres no such thing as public opinion.

BALSQUITH. No such thing as public opinion!!

MITCHENER. Absolutely no such thing. There are certain persons who entertain certain opinions. Well, shoot them down. When you have shot them down, there are no longer any persons entertaining those opinions alive; consequently there is no longer any more of the public opinion you are so much afraid of. Grasp that fact, my dear Balsquith; and you have grasped the secret of government. Public opinion is mind. Mind is inseparable from matter. Shoot down the matter and you kill the mind.

BALSQUITH. But hang it all—

MITCHENER [*intolerantly*] No I wont hang it all. It's no use coming to me and talking about public opinion. You have put yourself into the hands of the army; and you are committed to military methods. And the basis of all military methods is that when people wont do what theyre told to do, you shoot them down.

BALSQUITH. Oh yes; it's all jolly fine for you and Old Red. You dont depend on votes for your places. What do you suppose would happen at the next election?

MITCHENER. Have no next election. Bring in a Bill at once repealing all the Reform Acts and vesting the Government in a properly trained magistracy responsible only to a Council of War. It answers perfectly in India. If anyone objects, shoot him down.

BALSQUITH. But none of the members of my party would be on the Council of War. Neither should I. Do you expect us to vote for making ourselves nobodies?

MITCHENER. Youll have to, sooner or later, or the Socialists will make nobodies of the lot of you by collaring every penny you possess. Do you suppose this damned democracy can be allowed to go on now that the mob is beginning to take it seriously and using its power to lay hands on property? Parliament must abolish itself. The Irish parliament voted for its own extinction. The English parliament will do the same if the same means are taken to persuade it.

BALSQUITH. That would cost a lot of money.

MITCHENER. Not money necessarily. Bribe them with titles.

BALSQUITH. Do you think we dare?

MITCHENER [*scornfully*] Dare! Dare! What is life but daring, man? "To dare, to dare, and again to dare—"

FEMALE VOICE IN THE STREET. Votes for Women! [*Mitchener, revolver in hand, rushes to the door and locks it. Balsquith hides under the table*]. Votes for Women!

A shot is heard.

BALSQUITH [*emerging in the greatest alarm*] Good heavens, you havent given orders to fire on them: have you?

MITCHENER. No: but it's a sentinel's duty to fire on anyone who persists in attempting to pass without giving the word.

BALSQUITH [*wiping his brow*] This military business is really awful.

MITCHENER. Be calm, Balsquith. These things must happen: they save bloodshed in the long run, believe me. Ive seen plenty of it; and I know.

BALSQUITH. I havnt; and I dont know. I wish those guns didnt make such a devil of a noise. We must adopt Maxim's Silencer for the army rifles if we're going to shoot women. I really couldnt stand hearing it. [*Someone outside tries to open the door and then knocks*]. Whats that?

MITCHENER. Who's there?

THE ORDERLY. It's only me, governor. It's all right.

MITCHENER [*unlocking the door and admitting the Orderly, who comes between them*] What was it?

THE ORDERLY. Suffraget, sir.

BALSQUITH. Did the sentry shoot her?

[232]

THE ORDERLY. No, sir: she shot the sentry.

BALSQUITH [*relieved*] Oh: is that all?

MITCHENER [*most indignantly*] All! A civilian shoots
down one of His Majesty's soldiers on duty; and the
Prime Minister of England asks, Is that all?!!! Have
you no regard for the sanctity of human life?

BALSQUITH [*much relieved*] Well, getting shot is what
a soldier is for. Besides, he doesnt vote.

MITCHENER. Neither do the Suffragets.

BALSQUITH. Their husbands do. [*To the Orderly*]
Did she kill him?

THE ORDERLY. No, sir. He got a stinger on his
trousers, sir; but it didnt penetrate. He lost his
temper a bit and put down his gun and clouted her
head for her. So she said he was no gentleman; and
we let her go, thinking she'd had enough, sir.

MITCHENER [*groaning*] Clouted her head! These
women are making the army as lawless as themselves. Clouted her head indeed! A purely civil pro-
cedure.

THE ORDERLY. Any orders, sir?

MITCHENER. No. Yes. No. Yes: send everybody who
took part in this disgraceful scene to the guard-room.
No. I'll address the men on the subject after lunch.
Parade them for that purpose: full kit. Dont grin at
me, sir. Right about face. March.

The Orderly obeys and goes out.

BALSQUITH [*taking Mitchener affectionately by the
arm and walking him persuasively to and fro*] And now,
Mitchener, will you come to the rescue of the Government and take the command that Old Red has thrown
up?

MITCHENER. How can I? You know that the people
are devoted heart and soul to Sandstone. He is only

bringing you "on the knee," as we say in the army. Could any other living man have persuaded the British nation to accept universal compulsory military service as he did last year? Why, even the Church refused exemption. He is supreme—omnipotent.

BALSQUITH. He was, a year ago. But ever since your book of reminiscences went into two more editions than his, and the rush for it led to the wrecking of the Times Book Club, you have become to all intents and purposes his senior. He lost ground by saying that the wrecking was got up by the booksellers. It shewed jealousy; and the public felt it.

MITCHENER. But I cracked him up in my book—you see I could do no less after the handsome way he cracked me up in his —and I cant go back on it now. [Breaking loose from Balsquith] No: it's no use, Balsquith: he can dictate his terms to you.

BALSQUITH. Not a bit of it. That affair of the curate—

MITCHENER [impatiently] Oh, damn that curate. Ive heard of nothing but that wretched mutineer for a fortnight past. He's not a curate: whilst he's serving in the army he's a private soldier and nothing else. I really havnt time to discuss him further. I'm busy. Good morning. [He sits down at his table and takes up his letters].

BALSQUITH [near the door] I'm sorry you take that tone, Mitchener. Since you do take it, let me tell you frankly that I think Lieutenant Chubbs-Jenkinson shewed a great want of consideration for the Government in giving an unreasonable and unpopular order, and bringing compulsory military service into disrepute.

MITCHENER. No order is unreasonable; and all orders are unpopular.

BALSQUITH. When the leader of the Labor Party

appealed to me and to the House last year not to throw away all the liberties of Englishmen by accepting compulsory military service without full civil rights for the soldier—

MITCHENER. Rot.

BALSQUITH. —I said that no British officer would be capable of abusing the authority with which it was absolutely necessary to invest him.

MITCHENER. Quite right.

BALSQUITH. That carried the House;—

MITCHENER. Naturally.

BALSQUITH. —and the feeling was that the Labor Party were soulless cads.

MITCHENER. So they are.

BALSQUITH. And now comes this unmannerly young whelp Chubbs-Jenkinson, the only son of what they call a soda king, and orders a curate to lick his boots. And when the curate punches his head, you first sentence him to be shot; and then make a great show of clemency by commuting it to a flogging. What did you expect the curate to do?

MITCHENER [*throwing down his pen and his letters and jumping up to confront Balsquith*] His duty was perfectly simple. He should have obeyed the order; and then laid his complaint against the officer in proper form. He would have received the fullest satisfaction.

BALSQUITH. What satisfaction?

MITCHENER. Chubbs-Jenkinson would have been reprimanded. In fact, he was reprimanded. Besides, the man was thoroughly insubordinate. You cant deny that the very first thing he did when they took him down after flogging him was to walk up to Chubbs-Jenkinson and break his jaw. That shewed there was no use flogging him; so now he will get two years' hard labor; and serve him right!

BALSQUITH. I bet you a guinea he wont get even a week. I bet you another that Chubbs-Jenkinson apologizes abjectly. You evidently havnt heard the news.

MITCHENER. What news?

BALSQUITH. It turns out that the curate is well connected. [*Mitchener staggers at the shock. He reels into his chair and buries his face in his hands over the blotter*]. He has three aunts in the peerage; Lady Richmond's one of them [*Mitchener punctuates these announcements with heartrending groans*]; and they all adore him. The invitations for six garden parties and fourteen dances have been cancelled for all the subalterns in Chubbs's regiment. [*Mitchener attempts to shoot himself*].

BALSQUITH [*seizing the pistol*] No: your country needs you, Mitchener.

MITCHENER [*putting down the pistol*] For my country's sake. [*Balsquith, reassured, sits down*]. But what an infernal young fool Chubbs-Jenkinson is, not to know the standing of his man better! Why didnt he know? It was his business to know. He ought to be flogged.

BALSQUITH. Probably he will be, by the other subalterns.

MITCHENER. I hope so. Anyhow, out he goes. Out of the army. He or I.

BALSQUITH. Steady, steady. His father has subscribed a million to the party funds. We owe him a peerage.

MITCHENER. I dont care.

BALSQUITH. I do. How do you think parties are kept up? Not by the subscriptions of the local associations, I hope. They dont pay for the gas at the meetings.

MITCHENER. Man: can you not be serious? Here are

we, face to face with Lady Richmond's grave displeasure; and you talk to me about gas and subscriptions. Her own nephew!!!!!

BALSQUITH [*gloomily*] It's unfortunate. He was at Oxford with Bobby Bessborough.

MITCHENER. Worse and worse. What shall we do?

A VOICE IN THE STREET. Votes for Women! Votes for Women!

A terrific explosion shakes the building. They take no notice.

MITCHENER [*breaking down*] You dont know what this means to me, Balsquith. I love the army. I love my country.

BALSQUITH. It certainly is rather awkward.

The Orderly comes in.

MITCHENER [*angrily*] What is it? How dare you interrupt us like this?

THE ORDERLY. Didnt you hear the explosion, sir?

MITCHENER. Explosion. What explosion? No: I heard no explosion: I have something more serious to attend to than explosions. Great Heavens! Lady Richmond's nephew has been treated like any common laborer; and while England is reeling under the shock, a private walks in and asks me if I heard an explosion.

BALSQUITH. By the way, what was the explosion?

THE ORDERLY. Only a sort of bombshell, sir.

BALSQUITH. Bombshell!

THE ORDERLY. A pasteboard one, sir. Full of papers with Votes for Women in red letters. Fired into the yard from the roof of the Alliance Office.

MITCHENER. Pooh! Go away. GO away.

The Orderly, bewildered, goes out.

BALSQUITH. Mitchener: you can save the country yet. Put on your full dress uniform and your medals

and orders and so forth. Get a guard of honor—
something showy—horse guards or something of that
sort; and call on the old girl—

MITCHENER. The old girl?

BALSQUITH. Well, Lady Richmond. Apologize to
her. Ask her leave to accept the command. Tell her
that youve made the curate your adjutant or your
aide-de-camp or whatever is the proper thing. By the
way, what can you make him?

MITCHENER. I might make him my chaplain. I dont
see why I shouldnt have a chaplain on my staff. He
shewed a very proper spirit in punching that young
cub's head. I should have done the same myself.

BALSQUITH. Then Ive your promise to take command if Lady Richmond consents?

MITCHENER. On condition that I have a free hand.
No nonsense about public opinion or democracy.

BALSQUITH. As far as possible, I think I may say yes.

MITCHENER [rising intolerantly and going to the
hearthrug] That wont do for me. Dont be weak-
kneed, Balsquith. You know perfectly well that the
real government of this country is and always must
be the government of the masses by the classes. You
know that democracy is damned nonsense, and that
no class stands less of it than the working class. You
know that we are already discussing the steps that will
have to be taken if the country should ever be face to
face with the possibility of a Labor majority in Parliament. You know that in that case we should disfran-
chise the mob, and if they made a fuss, shoot them
down. You know that if we need public opinion to
support us, we can get any quantity of it manufactured
in our papers by poor devils of journalists who will sell
their souls for five shillings. You know—

BALSQUITH. Stop. Stop, I say. I dont know. That is

the difference between your job and mine, Mitchener. After twenty years in the army a man thinks he knows everything. After twenty months in the Cabinet he knows that he knows nothing.

MITCHENER. We learn from history—

BALSQUITH. We learn from history that men never learn anything from history. That's not my own: it's Hegel.

MITCHENER. Who's Hegel?

BALSQUITH. Dead. A German philosopher. [*He half rises, but recollects something and sits down again*]. Oh, confound it: that reminds me. The Germans have laid down four more Dreadnoughts.

MITCHENER. Then you must lay down twelve.

BALSQUITH. Oh yes: it's easy to say that; but think of what theyll cost.

MITCHENER. Think of what it would cost to be invaded by Germany and forced to pay an indemnity of five hundred millions.

BALSQUITH. But you said that if you got compulsory military service there would be an end of the danger of invasion.

MITCHENER. On the contrary, my dear fellow, it increases the danger tenfold, because it increases German jealousy of our military supremacy.

BALSQUITH. After all, why should the Germans invade us?

MITCHENER. Why shouldnt they? What else has their army to do? What else are they building a navy for?

BALSQUITH. Well, we never think of invading Germany.

MITCHENER. Yes, we do. I have thought of nothing else for the last ten years. Say what you will, Balsquith, the Germans have never recognized, and until they get a stern lesson they never will recognize, the plain fact that the interests of the British Empire are paramount, and that the command of the sea belongs by nature to England.

BALSQUITH. But if they wont recognize it, what can I do?

MITCHENER. Shoot them down.

BALSQUITH. I cant shoot them down.

MITCHENER. Yes you can. You dont realize it; but if you fire a rifle into a German he drops just as surely as a rabbit does.

BALSQUITH. But dash it all, man, a rabbit hasnt got a rifle and a German has. Suppose he shoots you down.

MITCHENER. Excuse me, Balsquith; but that consideration is what we call cowardice in the army. A soldier always assumes that he is going to shoot, not to be shot.

BALSQUITH [*jumping up and walking about sulkily*] Oh come! I like to hear you military people talking of cowardice. Why, you spend your lives in an ecstasy of terror of imaginary invasions. I dont believe you ever go to bed without looking under it for a burglar.

MITCHENER [*calmly*] A very sensible precaution, Balsquith. I always take it; and, in consequence, Ive never been burgled.

BALSQUITH. Neither have I. Anyhow, dont you taunt me with cowardice. [*He posts himself on the hearthrug beside Mitchener, on his left*]. I never look under my bed for a burglar. I'm not always looking under the nation's bed for an invader. And if it comes to fighting, I'm quite willing to fight without being three to one.

MITCHENER. These are the romantic ravings of a Jingo civilian, Balsquith. At least youll not deny that the absolute command of the sea is essential to our security.

BALSQUITH. The absolute command of the sea is essential to the security of the principality of Monaco. But Monaco isnt going to get it.

MITCHENER. And consequently Monaco enjoys no security. What a frightful thing! How do the inhabitants sleep with the possibility of invasion, of bombardment, continually present to their minds? Would you have our English slumbers broken in the same way? Are we also to live without security?

BALSQUITH [*dogmatically*] Yes. Theres no such thing as security in the world; and there never can be as long as men are mortal. England will be secure when England is dead, just as the streets of London will be safe when theres no longer a man in her streets to be run over or a vehicle to run over him. When you military chaps ask for security you are crying for the moon.

MITCHENER [*very seriously*] Let me tell you, Balsquith, that in these days of aeroplanes and Zeppelin airships the question of the moon is becoming one of the greatest importance. It will be reached at no very distant date. Can you, as an Englishman, tamely contemplate the possibility of having to live under a German moon? The British flag must be planted there at all hazards.

BALSQUITH. My dear Mitchener, the moon is outside practical politics. I'd swop it for a coaling-station tomorrow with Germany or any other Power sufficiently military in its way of thinking to attach any importance to it.

MITCHENER [*losing his temper*] You are the friend of every country but your own.

BALSQUITH. Say nobody's enemy but my own. It

sounds nicer. You really neednt be so horribly afraid of the other countries. Theyre all in the same fix as we are. I'm much more interested in the death-rate in Lambeth than in the German fleet.

MITCHENER. You darent say that in Lambeth.

BALSQUITH. I'll say it the day after you publish your scheme for invading Germany and repealing all the Reform Acts.

The Orderly comes in.

MITCHENER. What do you want?

THE ORDERLY. I dont want anything, governor, thank you. The secretary and president of the Anti-Suffraget League says they had an appointment with the Prime Minister, and that theyve been sent on here from Downing Street.

BALSQUITH [*going to the table*] Quite right. I forgot them. [*To Mitchener*] Would you mind my seeing them here? I feel extraordinarily grateful to these women for standing by us and facing the Suffragets, especially as they are naturally the gentler and timider sort of women. [*The Orderly moans*]. Did you say anything?

THE ORDERLY. No, sir.

BALSQUITH. Did you catch their names?

THE ORDERLY. Yes, sir. The president is Lady Corinthia Fanshawe; and the secretary is Mrs Banger.

MITCHENER [*abruptly*] Mrs what?

THE ORDERLY. Mrs Banger.

BALSQUITH. Curious that quiet people always seem to have violent names.

THE ORDERLY. Not much quiet about her, sir.

MITCHENER [*outraged*] Attention! Speak when youre spoken to. Hold your tongue when youre not. Right about face. March. [*The Orderly obeys*]. Thats the way to keep these chaps up to the mark. [*The Orderly returns*]. Back again! What do you mean by this mutiny?

THE ORDERLY. What am I to say to the ladies, sir?

BALSQUITH. You dont mind my seeing them somewhere, do you?

MITCHENER. Not at all. Bring them in to see me when youve done with them. I understand that Lady Corinthia is a very fascinating woman. Who is she, by the way?

BALSQUITH. Daughter of Lord Broadstairs, the automatic turbine man. Gave quarter of a million to the party funds. She's musical and romantic and all that—dont hunt: hates politics: stops in town all the year round: one never sees her except at the opera and at musical at-homes and so forth.

MITCHENER. What a life! [*To the Orderly*] Where are the ladies?

THE ORDERLY. In No. 17, sir.

MITCHENER. Shew Mr Balsquith there; and send Mrs Farrell here.

THE ORDERLY [*calling into the corridor*] Mrs Farrell! [*To Balsquith*] This way, sir. [*He goes out with Balsquith*].

Mrs Farrell, a lean, highly respectable Irish charwoman of about fifty, comes in.

MITCHENER. Mrs Farrell: Ive a very important visit to pay: I shall want my full dress uniform and all my medals and orders and my presentation sword. There was a time when the British Army contained men capable of discharging these duties for their commanding officer. Those days are over. The compulsorily enlisted soldier runs to a woman for everything. I'm therefore reluctantly obliged to trouble you.

MRS FARRELL. Your meddles n ordhers n the crooked

sword widh the ivory handle n your full dress uniform is in the waxworks in the Chamber o Military
Glory over in the place they used to call the Banquetin
Hall. I told you youd be sorry for sendin them away;
and you told me to mind me own business. Youre
wiser now.

MITCHENER. I am. I had not at that time discovered
that you were the only person in the whole military
establishment of this capital who could be trusted to
remember where anything was, or to understand an
order and obey it.

MRS FARRELL. It's no good flattherin me. I'm too old.

MITCHENER. Not at all, Mrs Farrell. How is your
daughter?

MRS FARRELL. Which daughter?

MITCHENER. The one who has made such a gratify-
ing success in the Music Halls.

MRS FARRELL. Theres no Music Halls nowadays:
theyre Variety Theatres. She's got an offer of marriage
from a young jook.

MITCHENER. Is it possible? What did you do?

MRS FARRELL. I told his mother on him.

MITCHENER. Oh! What did she say?

MRS FARRELL. She was as pleased as Punch. Thank
Heaven, she says, he's got somebody thatll be able to
keep him when the supertax is put up to twenty
shillings in the pound.

MITCHENER. But your daughter herself? What did
she say?

MRS FARRELL. Accepted him, of course. What else
would a young fool like her do? He inthrojooced her
to the Poet Laureate, thinkin she'd inspire him.

MITCHENER. Did she?

MRS FARRELL. Faith, I dunna. All I know is she
walked up to him as bold as brass n said, "Write me

a sketch, dear." Afther all the throuble Ive took with that child's manners she's no more notion how to behave herself than a pig. Youll have to wear General Sandstone's uniform: it's the only one in the place, because he wont lend it to the shows.

MITCHENER. But Sandstone's clothes wont fit me.

MRS FARRELL [*unmoved*] Then youll have to fit them. Why shouldnt they fitchya as well as they fitted General Blake at the Mansion House?

MITCHENER. They didnt fit him. He looked a frightful guy.

MRS FARRELL. Well, you must do the best you can with them. You cant exhibit your clothes and wear them too.

MITCHENER. And the public thinks the lot of a commanding officer a happy one! Oh, if they could only see the seamy side of it. [*He returns to his table to resume work*].

MRS FARRELL. If they could only see the seamy side o General Sandstone's uniform, where his flask rubs agen the buckle of his braces, theyd tell him he ought to get a new one. Let alone the way he swears at me.

MITCHENER. When a man has risked his life on eight battlefields, Mrs Farrell, he has given sufficient proof of his self-control to be excused a little strong language.

MRS FARRELL. Would you put up with bad language from me because Ive risked me life eight times in childbed?

MITCHENER. My dear Mrs Farrell, you surely would not compare a risk of that harmless domestic kind to the fearful risks of the battlefield.

MRS FARRELL. I wouldnt compare risks run to bear livin people into the world to risks run to blow dhem out of it. A mother's risk is jooty: a soldier's is nothin but divilmint.

MITCHENER [*nettled*] Let me tell you, Mrs Farrell, that if the men did not fight, the women would have to fight themselves. We spare you that at all events.

MRS FARRELL. You cant help yourselves. If three-quarters of you was killed we could replace you with the help of the other quarter. If three-quarters of us was killed how many people would there be in England in another generation? If it wasnt for that, the men'd put the fightin on us just as they put all the other dhrudgery. What would y o u do if we was all kilt? Would you go to bed and have twins?

MITCHENER. Really, Mrs Farrell, you must discuss these questions with a medical man. You make me blush, positively.

MRS FARRELL [*grumbling to herself*] A good job too. If I could have made Farrell blush I wouldnt have had to risk me life so often. You n your risks n your bravery n your self-conthrol indeed. "Why dont you conthrol yourself?" I sez to Farrell. "It's agen me religion," he sez.

MITCHENER [*plaintively*] Mrs Farrell: youre a wo-man of very powerful mind. I'm not qualified to argue these delicate matters with you. I ask you to spare me, and to be good enough to take these clothes to Mr Balsquith when the ladies leave.

The Orderly comes in.

THE ORDERLY. Lady Corinthia Fanshawe and Mrs Banger want to see you, sir. Mr Balsquith told me to tell you.

MRS FARRELL. Theyve come about the vote. I dont know whether it's dhem dhat want it or dhem dhat doesnt want it: anyhow, theyre all alike when they get into a state about it. [*She goes out, having gathered Balsquith's Suffraget disguise from the desk*].

MITCHENER. Is Mr Balsquith not with them.

THE ORDERLY. No, sir. Couldnt stand Mrs Banger, I expect. Fair caution she is. [*Chuckling*] Couldnt help larfin when I sor im op it.

MITCHENER [*highly incensed*] How dare you indulge in this unseemly mirth in the presence of your commanding officer? Have you no sense of a soldier's duty?

THE ORDERLY [*sadly*] I'm afraid I shant ever get the ang of it, sir. You see, my father has a tidy little barber's business down off Shoreditch; and I was brought up to be chatty and easy-like with everybody. I tell you, when I drew the number in the conscription it gev my old mother the needle and it gev me the ump. I should take it very kind, sir, if youd let me off the drill and let me shave you instead. Youd appreciate my qualities then: you would indeed, sir. I shant never do myself jastice at soljerin, sir. I cant bring myself to think of it as proper work for a man with an active mind, as you might say, sir. Arf of it's only ousemaidin; and tother arf is dress-up and make-believe.

MITCHENER. Stuff, sir. It's the easiest life in the world. Once you learn your drill, all you have to do is to hold your tongue and obey your orders.

THE ORDERLY. But I do assure you, sir, arf the time theyre the wrong orders; and I get into trouble when I obey them. The sergeant's orders is all right; but the officers dont know what theyre talkin about. Why, the orses knows better sometimes. "Fours," says Lieutenant Trevor at the gate of Buckingham Palace only this mornin when we was on dooty for a State visit to the Coal Trust. I was fourth man like in the first file; and when I started the orse eld back; and the sergeant was on to me straight. Threes, you bally

fool, e whispers. An e was on to me again about it
when we come back, and called me a fathead, e did.
What am I to do, I says: the lieutenant's orders was
fours, I says. I'll shew you who's lieutenant here, e
says. In future you attend to my orders and not to iz,
e says: what does e know about it? e says. You didnt
give me any orders, I says. Couldnt you see for yourself there wasnt room for fours, e says: why cant you
think? General Mitchener tells me I'm not to
think, but to obey orders, I says. Is Mitchener your
sergeant or am I? e says in his bullyin way. You are, I
says. Well, e says, you got to do what your sergeant
tells you: thats discipline, e says. And what am I to do
for the General? I says. Youre to let him talk, e says:
thats what e's for.

MITCHENER [groaning] It is impossible for the
human mind to conceive anything more dreadful
than this. Youre a disgrace to the service.

THE ORDERLY [deeply wounded] The service is a
disgrace to me. When my mother's people pass me in
the street with this uniform on, I ardly know which
way to look. There never was a soldier in my family
before.

MITCHENER. There never was anything else in mine,
sir.

THE ORDERLY. My mother's second cousin was one
of the Parkinsons o Stepney. [Almost in tears] What
do you know of the feelings of a respectable family
in the middle station of life? I cant bear to be looked
down on as a common soldier. Why cant my father
be let buy my discharge? Youve done away with the
soldier's right to ave his discharge bought for him by
his relations. The country didnt know you were going
to do that or it'd never ave stood it. Is an Englishman
to be made a mockery like this?

MITCHENER. Silence. Attention. Right about face. March.

THE ORDERLY [*retiring to the standing desk and bedewing it with passionate tears*] Oh that I should have lived to be spoke to as if I was the lowest of the low! Me! that has shaved a City o London alderman wiv me own and.

MITCHENER. Poltroon. Crybaby. Well, better disgrace yourself here than disgrace your country on the field of battle.

THE ORDERLY [*angrily coming to the table*] Who's going to disgrace his country on the field of battle? It's not fightin I object to: it's soljerin. Shew me a German and I'll ave a go at him as fast as you or any man. But to ave me time wasted like this, an be stuck in a sentry-box at a street corner for an ornament to be stared at; and to be told "right about face: march," if I speak as one man to another: that aint pluck: that aint fightin: that aint patriotism: it's bein made a bloomin sheep of.

MITCHENER. A sheep has many valuable military qualities. Emulate them, dont disparage them.

THE ORDERLY. Oh, wots the good of talkin to you? If I wasnt a poor soldier I could punch your ed for forty shillins or a month. But because youre my commandin officer you deprive me of my right to a magistrate, and make a compliment of giving me two years ard stead o shootin me. Why cant you take your chance the same as any civilian does?

MITCHENER [*rising majestically*] I search the pages of history in vain for a parallel to such a speech made by a private to a General. But for the coherence of your remarks I should conclude that you were drunk. As it is, you must be mad. You shall be placed under restraint at once. Call the guard.

THE ORDERLY. Call your grandmother. If you take one man off the doors the place'll be full of Suffragets before you can wink.

MITCHENER. Then arrest yourself; and off with you to the guard-room.

THE ORDERLY. What am I to arrest myself for?

MITCHENER. Thats nothing to you. You have your orders: obey them. Do you hear? Right about face. March.

THE ORDERLY. How would you feel if you was told to right-about-face and march as if you was a door-mat?

MITCHENER. I should feel as if my country had spoken through the voice of my officer. I should feel proud and honored to be able to serve my country by obeying its commands. No thought of self, no vulgar preoccupation with my own petty vanity, could touch my mind at such a moment. To me my officer would not be a mere man: he would be for the moment—whatever his personal frailties—the incarnation of our national destiny.

THE ORDERLY. What I'm saying to you is the voice of old England a jolly sight more than all this rot that you get out of books. I'd rather be spoke to by a ser-geant than by you. He tells me to go to hell when I challenges him to argue it out like a man. It aint polite; but it's English. What you say aint anything at all. You dont act on it yourself. You dont believe in it. Youd punch my head if I tried it on you; and serve me right. And look here. Heres another point for you to argue—

MITCHENER [with a shriek of protest] No—

Mrs Banger comes in followed by Lady Corinthia Fanshawe. Mrs Banger is a masculine woman of forty with a powerful voice and great physical strength. Lady

Corinthia, who is also over thirty, is beautiful and romantic.

MRS BANGER [*throwing the door open decisively and marching straight to Mitchener*) Pray how much longer is the Anti-Suffraget League to be kept waiting? [*She passes him contemptuously and sits down with impressive confidence in the chair next the fireplace Lady Corinthia takes the chair on the opposite side of the table with equal aplomb*].

MITCHENER. I'm extremely sorry. You really do not know what I have to put up with. This imbecile, incompetent, unsoldierly disgrace to the uniform he should never have been allowed to put on, ought to have shewn you in fifteen minutes ago.

THE ORDERLY. All I said was—

MITCHENER. Not another word. Attention. Right about face. March. [*The Orderly sits down doggedly*]. Get out of the room this instant, you fool; or I'll kick you out.

THE ORDERLY [*civilly*] I dont mind that, sir. It's human. It's English. Why couldnt you have said it before? [*He goes out*].

MITCHENER. Take no notice, I beg: these scenes are of daily occurrence now that we have compulsory service under the command of the halfpenny papers. Pray sit down.

LADY CORINTHIA AND MRS BANGER} [*rising*] {Thank you. [*They sit down again*].

MITCHENER [*sitting down with a slight chuckle of satisfaction*] And now, ladies, to what am I indebted—

MRS BANGER. Let me introduce us. I am Rosa Carmina Banger: Mrs Banger, organizing secretary of the Anti-Suffraget League. This is Lady Corinthia Fanshawe, the president of the League, known in musical circles—*I am not musical*—as the Richmond

Park nightingale. A soprano. I am myself said to be almost a baritone; but I do not profess to understand these distinctions.

MITCHENER [*murmuring politely*] Most happy, I'm sure.

MRS BANGER. We have come to tell you plainly that the Anti-Suffragets are going to fight.

MITCHENER [*gallantly*] Oh, pray leave that to the men, Mrs Banger.

LADY CORINTHIA. We can no longer trust the men.

MRS BANGER. They have shewn neither the strength, the courage, nor the determination which are needed to combat women like the Suffragets.

LADY CORINTHIA. Nature is too strong for the combatants.

MRS BANGER. Physical struggles between persons of opposite sexes are unseemly.

LADY CORINTHIA. Demoralizing.

MRS BANGER. Insincere.

LADY CORINTHIA. They are merely embraces in disguise.

MRS BANGER. No such suspicion can attach to combats in which the antagonists are of the same sex.

LADY CORINTHIA. The Anti-Suffragets have resolved to take the field.

MRS BANGER. They will enforce the order of General Sandstone for the removal of all women from the two-mile radius—that is, all women except themselves.

MITCHENER. I am sorry to have to inform you, madam, that the Government has given up that project, and that General Sandstone has resigned in consequence.

MRS BANGER. That does not concern us in the least. We approve of the project and will see that it is carried out. We have spent a good deal of money arming ourselves; and we are not going to have that money thrown away through the pusillanimity of a Cabinet of males.

MITCHENER. Arming yourselves! But, my dear ladies, under the latest proclamation women are strictly forbidden to carry chains, padlocks, tracts on the franchise, or weapons of any description.

LADY CORINTHIA [*producing an ivory-handled revolver and pointing it at his nose*] You little know your countrywomen, General Mitchener.

MITCHENER [*without flinching*] Madam: it is my duty to take possession of that weapon in accordance with the proclamation. Be good enough to put it down.

MRS BANGER [*producing an XVIII century horse pistol*] Is it your duty to take possession of this also?

MITCHENER. That, madam, is not a weapon: it is a curiosity. If you would be kind enough to place it in some museum instead of pointing it at my head, I should be obliged to you.

MRS BANGER. This pistol, sir, was carried at Waterloo by my grandmother.

MITCHENER. I presume you mean your grandfather.

MRS BANGER. You presume unwarrantably.

LADY CORINTHIA. Mrs Banger's grandmother commanded a canteen at that celebrated battle.

MRS BANGER. Who my grandfather was is a point that has never been quite clearly settled. I put my trust, not in my ancestors, but in my good sword, which is at my lodgings.

MITCHENER. Your sword!

MRS BANGER. The sword with which I slew five Egyptians with my own hand at Kassassin, where I served as a trooper.

MITCHENER. Lord bless me! But was your sex never discovered?

[253]

MRS BANGER. It was never even suspected. I had a comrade—a gentleman ranker—whom they called Fanny. They never called me Fanny.

LADY CORINTHIA. The Suffragets have turned the whole woman movement on to the wrong track. They ask for a vote.

MRS BANGER. What use is a vote? Men have the vote.

LADY CORINTHIA. And men are slaves.

MRS BANGER. What women need is the right to military service. Give me a well-mounted regiment of women with sabres, opposed to a regiment of men with votes. We shall see which will go down before the other. No: we have had enough of these gentle pretty creatures who merely talk and cross-examine ministers in police courts, and go to prison like sheep, and suffer and sacrifice themselves. This question must be solved by blood and iron, as was well said by Bismarck, whom I have reason to believe was a woman in disguise.

MITCHENER. Bismarck a woman!

MRS BANGER. All the really strong men of history have been disguised women.

MITCHENER [remonstrating] My dear lady!

MRS BANGER. How can you tell? You never knew that the hero of the charge at Kassassin was a woman: yet she was: it was I, Rosa Carmina Banger. Would Napoleon have been so brutal to women, think you, had he been a man?

MITCHENER. Oh, come, come! Really! Surely female rulers have often shewn all the feminine weaknesses. Queen Elizabeth, for instance. Her vanity, her levity—

MRS BANGER. Nobody who has studied the history of Queen Elizabeth can doubt for a moment that she was a disguised man.

LADY CORINTHIA [admiring Mrs Banger] Isnt she splendid!

MRS BANGER [*rising with a large gesture*] This very afternoon I shall cast off this hampering skirt for ever; mount my charger; and with my good sabre lead the Anti-Suffragets to victory. [*She strides to the other side of the room, snorting*].

MITCHENER. But I cant allow anything of the sort, madam. I shall stand no such ridiculous nonsense. I'm perfectly determined to put my foot down—

LADY CORINTHIA. Dont be hysterical, General.

MITCHENER. Hysterical!

MRS BANGER. Do you think we are to be stopped by these childish exhibitions of temper? They are useless; and your tears and entreaties—a man's last resource—will avail you just as little. I sweep them away, just as I sweep your plans of campaign "made in Germany"—

MITCHENER [*flying into a transport of rage*] How dare you repeat that infamous slander! [*He rings the bell violently*]. If this is the alternative to votes for women, I shall advocate giving every woman in the country six votes. [*The Orderly comes in*]. Remove that woman, See that she leaves the building at once.

The Orderly forlornly contemplates the iron front presented by Mrs Banger.

THE ORDERLY [*propitiatorily*] Would you ave the feelin art to step out, madam?

MRS BANGER. You are a soldier. Obey your orders. Put me out. If I got such an order I should not hesitate.

THE ORDERLY [*to Mitchener*] Would you mind lendin me a and, Guvner?

LADY CORINTHIA [*raising her revolver*] I shall be obliged to shoot you if you stir, General.

MRS BANGER [*to the Orderly*] When you are ordered to put a person out you should do it like this. [*She hurls him from the room. He is heard falling headlong downstairs and crashing through a glass door*]. I shall now wait on General Sandstone. If he shews any sign of weakness, he shall share that poor wretch's fate. [*She goes out*].

LADY CORINTHIA. Isnt she magnificent?

MITCHENER. Thank heaven she's gone. And now, my dear lady, is it necessary to keep that loaded pistol to my nose all through our conversation?

LADY CORINTHIA. It's not loaded. It's heavy enough, goodness knows, without putting bullets in it.

MITCHENER [*triumphantly snatching his revolver from the drawer*] Then I am master of the situation. This is loaded. Ha, ha!

LADY CORINTHIA. But since we are not really going to shoot one another, what difference can it possibly make?

MITCHENER [*putting his pistol down on the table*] True. Quite true. I recognize there the practical good sense that has prevented you from falling into the snares of the Suffragets.

LADY CORINTHIA. The Suffragets, General, are the dupes of dowdies. A really attractive and clever woman—

MITCHENER [*gallantly*] Yourself, for instance.

LADY CORINTHIA. [*snatching up his revolver*] Another step and you are a dead man.

MITCHENER [*amazed*] My dear lady!

LADY CORINTHIA. I am not your dear lady. You are not the first man who has concluded that because I am devoted to music and can reach F in alt with the greatest facility—Patti never got above E flat—I am marked out as the prey of every libertine. You think I am like the thousands of weak women whom you have ruined—

MITCHENER. I solemnly protest—

[256]

LADY CORINTHIA. Oh, I know what you officers are. To you a woman's honor is nothing, and the idle pleasure of the moment is everything.

MITCHENER. This is perfectly ridiculous. I never ruined anyone in my life.

LADY CORINTHIA. Never! Are you in earnest?

MITCHENER. Certainly I am in earnest. Most indignantly in earnest.

LADY CORINTHIA [*throwing down the pistol contemptuously*] Then you have no temperament: you are not an artist. You have no soul for music.

MITCHENER. Ive subscribed to the regimental band all my life. I bought two sarrusophones for it out of my own pocket. When I sang Tosti's Goodbye for Ever at Knightsbridge in 1880 the whole regiment wept. You are too young to remember that.

LADY CORINTHIA. Your advances are useless. I—

MITCHENER. Confound it, madam, can you not receive an innocent compliment without suspecting me of dishonorable intentions?

LADY CORINTHIA. Love—real love—makes all intentions honorable. But you could never understand that.

MITCHENER. I'll not submit to the vulgar penny-novelette notion that an officer is less honorable than a civilian in his relations with women. While I live I'll raise my voice—

LADY CORINTHIA. Tush!

MITCHENER. What do you mean by tush?

LADY CORINTHIA. You cant raise your voice above its natural compass. What sort of voice have you?

MITCHENER. A tenor. What sort had you?

LADY CORINTHIA. Had! I have it still. I tell you I am the highest living soprano. [*Scornfully*] What was your highest note, pray?

[257]

MITCHENER. B flat—once—in 1879. I was drunk at the time.

LADY CORINTHIA [*gazing at him almost tenderly*] Though you may not believe me, I find you are more interesting when you talk about music than when you are endeavoring to betray a woman who has trusted you by remaining alone with you in your apartment.

MITCHENER [*springing up and fuming away to the fireplace*] Those repeated insults to a man of blameless life are as disgraceful to you as they are undeserved by me, Lady Corinthia. Such suspicions invite the conduct they impute. [*She raises the pistol*]. You need not be alarmed: I am only going to leave the room.

LADY CORINTHIA. Fish.

MITCHENER. Fish! This is worse than tush. Why fish?

LADY CORINTHIA. Yes, fish: cold-blooded fish.

MITCHENER. Dash it all, madam, do you want me to make advances to you?

LADY CORINTHIA. I have not the slightest intention of yielding to them; but to make them would be a tribute to romance. What is life without romance?

MITCHENER [*making a movement towards her*] I tell you—

LADY CORINTHIA. Stop. No nearer. No vulgar sensuousness. If you must adore, adore at a distance.

MITCHENER. This is worse than Mrs Banger. I shall ask that estimable woman to come back.

LADY CORINTHIA. Poor Mrs Banger! Do not for a moment suppose, General Mitchener, that Mrs Banger represents my views on the suffrage question. Mrs Banger is a man in petticoats. I am every inch a woman; but I find it convenient to work with her.

MITCHENER. Do you find the combination comfortable?

LADY CORINTHIA. I do not wear combinations, General: [*with dignity*] they are unwomanly.

MITCHENER [*throwing himself despairingly into the chair next the hearthrug*] I shall go mad. I never for a moment dreamt of alluding to anything of the sort.

LADY CORINTHIA. There is no need to blush and become self-conscious at the mention of underclothing. You are extremely vulgar, General.

MITCHENER. Lady Corinthia: you have my pistol. Will you have the goodness to blow my brains out? I should prefer it to any other effort to follow the gyrations of the weathercock you no doubt call your mind. If you refuse, then I warn you that youll not get another word out of me—not if we sit here until doomsday.

LADY CORINTHIA. I dont want you to talk. I want you to listen. You do not understand my views on the question of the suffrage. [*She rises to make a speech*]. I must preface my remarks by reminding you that the Suffraget movement is essentially a dowdy movement. The Suffragets are not all dowdies; but they are mainly supported by dowdies. Now I am not a dowdy. Oh, no compliments—

MITCHENER. I did not utter a sound.

LADY CORINTHIA [*smiling*] It is easy to read your thoughts. I am one of those women who are accustomed to rule the world through men. Man is ruled by beauty, by charm. The men who are not have no influence. The Salic Law, which forbade women to occupy a throne, is founded on the fact that when a woman is on the throne the country is ruled by men, and therefore ruled badly; whereas when a man is on the throne the country is ruled by women, and therefore ruled well. The Suffragets would degrade women from being rulers to being voters, mere politicians, the drudges of the caucus and the polling booth. We should lose our influence completely under such a state of affairs. The New Zealand women have the vote. What is the result? No poet ever makes a New Zealand woman his heroine. One might as well be romantic about New Zealand mutton. Look at the Suffragets themselves. The only ones who are popular are the pretty ones, who flirt with mobs as ordinary women flirt with officers.

MITCHENER. Then I understand you to hold that the country should be governed by the women after all.

LADY CORINTHIA. Not by all the women. By certain women. I had almost said by one woman. By the women who have charm—who have artistic talent—who wield a legitimate, a refining influence over the men. [She sits down gracefully, smiling, and arranging her draperies with conscious elegance].

MITCHENER. In short, madam, you think that if you give the vote to the man, you give the power to the woman who can get round the man.

LADY CORINTHIA. That is not a very delicate way of putting it; but I suppose that is how you would express what I mean.

MITCHENER. Perhaps youve never had any experience of garrison life. If you had, youd have noticed that the sort of woman who's clever at getting round men is sometimes rather a bad lot.

LADY CORINTHIA. What do you mean by a bad lot?

MITCHENER. I mean a woman who would play the very devil if the other women didnt keep her in pretty strict order. I dont approve of democracy, because it's rot; and I'm against giving the vote to women, because I'm not accustomed to it, and therefore am able to see with an unprejudiced eye what infernal nonsense it is. But I tell you plainly, Lady Corinthia, that there is one game that I dislike more than either democracy or votes for women; and that is the game of Antony and Cleopatra. If I must be ruled by women, let me have decent women, and not—well, not the other sort.

LADY CORINTHIA. You have a coarse mind, General Mitchener.

MITCHENER. So has Mrs Banger. And, by George! I prefer Mrs Banger to you!

LADY CORINTHIA. [bounding to her feet] You prefer Mrs Banger to me!!!

MITCHENER. I do. You said yourself she was splendid.

LADY CORINTHIA. You are no true man. You are one of those unsexed creatures who have no joy in life, no sense of beauty, no high notes.

MITCHENER. No doubt I am, madam. As a matter of fact, I am not clever at discussing public questions, because, as an English gentleman, I was not brought up to use my brains. But occasionally, after a number of remarks which are perhaps sometimes rather idiotic, I get certain convictions. Thanks to you, I have now got a conviction that this woman question is not a question of lovely and accomplished females, but of dowdies. The average Englishwoman is a dowdy and never has half a chance of becoming anything else. She hasnt any charm; and she has no high notes, except when she's giving her husband a piece of her mind, or calling down the street for one of the children.

LADY CORINTHIA. How disgusting!

MITCHENER. Somebody must do the dowdy work! If we had to choose between pitching all the dowdies into the Thames and pitching all the lovely and accomplished women, the lovely ones would have to go.

LADY CORINTHIA. And if you had to do without

Wagner's music or do without your breakfast, you would do without Wagner. Pray does that make eggs and bacon more precious than music, or the butcher and baker better than the poet and philosopher? The scullery may be more necessary to our bare existence than the cathedral. Even humbler apartments might make the same claim. But which is the more essential to the higher life?

MITCHENER. Your arguments are so devilishly ingenious that I feel convinced you got them out of some confounded book. Mine—such as they are—are my own. I imagine it's something like this. There is an old saying that if you take care of the pence, the pounds will take care of themselves. Well, perhaps if we take care of the dowdies and the butchers and the bakers, the beauties and the bigwigs will take care of themselves. [*Rising and facing her determinedly*] Anyhow, I dont want to have things arranged for me by Wagner. I'm not Wagner. How does h e know where the shoe pinches m e? How do y o u know where the shoe pinches your washerwoman? you and your high F in alt! How are you to know when you havnt made her comfortable unless she has a vote? Do you want her to come and break your windows?

LADY CORINTHIA. Am I to understand that General Mitchener is a Democrat and a Suffraget?

MITCHENER. Yes: you have converted me—you and Mrs Banger.

LADY CORINTHIA. Farewell, creature. [*Balsquith enters hurriedly*]. Mr Balsquith: I am going to wait on General Sandstone. He, at least, is an officer and a gentleman. [*She sails out*].

BALSQUITH. Mitchener: the game is up.

MITCHENER. What do you mean?

BALSQUITH. The strain is too much for the Cabinet.

The old Liberal and Unionist Free Traders declare that if they are defeated on their resolution to invite tenders from private contractors for carrying on the Army and Navy, they will go solid for votes for women as the only means of restoring the liberties of the country which we have destroyed by compulsory military service.

MITCHENER. Infernal impudence!

BALSQUITH. The Labor Party is taking the same line. They say the men got the Factory Acts by hiding behind the women's petticoats, and that they will get votes for the army in the same way.

MITCHENER. Balsquith: we must not yield to clamor. I have just told that woman that I am at last convinced—

BALSQUITH [*joyfully*]—that the Suffragets must be supported?

MITCHENER. No: that the Anti-Suffragets must be put down at all hazards.

BALSQUITH. Same thing.

MITCHENER. No. For you now tell me that the Labor Party demands votes for women. That makes it impossible to give them, because it would be yielding to clamor. The one condition on which we can consent to grant anything in this country is that nobody shall presume to ask for it.

BALSQUITH [*earnestly*] Mitchener: it's no use. You cant have the conveniences of Democracy without its occasional inconveniences.

MITCHENER. What are its conveniences, I should like to know?

BALSQUITH. Well, when you tell people that they are the real rulers and they can do what they like, nine times out of ten they say "All right: tell us what to do." But it happens sometimes that they get an idea of their own; and then of course youre landed.

MITCHENER. Sh—

BALSQUITH [*desperately shouting him down*] No: it's no use telling me to shoot them down: I'm not going to do it. After all, I dont suppose votes for women will make much difference. It hasnt in the other countries in which it has been tried.

MITCHENER. I never supposed it would make any difference. What I cant stand is giving in to that Pankhurst lot. Hang it all, Balsquith, it seems only yesterday that we put them in quad for a month. I said at the time that it ought to have been ten years. If my advice had been taken this wouldnt have happened. It's a consolation to me that events are proving how thoroughly right I was.

The Orderly rushes in.

THE ORDERLY. Look 'ere, sir: Mrs Banger's locked the door of General Sandstone's room on the inside; an she's sittin on his ed til he signs a proclamation for women to serve in the army.

MITCHENER. Put your shoulder to the door and burst it open.

THE ORDERLY. It's only in story books that doors burst open as easy as that. Besides, I'm only too thankful to av a locked door between me and Mrs B.; and so is all the rest of us.

MITCHENER. Cowards. Balsquith: to the rescue! [*He dashes out*].

BALSQUITH [*ambling calmly to the hearth*] This is the business of the Sergeant-at-Arms rather than of the leader of the House. Theres no use in my tackling Mrs Banger: she would only sit on my head too.

THE ORDERLY. You take my tip, Mr Balsquith. Give the women the vote and give the army civil rights; and av done with it.

Mitchener returns and comes between them.

MITCHENER. Balsquith: prepare to hear the worst.

BALSQUITH. Sandstone is no more?

MITCHENER. On the contrary, he is particularly lively. He has softened Mrs Banger by a proposal of marriage in which he appears to be perfectly in earnest. He says he has met his ideal at last, a really soldierly woman. She will sit on his head for the rest of his life; and the British Army is now to all intents and purposes commanded by Mrs Banger. When I remonstrated with Sandstone she positively shouted "Right about face. March" at me in the most offensive tone. If she hadnt been a woman I should have punched her head. I precious nearly punched Sandstone's. The horrors of martial law administered by Mrs Banger are too terrible to be faced. I demand civil rights for the army.

THE ORDERLY [*chuckling*] Wot oh, General! Wot oh!

MITCHENER. Hold your tongue. [*He goes to the door and calls*] Mrs Farrell! [*He returns, and again addresses the Orderly*]. Civil rights dont mean the right to be uncivil. [*Pleased with his own wit*] Almost a pun. Ha ha!

MRS FARRELL [*entering*] Whats the matther now? [*She comes to the table*].

MITCHENER [*to the Orderly*] I have private business with Mrs Farrell. Outside, you infernal blackguard.

THE ORDERLY [*arguing, as usual*] Well, I didnt ask to— [*Mitchener seizes him by the nape; marches him out; slams the door; and comes solemnly to Mrs Farrell*].

MITCHENER. Excuse the abruptness of this communication, Mrs Farrell; but I know only one woman in the country whose practical ability and force of character can maintain her husband in competition with the husband of Mrs Banger. I have the honor to propose for your hand.

MRS FARRELL. D'ye mean you want to marry me?

MITCHENER. I do.

MRS FARRELL. No thank you. I'd have to work for you just the same; only I shouldnt get any wages for it.

BALSQUITH. That will be remedied when women get the vote. Ive had to promise that.

MITCHENER [*winningly*] Mrs Farrell: you have been charwoman here now ever since I took up my duties. Have you really never, in your more romantic moments, cast a favorable eye on my person?

MRS FARRELL. Ive been too busy casting an unfavorable eye on your cloze an on the litther you make with your papers.

MITCHENER [*wounded*] Am I to understand that you refuse me?

MRS FARRELL. Just wait a bit. [*She takes Mitchener's chair and rings up the telephone*] Double three oh seven Elephant.

MITCHENER. I trust youre not ringing for the police, Mrs Farrell. I assure you I'm perfectly sane.

MRS FARRELL [*into the telephone*] Is that you, Eliza? [*She listens for the answer*]. Not out o bed yet! Go and pull her out be the heels, the lazy sthreel; an tell her her mother wants to speak to her very particularly about General Mitchener. [*To Mitchener*] Dont you be afeard: I know youre sane enough when youre not talkin about the Germans. [*Into the telephone*] Is that you, Eliza? [*She listens for the answer*]. D'ye remember me givin you a clout on the side of the head for tellin me that if I only knew how to play me cards I could marry any General on the staff instead o disgracin you be bein a charwoman? [*She listens for the answer*]. Well, I can have General Mitchener without playin any cards at all. What d'ye think I ought to say? [*She listens*]. Well, I'm no chicken meself. [*To Mitchener*] How old are you?

MITCHENER [*with an effort*] Fifty-two.

MRS FARRELL [*into the telephone*] He says he's fifty-two. [*She listens; then, to Mitchener*] She says youre down in Who's Who as sixty-one.

MITCHENER. Damn Who's Who!

MRS FARRELL [*into the telephone*] Anyhow I wouldnt let that stand in the way. [*She listens*]. If I really what? (She listens). I cant hear you. If I really what? (She listens). Who druv him? I never said a word to—Eh? (She listens). Oh, love him. Arra, dont be a fool, child. [*To Mitchener*] She wants to know do I really love you. [*Into the telephone*] It's likely indeed I'd frighten the man off with any such nonsense at my age. What? [*She listens*]. Well, thats just what I was thinkin.

MITCHENER. May I ask what you were thinking, Mrs Farrell? This suspense is awful.

MRS FARRELL. I was thinkin that praps the Duchess might like her daughter-in-law's mother to be a General's lady bether than to be a charwoman. [*Into the telephone*] Waitle youre married yourself, me fine lady: youll find out that every woman's a charwoman from the day she's married. [*She listens*]. Then you think I might take him? [*She listens*]. G'lang, you young scald: if I had you here I'd teach you manners. [*She listens*]. Thats enough now. Back wid you to bed; and be thankful I'm not there to put me slipper across you. [*She rings off*]. The impudence! [*To Mitchener*] Bless you, me childher, may you be happy, she says. [*To Balsquith, going to his side of the room*] Give dear old Mitch me love, she says.

The Orderly opens the door, ushering in Lady Corinthia.

THE ORDERLY. Lady Corinthia Fanshawe to speak to you, sir.

LADY CORINTHIA. General Mitchener: your designs on Mrs Banger are defeated. She is engaged to General Sandstone. Do you still prefer her to me?

MRS FARRELL. He's out o the hunt. He's engaged to me.

The Orderly, overcome by this news, reels from the door to the standing desk and clutches the stool to save himself from collapsing.

MITCHENER. And extremely proud of it, Lady Corinthia.

LADY CORINTHIA [*contemptuously*] She suits you exactly. [*Coming to Balsquith*] Mr Balsquith: you, at least, are not a Philistine.

BALSQUITH. No, Lady Corinthia; but I'm a confirmed bachelor. I dont want a wife; but I want an Egeria.

MRS FARRELL. More shame for you!

LADY CORINTHIA. Silence, woman. The position and functions of a wife may suit your gross nature. An Egeria is exactly what I desire to be. [*To Balsquith*] Can you play accompaniments?

BALSQUITH. Melodies only, I regret to say. With one finger. But my brother, who is a very obliging fellow, and not unlike me personally, is acquainted with three chords, with which he manages to accompany most of the comic songs of the day.

LADY CORINTHIA. I do not sing comic songs. Neither will you when I am your Egeria. You must come to my musical at-home this afternoon. I will allow you to sit at my feet.

BALSQUITH [*doing so*] That is my ideal of romantic happiness. It commits me exactly as far as I desire to venture. Thank you.

THE ORDERLY. Wot price me, General? Wont you

celebrate your engagement by doin somethin for me?
Maynt I be promoted to be a sergeant?

MITCHENER. Youre too utterly imcompetent to discharge the duties of a sergeant. You are only fit to be
a lieutenant. I shall recommend you for a commission.

THE ORDERLY. Hooray! The Parkinsons o Stepney'll
be proud to have me call on em now. I'll go and tell the
sergeant what I think of him. Hooray! [*He rushes out*].

MRS FARRELL [*going to the door and calling after him*]
You might have the manners to shut the door afther
you. [*She shuts it and comes between Mitchener and
Lady Corinthia*].

MITCHENER. Poor wretch! the day after civil rights
are conceded to the army he and Chubbs-Jenkinson
will be found incapable of maintaining discipline.
They will be sacked and replaced by really capable
men. Mrs Farrell: as we are engaged, and I am anxious
to do the correct thing in every way, I am quite
willing to kiss you if you wish it.

MRS FARRELL. Youd only feel like a fool; and so
would I.

MITCHENER. You are really the most sensible woman.
Ive made an extremely wise choice. [*He kisses her hand*].

LADY CORINTHIA [*to Balsquith*] You may kiss my
hand, if you wish.

BALSQUITH [*cautiously*] I think we had better not
commit ourselves too far. Let us change a subject
which threatens to become embarrassing. [*To
Mitchener*] The moral of the occasion for you,
Mitchener, appears to be that youve got to give up
treating soldiers as if they were schoolboys.

MITCHENER. The moral for you, Balsquith, is that
youve got to give up treating women as if they were
angels. Ha ha!

MRS FARRELL. It's a mercy youve found one another
out at last. Thats enough now.

FOR THE BEST IN PAPERBACKS, LOOK FOR THE 🐧

In every corner of the world, on every subject under the sun, Penguin represents quality and variety – the very best in publishing today.

For complete information about books available from Penguin – including Puffins, Penguin Classics and Arkana – and how to order them, write to us at the appropriate address below. Please note that for copyright reasons the selection of books varies from country to country.

In the United Kingdom: Please write to *Dept E.P., Penguin Books Ltd, Harmondsworth, Middlesex, UB7 0DA.*

If you have any difficulty in obtaining a title, please send your order with the correct money, plus ten per cent for postage and packaging, to *PO Box No 11, West Drayton, Middlesex*

In the United States: Please write to *Dept BA, Penguin, 299 Murray Hill Parkway, East Rutherford, New Jersey 07073*

In Canada: Please write to *Penguin Books Canada Ltd, 2801 John Street, Markham, Ontario L3R 1B4*

In Australia: Please write to the *Marketing Department, Penguin Books Australia Ltd, P.O. Box 257, Ringwood, Victoria 3134*

In New Zealand: Please write to the *Marketing Department, Penguin Books (NZ) Ltd, Private Bag, Takapuna, Auckland 9*

In India: Please write to *Penguin Overseas Ltd, 706 Eros Apartments, 56 Nehru Place, New Delhi, 110019*

In the Netherlands: Please write to *Penguin Books Netherlands B.V., Postbus 195, NL–1380AD Weesp*

In West Germany: Please write to *Penguin Books Ltd, Friedrichstrasse 10–12, D–6000 Frankfurt/Main 1*

In Spain: Please write to *Longman Penguin España, Calle San Nicolas 15, E–28013 Madrid*

In Italy: Please write to *Penguin Italia s.r.l., Via Como 4, I-20096 Pioltello (Milano)*

In France: Please write to *Penguin Books Ltd, 39 Rue de Montmorency, F-75003 Paris*

In Japan: Please write to *Longman Penguin Japan Co Ltd, Yamaguchi Building, 2–12–9 Kanda Jimbocho, Chiyoda-Ku, Tokyo 101*

Bernard Shaw in Penguin

'Shaw has redeemed and embellished our fantasies'
– Raymond Williams
The complete dramatic works of Bernard Shaw are now
published in paperback for the first time. Definitive text under
the editorial supervision of Dan H. Laurence.

THE BERNARD SHAW LIBRARY
Androcles and the Lion
The Doctor's Dilemma
Getting Married/Press Cuttings
Heartbreak House
Major Barbara
Plays Pleasant
(Arms and the Man, Candida, The Man of Destiny,
You Never Can Tell)
Plays Unpleasant
(Widowers' Houses, The Philanderer,
Mrs Warren's Profession)
Saint Joan
Selected Short Plays
(including The Admirable Bashville and Great Catherine)
The Shewing-Up of Blanco Posnet and Fanny's First Play
(in one volume)
Back to Methuselah

Published in Penguin Plays
The Apple Cart
Last Plays
('In Good King Charles's Golden Days', Buoyant Billions,
Farfetched Fables, Shakes Versus Shav, Why She Would Not)
Misalliance *and* The Fascinating Foundling
Plays Political
(The Apple Cart, On the Rocks, Geneva)
John Bull's Other Island
Man and Superman
Plays Extravagant
(The Millionairess, Too True to be Good,
The Simpleton of the Unexpected Isles)
Three Plays for Puritans
(The Devil's Disciple, Caesar and Cleopatra,
Captain Brassbound's Conversion)

Fiction
The Black Girl in Search of God and some lesser tales
Cashel Byron's Profession

And in Pelican
The Intelligent Woman's Guide to
Socialism, Capitalism, Sovietism and Fascism
Major Critical Essays (The Quintessence of Ibsenism,
The Perfect Wagnerite, the Sanity of Art)